Case Files of a Spirit Talker

Lela E. Buis

Case Files of a Spirit Talker

That Ridge ~ Knoxville

This is a work of fiction. All characters and events are products of the author's imagination, or are used fictitiously.

Case Files of a Spirit Talker

ISBN 978-0-9850190-4-4 (Paperback)
ISBN 978-0-9850190-0-6 (E-book)

Published by That Ridge Publishing, Knoxville TN

First Edition 2020
Printed in the United States of America

Cover photo by goodCoverDesign.

Acknowledgments

Some of the chapters in this book have been previously published as short stories in magazines and anthologies. Grateful acknowledgement is made to the editors.

"Death in Nairobi,"*Afromyth: A Fantasy Collection*, ed. J.S. Emuakpor, Afrocentric Books, 2017.

"Souls," *Storm and Shadow,* That Ridge Press, 2013, and *Moonshadows: A Collection of Short Stories*, That Ridge Press, 2019.

Contents

Dedication

For Roger Zelazny, who inspired all of this.

*"Life isn't about waiting for the storm to pass...
It's about learning to dance in the rain."*

--Vivian Greene

Prologue

I'm Anna Detroyer, private investigator. I've got a little detective business in Miami, Florida, that will take on your case if you need help—just give me a call. Incidentally, I'm also Black Seminole and a spirit talker. The first part means I'm racially mixed. The last part means I can see spirits and creatures other people just dismiss as unreal. I was ten years old when I found that out. I was at my Aunt Patti's house, where I met my grandfather for the first time.

Aunt Patti lived in Hollywood, Florida, just then, and she had about ten acres of land where she kept horses and a few cows. I always went to stay with her for a while when my mother was in the hospital for chemo. I was sitting under a live oak that day, my back to the rough bark, watching Aunt Patti's pinto mare graze in the straggly grass. Summer heat lay on the scene like a blanket, and a slight haze made it all seem a bit unreal.

After a while, I saw a man walking toward me out of the slash pines off to the left. He was about medium height, with a dark face and gray-threaded black hair. He was wearing a hat, jeans and the kind of quilted shirts that Seminoles sometimes wear. He walked on up and stopped in the shade of the tree.

"Hello, little one," he said.

I looked up at him.

"Who are you?" I asked.

"I'm your grandfather," he said.

I sized him up.

"How do you know?" I asked. "You've never seen me before."

"You're Anna Detroyer, aren't you?" he asked.

"Yes," I said. "You're Amos Chupco?"

He did look something like my mother—and like me, too, high cheekbones and warm brown eyes set deep into the sockets. His skin was creased and wrinkled with age.

"Yes," he said. He sat down cross-legged under the tree, looked out to where the spotted mare was switching her tail against the flies. "Nice day, isn't it?"

"It could be better," I said.

"Your mother's in the hospital again?" he asked.

"Yes," I said. "Her cancer's getting worse."

"That's a shame," he said. "She's always been a good daughter. She tries hard."

In the silence that followed, I twisted a strand of grass, tore it into shreds. I looked over at him.

"Is she going to die?" I asked.

"Yes," he said. "I'm sorry to tell you that, but I'm sure you had an idea about it already."

I pulled my knees up, dropped my head against them.

"Do you have somewhere to go?" he asked.

"Maybe I can stay with Aunt Patti," I said.

"You will need strength to grow up straight and true without your mother," he said. "I've brought you something to help."

He reached into his shirt then, pulled out a pouch that looked to be made of deerskin. He took off his hat, lifted the thong that held the pouch over his head. He laid it against his thigh, stroked one hand over the beaded design.

"This is a medicine pouch," he said.

"What's it for?" I asked.

"It is a source of power," he said. "There are objects inside that seem ordinary, but they are invested with strong medicine. I gathered these over my lifetime through personal spirit quests. They will increase your hunting skills, fighting skills, healing abilities, the power to overcome enemies…"

"Can I see what's inside?" I asked.

"Not until you can control the objects," he said. "Their power is attuned to the owner. Usually people are buried with their medicine pouch, but sometimes they pass it on to others of their kin."

"And this is for me?"

"Yes," he said. "I've brought it for you."

He looped the thong over my head then, lifted my hair over it.

"Wear it inside your shirt," he said, "against your heart. After a while the fetishes will retune to you."

"Thank you," I said.

I tucked the pouch inside my tee-shirt so it lay against my skin. Amos touched my hair again, like a blessing.

"I have to go," he said, "but I will come any time if you need me."

He got up then, walked across the field and back into the stand of pines. I sat there for a while with my hand on the pouch under my shirt, but then an afternoon shower of rain blew up, so I pushed up to my feet and started off for the house.

Aunt Patti was dusky shadow against the light, busy making a raisin pie on the kitchen counter. She glanced around as I opened the door from the porch.

"There you are," she said. "Didn't the school bus run an hour ago?"

"Yes, ma'am," I said. "I've been out in the field."

"Honey," she said, "what were you doing out there?"

"I've been talking to Grandpa," I said.

She turned all the way around and looked at me then, propped one floured fist on her hip—just like my grandma used to do.

"Anna," she said. "You know your grandpa's been dead for fifteen years."

"Yes, ma'am," I said. "I know."

That's how I came to know I was a spirit talker. I see ghosts, spirits, things that aren't material to most other people. I wore the medicine bundle like Grandpa told me to, waiting until I could feel the fetishes of power attune to me. I've still got it, still wear it—a reminder that I'm never really alone in the world—however much I might feel that way.

My mother died. I grew up to be a lot like her.

Here are my case files.

Chapter 1

THE FOX

It's late afternoon. I'm an origami woman by this time, crumpled and stiff, watching Chiba City flash past the train windows. I'm creased permanently into fetal shape, sculpted into a paper caricature of life. I'm also spent and cross, and just waiting for jet lag to set in. The reflection in the window shows a sturdy girl with tired eyes.

"Anna," I ask myself, "what the hell are you doing here?"

Paul and his buddy Colin Wentworth are huddled in the seats ahead of me, oblivious to anything. The coach rattles on, clean and worn, full but not sardine tight like the crush in immigration at Narita Airport. The train rocks and clatters through a cityscape of strong verticals, bound together by electrical wires and wash, ornamented by futons hung on the balconies to air.

Paul and I are partners in a little detective business in Miami, and we're here to look for missing securities that belong to a small pension fund back home. After weeks of song and dance from the Tokyo bank, the American brokerage firm has finally dispatched someone to see what's going on. That someone is Colin, and he's brought Paul along. Paul's brought me—the rest of Detroyer and Angstrom, P.I.'s. It's been eighteen hours of travel to get here, and the time is now thirteen hours off. At home it's dark. I should be sleeping.

The train finally squeals to a halt at Tokyo Station, and we're hit by another blast of confusion as it empties out onto the platform. Somehow we get a taxi that takes us to the Tokyo Hilton, where we snag on a final reservations glitch. Bone tired, I hold up the wall and let the guys handle it. I remember it's supposed to be okay in Japan to take your shoes off indoors, but I don't see anybody doing it here. That's too bad. My feet are killing me.

It's a nice hotel. I can tell from the *yen* it takes to get in. I'm pleased with the room, but not the arrangements—Paul and Colin are together, and I'm rooming solo. I'd prefer that it was Colin solo, but somehow that seldom happens for me anymore. The room looks comfortable enough. The furniture is functional, and the carpeting is lush. I drop my single suitcase onto the stand and grab a quick shower. At dinner I doze through American style prime rib, feeling like the third wheel of a rundown rickshaw. When were done, I'm wide-awake.

"What happened?" I ask, rubbing my eyes.

"It's the green tea," snipes Colin. "It has so much more caffeine than coffee, my dear." He's dark-haired and terribly British, with a terribly correct, fine pencil line of mustache.

"Oh, damn," I groan. "Somebody should have warned me."

"I?" He raises disapproving brows. "Heaven forbid that I should interfere with your gastronomic errors."

This is standard chitchat for the trip. I grimace. He smirks visibly, sips an appropriate wine. Paul is applying himself to the check—it looks like Detroyer and Angstrom is going to pay. Again.

"I hope you're going to wear more fashionable clothing tomorrow," says Colin. He brushes imaginary lint off one sleeve. "In Marunouchi district no one wears tee-shirts and jeans. Not even the vagrants."

I grit my teeth.

"Paul," I say, "what time is our appointment in the morning?"

"Colin's in charge," he says. He's still absorbed in the check.

"It's at ten," Colin says, taking the hand-off smoothly. His eyebrows twitch upward again. "Will you need extra time getting dressed?"

"No," I snarl. "Will you?"

The next morning I'm dressed at nine in the one business suit I've got—to spite Colin, if nothing else. I twitch and tug at the skirt as we launch our first assault on the subway. Colin says this is past rush hour, but still there's standing room only on the Chiyoda line.

I'm beginning to work up an interest in the place now, sleep-deprived as I am. We're clearly a long way from Miami. The hotel is in Shinjuku, which has the same upward tendency to the buildings, the same pocket stores I saw coming in—with only a workman's width between. Land here sells by the square foot, I recall, with hundred-year mortgages the standard thing. The average street seems hardly more than a sidewalk wide, crowded by bikes and awnings and bobbing with masses of people. Power lines and *kanji* scrawlings obscure every view. The subway speeds us along—and deposits us in a different world.

Marunouchi is all Western style high-rises, broad streets and a lake with tended landscaping. We hike from the subway stop to the bank. It's tiny, tucked into the corner of a block of office towers, faced with cracked stucco and narrow concrete steps. Inside, the carpets are worn and the ceiling is stained. That's a surprise again. I'm used to posh American banks.

My feet hurt again from the high heel pumps, but it's a more focused pain now. I'm happy enough to sit in the lobby and wait, but Colin gets edgy fast. He thinks we're being stalled, makes a scene. We're promptly ejected from the waiting area and into the president's suite.

The man inside gets up from the desk and charges toward us.

"*Ohayo gozaimasu!*" he insists.

He's younger than I expected. This is apparently Hanada-san himself, the bank president. He's about five-six and balding, wearing heavy glasses and a standard salaryman's black suit and tie. He shakes hands Western style, bobs up and down in a Japanese accompaniment.

He regards me with a faint surprise—skin as dark as mine is unusual in Japan—but clearly it's Colin and Paul he's terrified of. He's sweating visibly as he goes into his explanation about the securities. The delay in delivery is inexcusable, he declares, but it's not his fault. The securities were to be forwarded from the branch in Yokohama.

"Where in Yokohama?" asks Colin.

Hanada-san calls for a uniformed girl, who sends another to get the address. It comes back the same way, and it's comprehensible to Colin, at least. Still another girl bows and smiles us out the door, and then we're squashed again on the Chiyoda line, headed back to Shinjuku. So much for our visit to the bank.

Back in my room, I shed the skirt and yank on my jeans in time to answer the door. It's Paul. It damn well better be. Otherwise, I'd be over there to find him, myself.

"What the hell's gotten into you?" I snarl.

"What do you mean?" he asks.

Paul is tall and blond, and his face acquired a certain tough quality during ten years with the Miami cops. He left the force to open his own P.I. business and picked me up as his partner. It's been a successful team for about fifteen years, but sometimes I wonder why. We've been partners long enough for me to be frank. So what if I always was?

"Complete stupidity!" I say. "It's all I can see."

"Now, Anna," he says, stepping into the room. His eyes have a pained quality. "Sweetheart, you're not going to make a scene, are you?"

"Don't you 'sweetheart' me—and you damn well know it," I say. Everything I've got pent up is threatening to spill out at once. "What do you want from this guy Colin anyhow?"

He frowns, catches his thumbs in his belt.

"Connections," he says.

"What for?" I ask.

"Business," he says.

The width of his shoulders strains at the shirt fabric as he settles on the bed.

"So you're going let him hustle us all over Japan," I complain, "all the way to Yokohama. You couldn't tell this

Hanada-type was lying? It likely the securities disappeared right there in Tokyo, and you know it."

His frown darkens.

"When did you get to be such an expert on Japanese banking?" he says.

I have to catch my breath.

"He was sweating bullets," I say. "Something's wrong. Listen, Paul. While you're off stroking Colin Wentworth, who's going to find the securities?"

He shrugs.

"Finding the securities isn't really what I came for."

"Paul," I say, "it's a small fund. Those investors have their whole life's savings tied up."

He shoves off the bed, catches my shoulders with both hands.

"Anna," he says, "just let me handle this. Okay?"

"So, we're going to Yokohama?" I ask.

"Colin and I are," he says.

"And not me, huh?"

"Anna," he says. For a second the man actually looks honest—actually looks like he cares what I think. "Look," he says. "You want me to apologize? I'm sorry. I didn't realize when I brought you along that Japan is still so damn conservative. And so is Colin—this is awkward. Just be a good girl. Stay here, and…we'll do some sightseeing after we wind up the investigation. Okay?"

What does he mean? Is he talking about racism? Sexism? It sets my teeth on edge, but he kneads my shoulders and then kisses me on the mouth, and I have to let it go. I let out my breath.

"Get lost," I say, and he does.

I refuse to go down to see them off. I have a solitary dinner and manage half a night's sleep. I'm wide-awake by three. The jet lag has set in with a vengeance.

I pace for a while after breakfast and look out the windows at the neighboring towers, watch indecipherable TV. I think about the missing securities and who's depending on them, and I wonder what it is Paul needs all these connections for. It pisses me off that he's not told me what he's up to. At ten a.m. there's a knock on my door. I expect it's the maid, but it's a porcelain doll instead.

"*Ohayo gozaimasu*," she says. "*Angstrom-sama?*"

I can't speak a word of Japanese, but I get the idea.

"No," I say. "I'm Anna Detroyer."

She looks surprised.

"*Ah so desu ka?*"

"Uh. Come in," I say.

This turns out to be Yukiko Hanada, and I gather the bank president saw the guys off last night. Now he's concerned that I'm languishing alone in my room while they're gone to Yokohama. I can't believe he'd send his wife out to entertain me—even in a country so polite that no one steals your luggage.

She's fifteen years younger than her husband, with glossy, crimped black hair and elegant painted eyes. She looks completely refined in a mint linen dress, and she clutches her purse and bobs repeatedly.

"*Shoppingu!*" she insists. "You come."

I'm on my own, so I'll have to play this by ear.

"Okay," I say. "I guess I can do that."

We get off the subway at Ginza, and soon I've gotten a basic line on the culture. The men ignore their wives twelve hours a day, minimum, so the women have their own hot little social life in the palatial department stores of Ginza—child care free on the roof.

Mrs. Hanada doesn't seem to mind my cotton shirt and jeans. She buys lunch and then later, cappuccino in a cozy, expensive, cinnamon-scented shop within the store.

I've bought a book called *Making Out in Japanese*, about making out, and a guidebook, and looked at a lot of other stuff. Of course, buying doesn't seem to be the point. It seems Mrs. Hanada really wants to drink coffee and chat.

"You go sightseeing?" She has an encouraging smile.

"Maybe," I say.

"You see Fuji-san?" she asks brightly.

"We haven't been here long enough."

"Go *onsen*?" she smiles.

It takes me a while to find that in my guidebook. It's a hot spring spa.

"I'd love to," I say.

"*Ah so!*" she says. "*Ito Onsen ichiban*—number one."

"Okay," I say. "I'll ask Paul about it when he gets back."

She doesn't seem to get that part, and chatters on about the attractions of Ito Onsen in broken English. After a while I gather she wants me to take something to her sister there.

"Gift," she insists, smiling. "You take."

It's a small box wrapped in tasteful paper and decorated with gray and black fans.

"I can't agree to that," I say. "Listen. I don't even know that I'm going."

"I pay," she says. "*Ichiban.*"

There's a ticket under the box.

She's still smiling, but now there's a shard of worry behind her eyes.

"I can't take this," I say carefully.

The worry grows visible and desperate, tightening her delicate face. She puts out her hand to push the gift back in my direction.

Maybe Hanada has sent her to buy us off, and I shouldn't touch this with a ten-foot pole. But why me? Colin's the guy who's going to sic the Ministry of Finance on him. Logic nets me nothing here.

"What's going on?" I ask.

She's forgotten her English, and her smile is frozen stiff.

"Listen," I decide finally. "I'll take the gift to your sister, but I'll pay for my own ticket. Will that suit you?"

"Please." She pushes the ticket at me again. "You take." But the desperation is gone now. I figure somehow I've translated this right.

I stick the gift in my pocket, leave the ticket there. It would be a conflict of interest. "Tell me your sister's name," I say. "And the address."

I'll have to add this up later. She says we've got to head back now—already we're seeing the rush hour traffic assemble around us. I work at figuring out the trains, the token machines, the colors and codes, the square *guchi* mouths of the exit signs. The rush and roar of the subways seems more familiar already, the crush, the big city clatter off concrete and tile.

Yukiko clicks along in her high-heeled pumps, looking serene and elegant. We get off the train at Shinjuku and head north toward the Hilton. I'm oriented already— skyscrapers, left, Kabuki-cho, right. The sidewalks are packed with people jostling through the impersonal crush of rush hour. Teens are crowding into the station, headed home from school. Businessmen are arriving for an evening in Kabuki-cho—famous for sleazy bars and strip clubs. The well-dressed women are coming and going, headed home for the night. The bar girls are easy to spot, standing out in their sexy, trendier clothes.

There's a major intersection north of us, Yasukuni-Dori, and Yukiko and I slow with the crowd for the light. There's no sign that anything's wrong, but something slams me from behind. I pitch forward. Stars and galaxies flash—I've hit my head on the concrete walk.

Yukiko screams.

A guy grabs me, tosses me into a car. He's made a mistake—there's no one else there. I'm only half tracking, but that's enough. I open the door and fall out the other side.

There's dim shouting behind me. It looks like guys are chasing Yukiko. I shake my head, hoping for clarity, but I'm too far gone. This appears to be a kidnapping, but no one interferes. Everyone gets politely out of the way. It's surreal.

I can't help her. Dusk is falling, but I'm not sure it's real. I lurch from behind the car and back to the safety of the sidewalk, dodge into an alleyway. I stagger, manage to stay upright. Fading, I get further than I expect, find handy steps to slide down.

It's a bar.

The hostess says something sharp. I have a confused vision of Japanese beauty. She's tall for a woman, auburn-haired, wearing a black leather jacket and a minimal skirt. She moves toward me, and I fall into darkness and Dior cologne.

I've been had by a porcelain doll. It's a luxury to sleep, but something nags at me—a pain in my head.

I struggle awake, find there's an ice pack on my face. I'm lying on a pallet in a curtained alcove, and something is lurching and bumping beyond my head. Remembering the bar and the woman, I drop the ice pack over my eyes again, and after a while the sound goes away.

The curtain rustles, and I start, lift the ice. The cologne is familiar, though, and the dramatic eyes, the chiseled bones.

"So," the woman says. "Does your head hurt?"

"Um," I grunt.

She smiles, amused. She's an alto, very decadent and un-Japanese, smoking perfumed tobacco. She slides into a chair beside the bed.

"I called the illegal abortion doctor around the corner," she says. "You have two lumps on your head, one in front and one in back. Maybe you have a concussion, he says, but you don't need a hospital."

"Um," I say again, and manage a husky question. "What happened?"

Her eyebrows arch like crane wings.

"You don't know? *Gaijin*, how long have you been in Japan?"

"Day and a half," I say.

She laughs. She's a curious madam, young and smooth-skinned under the paint, with an unmistakable poise. The red hair is long and straight. She reaches up, flips it back over her shoulder.

"They've already been here to ask for you," she says. "*Yakuza*. Do you know who that is?"

"Well damn," I say.

"That's right," she says, honey-voiced. "The local crime syndicate."

"What did you tell them?"

"Get out," she says. "Or else pay the cover."

I laugh this time, but it hurts my head.

"I'll have to report a kidnapping," I say. "A woman was with me, Mrs. Yukiko Hanada. I'm sure they got her."

"You can report it, but it may not do much good," she says. "Do you want to go back to your hotel?"

I try to think, but the going's tough. Somehow it doesn't sound safe.

"No," I decide. "I have to go to Ito Onsen."

The painted brows take wing again, and her eyes flicker, alive under the paint.

"Why there?" she asks.

"I don't know," I say.

She looks at the ceiling and smokes, legs crossed, one elbow propped on her knee. I have a curious take on reality that makes her hazy and indistinct. Smoke curls around her like a lazy dragon, caressing the sweep of calf and thigh, the rounded curves of her throat. The light strikes sparks from her hair.

"Do you have a ticket?" she asks.

"No," I say.

"You can't go tonight, then," she says. "It's Saturday, and you'll have to wait until Monday for the ticket office to open. Do you have anywhere else to go?"

"No," I say.

"You can come to my apartment."

It's half a challenge. Her eyes are level now, wry and amused.

"What does the invitation cost?" I ask, and she laughs, stubs out her cigarette on the floor.

"Nothing," she says. "Just a few hours of your life. But you'll have to walk there. I'm not going to call you a taxi."

"Okay," I say. "I'll come."

"I'll call the police for you," she says. "My name is Kitsune."

"Anna."

She's gone then, and I shift the ice to the back of my head.

Sometime later, she's ready to go, and we climb the steps again, set off walking. Night in Kabuki-cho is a different world from the staid, formulistic day. It's a floating world that officially doesn't exist. It's outlined in neon, and noise rebounds from the walls of the shops. Traffic squeals from somewhere close. A train rattles into the station, blocks away. Raucous crowds pour into the street, and clustered shadows flood the walks. Finally it grows quieter, but now the shadowed buildings seem to loom. With my head aching, I feel my way up a rickety stair into a dark hallway. Kitsune digs in her purse for a key.

It's not what I expected. The bar was western style, all garish chrome and red vinyl sin. This may be a slum, but it's a very traditional slum. Her apartment is one room, two tatami wide, with a scarred wood entry for shoes and slatted, elegant construction beyond. There's a storage wall, a window and a long niche with a vase that looks like bronze—a *tokonoma*. The room has a faint sandalwood smell.

"Are you hungry?" asks Kitsune. She folds back doors at the entry to expose a tiny kitchenette.

"If you don't mind," I say. "I'd rather just collapse. Where's the bathroom?"

"I'm sorry," she says, "there's not one in the apartment. It's down the hall."

She produces the necessities from a chest: slippers, a miniscule towel and a cotton robe. Down the hall, I find the toilet is a hole in the floor. There's a metal-clad sink, but no bath that I can see.

Back in the room, she's laid out a futon for me on the floor. The window is open, unscreened.

I'm a long way from the hotel, and I have a moment's concern that Paul will have called the room. Too bad. Things have gone wrong somehow, and until I know how, I'll be better off here.

I'm awakened by the faintest creak of the door. It's daylight, and I've slept through the jet lag. It must be the concussion.

The door's shut already, and I'm alone in the room. I lie there a while, and decide there's nothing wrong with me that a big jar of aspirin won't fix, so I get up and have a look around. The street below is brick and six feet wide, and there are more apartments across the way. In front of them somebody's tried to plant a whole garden in six square feet of space.

The door creaks open again. It's Kitsune, with a gray robe and damp hair falling over her shoulders, so I know there's a bath somewhere.

"Good morning," she says, and hangs her towel over a rack to dry.

Oddly, she's more exotic without makeup. I had thought the hair was bleached, but there's no sign of dark roots in the tangled mass. Instead it's streaked with natural variations. Her eyes are long and sharply slanted, and her skin has the pale china tint I expected. But the clear morning light picks out the heavy line of cheekbone and jaw, and the swell of too-wide shoulders.

I stand there, while he steps up on the tatami, reaches out to touch my cheek. But then I start, lurch backward against the wall.

He gives me the smile from last night, wry and amused, half a challenge.

"Your face is a mess," he says.

I manage to get my breath. The gray robe he's wearing is a kimono, and it's raw, nubby silk.

"The bath is in the building next door," he says. "Women's side to the right."

I retreat to the bath to regroup.

There are two other women in the bath, who stare surreptitiously. We scrub and soak in the basin, and then I put on my cotton robe and go resolutely back up the stairs. Hell if he's going to demoralize me. I said I'd stay and I will.

We have burnt minnows and raw eggs for breakfast, with rice. I inspect one of the minnows, which appears to have been parched, guts, feathers and all. Likely this is a popular snack, like popcorn.

"Sorry," says Kitsune. He's digging into his own breakfast like it's great stuff.

I sigh and pop the minnow, crunch away bravely, while mixing egg slime into my rice with slippery sticks.

"*Ohashi,*" he says.

"What?"

"Chopsticks," he says. "If you're going to curse effectively, you'll need to get the Japanese part right."

"Do you have a spoon?" I ask, and he laughs.

It took a lot of little dishes to serve breakfast, but it doesn't take long to clean up. They're lacquered wood, apparently, and not very washable. He only wipes them out.

Then he sits on the tatami, produces a box of the perfumed cigarettes and a bottle of Suntory Gold whisky. I take a glass myself. It's already afternoon.

He stretches like a sensual, sleepy animal, shoves back the mass of red hair.

"Now," he says, surveying me with those odd and disquieting eyes. "Tell me how you've arranged for the *yakuza's* attentions so quickly."

"Uh," I say, "I don't really know." I'm hedging, wondering if this shouldn't be confidential. But then, I need some help. I've got no idea what I'm doing here, and I'm lucky to find someone who's charitable—if I actually have. "I'm a private investigator," I hazard. "And I'm here with an American bank official."

"To investigate a Japanese bank?"

"Yes," I admit.

"Then it must be Tokkei Ginko."

So much for my caution. If he didn't know who Yukiko Hanada was last night, he's found out by now. The efficiency worries me. I'm obviously on the wrong side of the Shinjuku tracks.

He doesn't seem to notice what I'm thinking.

"So they're involved with the *yakuza*?" he says, almost to himself. "I've never heard that."

"What?" I say.

His eyes slide over. "The *yakuza* are well-known," he explains, "and the banks they do business with. I've never heard the Tokkei was one of them."

He says it like gangsters are just another *zaibatsu* conglomerate listed on the stock exchange. I have to sigh.

"Well," I say. Actually, I've hardly met the Hanadas, but they seemed like nice people. I've been hoping the target was Colin instead. "You think they're in trouble, then?"

"Yes," he says. "They got the husband, too, later last night."

"I'm sorry to hear that," I say.

"Why are you investigating the Tokkei?" he asks.

He seems to know a lot about the Hanadas, so I might as well tell him. "Missing securities," I say.

"And why do you want to go to Ito Onsen?" Without the paint his eyes are black onyx jewels, and just as unrevealing.

"Mrs. Hanada gave me something to take to her sister."

"Ah." He smiles obscurely. "And what is it?"

"A gift." I find it in my jacket pocket, then shake my head as he holds out his hand.

"You don't know what you're carrying?" he asks.

I frown, and he leans forward and snags it, slides a sharp nail beneath the tape. It's a small wooden box, lined with velvet, and inside is a carving I first take for resin. Then I remember where I am.

Holding the ivory in his hand, for the first time Kitsune looks completely real, deft and absorbed, with all the wry humor gone from his eyes.

"What is it?" I ask.

"*Hanko-wa.*"

"What's that?"

He glances up. "A registered seal for transferring property."

He puts it back in the box and sets it on the tatami, takes one of the cigarettes out and lights it with a golden lighter. His eyes narrow in the smoke from his cigarette, and now I'm getting that dragon effect from the smoke again, this time in broad daylight.

Abruptly he stubs out the cigarette, glides to his feet.

"Let's go," he says.

"Where?"

"To Marunouchi," he says.

"The bank's closed," I say.

He shrugs. "It doesn't matter."

He stands on the street corner and looks at it, seeing what I did before, the tiny bank against a backdrop of modern, high-rise, glass and steel-framed syndicates. But clearly the view means something to him. He laughs.

"What?"

"Nothing," he says. "Let's go somewhere and eat."

He picks a hole-in-the-wall shop with surprisingly excellent food. There are no burnt minnows tonight. It's shrimp and vegetables instead, over dark, sinuous noodles. I take it he's pleased with me.

"I'll go with you," he says, "to Ito Onsen."

We're finished eating and we're only drinking now. The little vials of *sake* go down like fire. I study him over my tiny cup, and find his eyes are mocking again.

"What for?" I ask.

"So we can meet your *yakuza* there," he says.

"Oh?"

Obviously he doesn't mean to elaborate. I'm not sure I like the basic plan.

"I don't know," I say. "Shouldn't we call the police?"

"What do you have to give them?" he asks.

Nothing, of course.

"Don't you have to work?" I ask.

"No," he says, slanting his auburn head to light another cigarette. "I own the bar. I can take off if I want."

Smoke circles above us, curls around his smile. He's transmuted again—into a capitalist—something else I didn't expect. That lighter he's got is real gold.

I frown.

"How will the *yakuza* know to meet us?" I ask.

"I'll call and invite them myself."

I think about that. At minimum, it sounds dangerous. "What if they follow us on the train?" I ask.

"No one will see us." His smile widens.

He's right. No one will admit this person actually exists in Japan. I'm still wondering about him myself—especially about his motives.

"Kitsune," I say. I turn the tiny cup and watch his reflection on the pale *sake* inside—at least the reflection is visible, I think. "Why are you doing this?"

"Are you suspicious?" he jeers, and then pouts. He shoves back his hair in a calculated, effeminate move. "How could you, my dear? I'm an honest businessman."

I have a coughing fit. My *sake* has gone down the wrong way.

It's late before we get back to his room, and by then I'm too drunk to worry about what we're planning, at least until morning.

We leave on the Shinkansen, the bullet train named *Echo* for the way it runs back and forth. Kitsune is dressed in a long, pleated skirt that turns out to be pants, and a charcoal silk jacket. He's done something ornate with his hair, and when I ask, he says it's *chonmage*, the chignon that only the *sumo* still wear. Somehow it goes with the clothes.

I watch the farms flash by, feeling the quick rock of adjustment as we careen through the curves. The western style toilet on the train has instructions for use. After a while Fuji-san towers over the landscape, its snow-capped summit dwarfing the industrial smokestacks that cluster below—something that never shows up in the tourist photos. Kitsune is right. No one's even glanced at us yet—we're too improper. Still, I'm worrying.

The town of Ito Onsen isn't much, only a small crush of shops and a harbor. The sea breaks on a black sand beach where a sign warns, "Beware of Tsunami." We have reservations at a hotel that costs an amazing count of yen. Obviously, it's several times nicer than the Hilton. But we don't go past the lobby, just now. Instead, we head out for what's apparently a stationery shop.

I can't follow the Japanese. Still, as the clerk takes Kitsune's order, for the first time I have a glimmer of what's in his mind. I have to laugh.

"So when are the *yakuza* coming?" I ask.

"Tomorrow," he says. "Let's find a place to eat lunch."

By evening we're back at the hotel. It looked like an ordinary place from the outside. Inside, somehow I've fallen back into time. The rooms are built of air and a sweet, grassland scent, a pale translucency of rice paper screens. Flowers in the *tokonoma* are nakedly artistic. Outside the rain doors, a tiered garden steps down to a pool of quicksilver koi. Kimono-clad maids arrange our dinner on six-inch bamboo tables. It's an exotic banquet for two, starting with *sashimi* and ending with plumb pickles in a piercing, salty brine. There's *sake* for an army.

It's late by then, and drunk again, I head on down to the bath. The women's side is a stone cavern, the entrance screened by woven reeds. A cataract of scalding mineral water tumbles down the rocks, risen from the depths of Fuji-san. Except for me and the mist, the place is empty.

In the anteroom I strip, check out my face in the mirror. Kitsune was right. The bruising on my forehead looks awful, and it aches, but the rest of me seems okay. I sit on a tiny bench, shampoo and scrub from a wooden bucket. Then I slide beneath the waterfall.

I've been there maybe ten minutes, and I'm thinking of climbing out, when an eddy swirls in the central pool. It's Kitsune.

Time was when everyone bathed together in Japan, but not anymore.

"How did you get in here," I demand.

"From the garden," he says. "The pools are connected beneath the walls.

I frown. "Well, I'm getting out."

"Don't," he says. "Anna, I want to talk privately. The room walls are thin."

I hesitate, turn to face him again. "About the *yakuza*?"

"Yes," he says. "This could be dangerous, you know."

"Well, yeah," I say, "I thought of that."

He studies me. "You don't care?"

"It depends," I say.

"On what?" he asks.

"You're planning something?"

He's closer now, reaches out to touch my cheek again like he did in his room, but I don't flinch away this time. His fingers are light, barely perceptible.

"Yes," he says. "You've figured it out?"

"Them, maybe, but not you."

He laughs, and shakes back the red, wet mass of his hair. His hands disappear beneath the water without a ripple.

"I'm an independent, myself," he says, "always under pressure—like the Hanadas—and I like baiting the *yakuza*. Is it enough motivation?"

"Okay," I say.

"I want you to help. Do you have the nerve for it?"

"As a back-up?" I ask. "It depends."

"Will you trust me?" he asks.

"Should I?" I ask.

"No."

The invisible hands close around my waist then and he slides forward, kisses me on the mouth. It's a surprise. I thrash, kick away from him.

He laughs.

"Damn you," I say, and he disappears under the water. Maybe he'll drown, I hope.

But he doesn't. He's asleep in the room when I get back. That makes me madder than anything.

Breakfast is exotic, but also delicious. I'm irritable, regardless.

"So what are we going to do?" I ask. "Trade the *hanko* for the Hanadas?"

He's serious and ordinary this morning, elegant in a green-tinted robe.

"That's the idea," he says.

"What's going on?"

"The seal is required to transfer any of their property. It's a small bank, and I'd guess the Hanadas are under duress to sell their property to a *yakuza* development syndicate. Now the *yakuza* have the Hanadas, but not the seal, because you had it in your pocket."

"A take-over?" I ask. "And the *yakuza* stole the securities to force a closing?"

He nods.

"In Tokyo it's called *jiage*," he says. "Forced eviction."

"Well, if I'm going along, I need to know what you're going to do," I say.

He shrugs, digs into his rice with the *ohashi*. "I don't know. I'll think about it on the way to the house."

"Think about it now," I say.

Clearly he doesn't, but somehow I find I'm going along anyhow. It turns out that I just like the Hanadas.

Outside the hotel, waiting in a cool morning mist for the taxi, I stare at the moisture that catches like jewels in Kitsune's red hair. Above us, fog shroud the hills, softens the trees.

"Kitsune," I ask, as the taxi materializes from nothingness, "are you really Japanese?"

"Of course," he says. "What else would I be?"

"God knows," I say.

This morning his jacket has extended shoulders, and he's wearing elevated wooden *geta* clogs. He looks completely out of time. The taxi man appears not to notice.

We pick up our package at the stationery shop and head out for the hills. The estates here are fenced off from the road, faced with walls and high, traditional *shomen* gates. In a little while the driver stops at the address Yukiko gave me.

Kitsune pays off the taxi, turns to look up the hill at the estate.

"Yukiko Hanada doesn't have a sister," he says. "That was a lie. So the house must belong to her, and she gave you the seal to keep it safe. Likely she meant to meet you here."

The house above us has a tile roof, a walled garden, a winding drive of water-smoothed stones. It's simple and traditional, but absolutely gorgeous in this setting, framed by twisted pines and perched on a ridge with a view of rooftops falling down to the sea.

I'm starting to worry, wondering what kind of back-up Kitsune wants.

"We're early," he says as his eyes measure the line of the drive. "I wanted to look around."

The house is locked up tight. There's visually more to the grounds than actually exists. Woods behind the house must be someone else's property—it's a modest estate, after all. In the shadow of the trees, Kitsune hands me a dark, ominous shape. It's a snub-nosed thirty-eight.

"Here," he says casually. "This is for you."

It's illegal here. I wonder what the penalties are in this country for shooting a *yakuza* with an illegal gun. It's not something I want to know about. I have my mouth open to object, but it's too late. There's a car growling up the access road and in through the trees.

"Ah. There they are," Kitsune says. He heads off at a leisurely pace.

The car is a stretch limo, black and mirror-waxed. I slide behind a tree as it turns through the gate. Wind whispers through the pines like the voice of hidden *kami* spirits, and I shiver at what they have to say.

Below me, three men climb out of the car. Two of them are deferential, so the other one must be the *oyabun*—the boss. They're all dressed in the standard uniform of black suit and tie, and they look at Kitsune like he's crazy. It's a great assessment.

Three shadows remain in the car—that's likely the Hanadas, and maybe a guard. I heft the gun and wish I'd had a chance to try out the sights. The short barrel is a hazard for marksmanship.

Kitsune bows sharply, elegant in the *hakama* skirt and coat, and the *oyabun* echoes his moves—just fractionally out of step. Kitsune wears the clothes impressively, without any posturing—he's mutated again. Against the backdrop of trees and indigenous house, he makes the other man look low class and cheap.

It's an eerie scene, the collision of times and styles. Kitsune and the *oyabun* stroll down the lane, apparently discussing terms, with the bodyguards trailing behind. I edge down closer through the trees, working for shorter range. I won't trust the gun to a long shot.

The faint click of a deer-knocker measures time in the garden. Wind groans in the pines. Finally I hear the harsh guttural of masculine Japanese returning along the path. There's shrubbery here, better cover, and I crouch quickly, peer through the leaves.

Negotiations don't seem to be going well. The two men stop at the car, and one of the lackeys opens the trunk to show something. The securities? I keep my head down—I don't need to know. I'm just supposed to be watching to make sure the deal goes the way it's planned.

Kitsune is dictating, I think. He reaches into his sleeve, produces the velvet box. There's a stir from within the car. Another gangster gets out. They've seen the seal—and don't mean to pay off. There's a quick shifting. They mean to catch Kitsune against the car.

He's good. Maybe he doesn't know I've moved, but I have the same line of fire. He keeps it open. Tension escalates. I don't know what to do. Finally they make a move on him—and then I make mine.

"Hold it!" I yell, jumping out.

They jerk and freeze—English or no. My gun is obvious. My tension is blatant. I'm berserk, of course, or I wouldn't be involved in this.

Technically, though, I'm in good shape. I'm sighting parallel to the car. I've got them all together—I'm in a great position. It's too far for them to rush me, and Kitsune is off to the side.

"Get the stuff out of the car," I yell, "and the Hanadas!"

Kitsune translates. Even I can tell it's snide.

One of the lackeys opens the car door and the Hanadas climb out. They're haggard and tense, staring at the gun, at Kitsune, at the *yakuza* boss—he's white and very cold. Kitsune hands him the seal, and he nearly spits. The lackeys throw down a briefcase. The boss leaps into the car, and the driver and the bodyguards follow. They squeal off down the drive.

It appears to be all over.

The Hanadas invite us inside the house. The living room is Western style, done in tints of pale pink with white leather couches. Hanada-san makes a call to the police, and his wife makes heavy-duty drinks.

"I am so sorry," Yukiko explains to me. She's sitting on the couch, demure and sorrowful. Her highball glass is empty already. "We can't keep the bank any longer." She swirls the ice, makes it click and slide along the crystal. "We had arrangement with legitimate syndicate, but now we can't sell. We have lost the seal."

"No, you haven't," says Kitsune.

Perched formally on the sofa, he smiles and reaches into his sleeve again. When he opens his hand, the fine yellowed ivory lies there like a breath from the past. He's given the *yakuza* a resin fake, made up at the shop in town.

Paul and Colin come trailing in from Yokohama late Thursday, but it's all wound up by then. The little Tokkei Ginko has spanking new owners; the Hanadas are making plans to move to Europe, and I've got the securities locked up in the hotel's safe. I run through the story, and Paul shakes his head at the sequence of events. Colin, as usual, has his own opinion.

"Kitsune?" he says. "It's some kind of joke. Fox is the Asian trickster." He sniffs. "It's only a damn myth."

I stare at him.

Spirit talker, I think. Welcome to Japan.

Chapter 2

THE DARK MIRROR

I'm dying, I think. My mouth tastes bitter. I'm hot and cold and doubled up tight around an agony in my gut. My teeth are chattering, and my clothes are wet with sweat. All I can see is red, and I'm not sure what I last remember.

I think the blood-tinted darkness around me is sky—desert, not a cityscape now—but I don't really know. The spray of stars looks lop-sided when I can get my eyes to focus at all, but mostly I'm not bothering. Instead, I'm trying to vomit.

There's an endless cycle of pain, and then I feel better. I'm detached from the agony, and sliding away from my body, as well. There's a burst of real bliss, and then I'm flying. Desert flows under me like wind, wafting me upward on billows of smoke. I've never felt such freedom, such liberty. I'm soaring, diving at wonderful speeds, and I can see forever—into the past, the future, all the great secrets of life...

It doesn't last. Nothing that great ever does. Some guy is shaking me.

"*Senorita!*" he says. "*Senorita!*"

I try to ignore it, but he slaps me on the face, so I have to come down at least enough to answer him.

"What?" I say. "What?"

In the confusion I've forgotten to put it into Spanish, but it doesn't matter—he shifts to English.

"Are you all right?" he asks.

That doesn't matter, either.

"Leave me alone," I say in Spanish. "I was flying."

He's a silhouette against the sky, silent now and not nearly so real as the blurred, ruby stars. I feel his fingers trail over my face, a cold touch that slides along my cheekbone, pauses beneath my chin.

"What do you see?" he asks. "What colors?"

"Red," I whisper. "Everything's red."

"Alright," he says. "Go back to flying."

I drift away. I'm back in Miami then, sitting in my office, listening to Idolina Almadera tell me about her missing stepdaughter.

"Ms. Detroyer," she says in a voice like whisky and silk. She's arrayed like a movie star against my office chair, svelte and decorative in a coral designer suit, her elegant hands fumbling with a cigarette and lighter. Her face doesn't show any tension, and there's none in her eyes. I suspect there's no actual substance to the woman, no bona fide reality. "The police say it's out of their jurisdiction," she continues. "I don't think the embassy has even tried." She snaps the lighter sharply. The tip of her cigarette flares, and she exhales a luxurious cloud. "The FBI insists they have to have some proof of a kidnapping before they can investigate a case."

"And you don't have any?" I ask.

"No," she says. "Of course we don't."

She's tall, a lush mouth, a severe hairstyle—but that doesn't matter a bit. The tight, pale upsweep of her hair only exposes the gorgeous bones of her face more clearly. The woman makes our office look cheap and rundown. Sometimes I feel like a decent-looking gal myself—but not today. Not with her sitting there in my office chair.

Her lips tighten faintly. "I'm so worried about my... my daughter," she says. "Elysia is...spoiled, perhaps, but she would never go off to Mexico with anyone, not even a boyfriend, without first letting her father and me know. We haven't heard from her in weeks."

Looking at the cool way Idolina sits there, at the clear, unmistakable evidence of trophy status, I wonder how much time she's actually spent with the girl.

"You have a photo?"

The daughter looks very much like her step-mother— about the same age, too, but shorter and smaller-breasted, less self-assured. In the snapshot a guy's got his arm around her shoulders.

"Is this her boyfriend?" I ask.

"Yes," says Idolina. "She met him at school here in Miami. That's why we thought we should hire private investigators here...locally, rather than so far away in New York. Your agency has come recommended."

"We do pretty well," I say. "Do you know anything about this guy?"

Traffic growls from the street outside, and she shifts her eyes to study the blinds that hide it from view. "Very little," she says. "Elysia wrote that his name was Edward Montoya."

"Mexican?"

"Columbian, I think."

It rang an alarm, even then.

"This is going to be a disaster," I say to Paul, falling into the chair in his office next door.

He only looks more obstinate. It's a minor change in his expression, the faintest of quirks around eyes and mouth—but I can read the signs by now. "Paul," I insist, "it's going to be about drugs. You know it as well as I do."

"That doesn't matter," he says. "We still have to do it." He goes on making notes, flipping through his calendar. He's switching his appointments around so he can go to Mexico.

I curse at him, and he glances up.

What's my issue with Paul Angstrom? Maybe it's just that he's an old habit. The office has his name and mine on the door, which ties us together tighter than marriage, in some ways. Or at least I've thought it did.

Our business has grown a lot since the first years. We started off with a few divorce cases and some missing heirs, and then expanded to take on some pretty interesting variations. We still do the divorces and missing heirs, of course, but we've become known for dealing with a lot of things other detective agencies wouldn't touch.

"The commissioner," he says, "has asked for a favor."

"The family is pulling strings?" I should have guessed that already. Almadera is a stockholder in a local restaurant chain and he's got a brand new, exclusive mansion down in Coral Gables, right on the water. "But why us?"

"Because we're here," Paul says. "And we know something about the trade."

"The drug trade? Paul, why don't they call the DEA? Isn't drug trafficking a government job?"

He shakes his head.

"All this is just preliminary," he says. "It won't be a problem. We go down like it's a vacation, ask around. If we think it's drugs, then we can call the government to go in." He shrugs his shoulders. "Look. The kids could just be having a good time—but whatever's going on, we have to get that girl back to Almadera before any trouble comes down. You can't say no to a man like that."

"Paul," I say, "do you think he cares? He didn't even come down here himself."

He looks up at me then. His eyes are sapphire chips in the brown of his face, and just as cold. The line of his jaw is clenched and hard, belying that reasonable tone.

"Anna, don't argue," he says. "We've got to do it." Then he adds, "Did you take care of your appointments?"

"Son-of-a-bitch," I say.

I think I was referring to him. There are more insights in hindsight, of course. It's a strange delusion, this dream, and now it turns vague and misty. I see a lot of people dead as I'm flying, but I'm not surprised by that. Blood and death seem to be everywhere. Then all of the sudden things start to close down on me. I'm not sure what's real and what's not—I start to panic, to breathe in hard, desperate gasps, to struggle and thrash.

Someone's holding me down. There are voices—I just can't hear what they're saying to me. Then the dream shifts again, so it doesn't matter anymore. I've got a rosy afterglow, and a terrible desire to sleep—so I do.

I wake up with a roof over my head. That item, not surprisingly, feels like it's going to explode. There are serious things wrong with it. My gut hurts, too, and periodically it clenches up in hard cramps that curl me tightly around inner space.

I open my eyes, shut them fast against a searing glare. It's morning. One glimpse is enough to tell me roughly where I am. It's not comforting.

I'm in a crude hut. It's a mud and stone structure with a dirt floor, a thatched roof. The door is the only opening I can see. It's half-closed by a blanket hooked off to the side. A mega-shaft of sun cuts through dancing dust motes in the opening and stabs into my eyes like a knife.

I'm lying on the ground, on another blanket. There's a battered chest of drawers in the room, a couple of baskets and two people. They're both *Indios*, I think, but they don't match.

The woman is praying, her fingers working down the beads of a rosary. She's dressed in white, the embroidered *huipil* smock that Mexican *Indios* wear. The man is sitting closer to me, cross-legged, and his shadow turns its head as I groan. The light plays across him, but fails to reveal. The effect only makes him darker and less visible.

"*Buenas, senorita,*" he says. "How are you feeling?"

"Is she praying because I'm going to die?" I ask.

"No," he says.

That confirms what I've been thinking. This is the worst hangover I've ever had in my life.

"How did I get here?" I ask.

He shifts one hand, sets down a dark pottery bowl.

"I found you on the road last night."

His voice is harsh and cool, almost familiar. It must be the voice from my dream.

"Uh. Well, thanks for dragging me out of the road," I say. I get one hand up to check my aching head. There is something worse than a hangover affecting it. There's a goose egg over my right ear, accompanied by a smear of sticky blood. I ease in a breath carefully, so as not to jar the world unnecessarily. "Do you have any idea how I got there?" I ask.

"No," he says, "don't you?"

I consider. I have vague notions, but I don't want to discuss them right now.

"What's your name?" he asks.

"Anna Detroyer," I say. The light's not so bad now, still blocked by my hand. I struggle carefully into a sitting position, slide backward out of the glare. "What's yours?"

"Espejo," he says, "Saturniño Espejo. Where have you come from?"

"Miami," I say. "I took a wrong turn. Is that coffee you have?"

"No," he says. "But it will have the same effect."

Getting my head out of the light has almost killed the aura that framed him. A better look at the man confirms what I'd guessed before. The woman matches the house, but he doesn't. He looks affluent as a slumming *yaqui*. Dressed in a knit polo, leather jacket and slacks, he's the picture of an upscale local yuppie. I remember headlights in the night, a nice car. Obviously he's not on the usual career path for a Mexican Native American, but still the face is unmistakable—more so even than the woman's.

She's like a statue, watching us. He glances at her and she starts, shuffles out. She goes to a fire and brings back another cup for me.

It's a dark, watery mixture, very black. I'd rather have my usual coffee, but I'm willing to try anything. I need some caffeine.

"God," I say, sorry at once. "What is this?"

"Cocoa."

"It needs sugar." I sigh. "Do you have any aspirin?"

"No," he says.

That's too bad. It would have helped a lot.

"So," I say, "what happened to me last night?"

"It was *datura*," he says. "Also known as devil's weed."

It rings a bell.

"Jimson?" I ask.

"Yes."

"Damn," I say, and fumble for his first question over an aching distance. "What else could I have seen besides red?"

"Black," he says.

"What would that have meant?"

"That you were dying. Apparently you have an affinity for the drug, *senorita*." He studies my face over the stained rim of his cup. The man is dark and cold, like his name. "Are you part *Indio*?" he asks.

There's nothing wrong with his eyes.

"Yes," I admit, "but not local."

"Ah," he says.

"Uh. Listen," I say, "I hate to impose on you any more, but would you mind giving me a lift back into Mexico City?"

"Of course," he says. "I had meant to offer. Do you need a doctor, *senorita*?"

I consider. I feel rotten, barely functional.

"No," I say. "I'll live."

I don't like the way the woman looks at him. She's scared. Her eyes follow us as we go outside, watching something I can't quite see. The sun glints off a late model Jaguar that's parked by the rude hut. It's very sleek and sporty. I lay one hand on the glossy roof, turn back to the woman.

"Thank you," I say, but she only stares at me impassively. Her black eyes are shuttered pools of darkness in a wide-boned *Indio* face.

Espejo gets the door for me, closes me into the car. He climbs in on his side, starts the engine to purring. For a while we jostle along a dirt track, and then intersect a better highway further on. The profile beside me is fierce and cruel—pre-Columbian—the hawk nose and almond eyes made even more dramatic by a flash of gold at wrist and throat. The man is quick, competent and very relaxed, driving over the highway. There's a lot of silence in the car.

"Are you visiting Mexico City alone?" he asks me finally.

"No," I say. "I've come with a...a friend."

Paul qualifies, I guess. I should have some other man in my life than a business partner, but I don't. I just don't have the time—or maybe it's inclination I lack. When he first asked me to work with him, I thought there could be a real spark between us. It wasn't long before I figured out he has more of an eye for advantage, but still...Well, maybe I'm just a masochist.

"Where are we headed?" I ask. By now I can see it's not straight into town. We're climbing into what looks like foothills.

"To my home," he says. "It's closer, and I thought you might want something for your headache."

"Thanks," I say.

I place the scenery then. We're in Bosque de las Lomas, an upscale district west of the main city. Ajusco looms above us, the shaft of an ancient volcano, smoky with pine and eucalyptus that clings like lace to the arc of the cone. Mansions built with oil money flash here and there through the trees. Climbing the winding road at dangerous speeds, we glimpse drives that wind into obscurity, gates posted with "Keep Out" signs. Eventually we turn into one of the drives. The house juts from the hill like an outcrop of indigenous stone, and there's a business-like steel gate. As we pass through it, I catch sight of uniformed guards sporting full automatics. The gentry are serious about those signs.

A *mozo* in a blue uniform helps me out of the car. The house is sheer-faced on this side, an archaic post and lintel construction ornamented with *Indio* designs. The shrubbery looks artfully accidental. The drive is already invisible as we step into the courtyard. It's all very simple, very expensive. Espejo leads the way up a low, smooth set of steps and in through a set of carved wooden doors.

Inside is a cool grotto of stone, dark as night after the blazing sun outdoors. We're met by the quiet shuffle of servants' feet.

"Something for the *senorita's* headache," says Saturniño. When my eyes adjust, he's already gone. A stoic *Indio* woman ushers me into a bath to freshen up, and then she plies me with aspirin. That done, she ushers me into a library to use the phone. Mine seems to be gone.

I try the hotel. Paul's not in his room. My host is still missing, and I'm afflicted by a sudden wave of vertigo. I ease down on the sofa, drop my head onto my knees. After a moment the sickness eases off, and I wonder who else I should call. The police?

Not yet.

I'm facing a glass wall that opens onto a breathtaking, empty plunge into space. That's the capital spread below me in all its smudged glory. Trapped in a dry lakebed, Mexico City accumulates pollution in a permanent, smoky cloud that makes it perpetually dim and eerie, a jumble of unreality, half-obscured by the haze.

Espejo still hasn't reappeared, but a maid shows up with a beer. It's cold and it helps—in a few minutes I feel nearly alive again. I heave to my feet and have a look around the room.

In some ways the house seems as ancient as the earth it's built on. The columns between the windows are carved like the outside in abstract low relief. The floors are dark flagstone, polished and smooth underfoot, and the walls are painted around the doorways with frescoes in bright colors. There's a maze of bookshelves, with glass cases set between them.

The first few are empty, the glass cracked and shattered. Beyond that lies the history of Ciudad de Mexico, laid out in artifacts beyond value.

I find a lustrous drum carved as a dying man, an ornate sacrificial knife, a collection of discolored bones and skulls set with turquoise and jet. There's actually a codex in one of the cases. Aztec priests dance across the leather pages— black robes, long hair, black-painted faces with ideograms on their cheeks. Other figures have black-painted faces with white bars over the eyes and mouth.

That takes me a minute of groping. These were the eight creator-born, I recall, four male and four female gods, holding up the four corners of the world. There's little information available on most of them—the Spaniards recording the lore considered them inconsequential. Instead, Feathered Serpent and his rival Tezcatlipoca get all of the press.

Emphasis on the two was a major split in Aztec philosophy from the rest of Mexico, and a major reason for the Aztecs' particular, bloodthirsty history. The Aztecs had just fulfilled a prophecy the year Hernán Cortés showed up, the unification of Mexico under one rule—and they knew all the time they were worshiping the wrong god. A hundred and twenty thousand sacrifices to consecrate Mexico City was an excess in anybody's book. Monteczuma just knew Cortés was Feathered Serpent come to punish him, and so he...

"Do you like my collection?"

I start and wince. My host has that misty aura again. He's silhouetted against the wall of glass.

"Yes," I say.

"Some of it's missing, as you can see from the broken cases. There was a robbery here just recently. Let me show you something else."

He turns, and I follow him without any thought.

It's a wall of black stone he's leading me to, a pool of darkness that roils with spectral ghosts and half-seen, inky images of luminous light. As I walk toward it, my reflection splinters and flashes like sun off cut diamonds. For an instant I feel the vertigo again, close my eyes against a wave of sickness. When I open them, it's only a wall again. I manage to suck in a breath.

"What's this stone," I ask. "Marble?"

"Obsidian," he says.

I swivel and turn my back to it, facing him instead.

"The Smoking Mirror?"

"Yes," he says.

My breath shudders out. Suddenly my heart is beating hard, and I feel the darkness descend in earnest, laced with the red haze of last night's bloody dream. There's a fortune lining the walls here, the masks and ornaments set with jewels, the jaguars of jade, the pottery and inlaid skulls. They're museum pieces if ever I saw them, hidden away here in a completely private collection. It's only the gold that's missing.

"Where did you get these things?" I ask slowly.

Caught in the cloudy light, Saturniño's face is indistinct. Only his eyes are visible, veiled and impassive as the obsidian behind me. His voice comes to me from a distance.

"I'm a conservator of history," he says.

"A what?" I ask.

"Do you think I have no right to these things?" he asks.

"You've bought them honestly?"

"I'm a rich man," he says. His outline turns to study the black, living face of the wall. "I speculate."

"In what?" I ask. "Souls?"

The question has risen out of nowhere. His eyes cut across at me—a dark glitter like the polished stone.

"All wealthy men deal in souls," he says.

I take a breath. "Not mine, I hope."

"I can hardly avoid it," he says.

That shudder within me rises again. I'm getting lost in this. I close my eyes and take another breath, groping for something real.

"I saw...faces in the mirror," I whisper. "Which of them do I believe?"

"All," he says. "The mirror is a continuum. It shows mortals their life."

Approaching it, he's had no reflection at all.

"I have to go back to the hotel," I say.

He gestures.

"You're welcome to stay here as long as you wish."

"I want to go now," I insist.

"Of course," he says, cool and dispassionate. Sunlight glints off the gold at his throat, catches a diamond-set Rolex. "I'll have my chauffeur to drive you in."

I sway on my feet. I'm not sure I believe him, and I don't until I'm in an actual car and headed down the drive. I turn to look behind us, but the house is gone by the time we reach the gate. Passing through it, I close my eyes and lean back against the seat of the sedan. I can feel the place there behind me, still heavy with the darkness I woke up with this morning.

We follow a winding parkway that eventually transforms to the twelve traffic-choked lanes of Paseo de la Reforma. Palm trees clutter the esplanade, broken by towering monuments and *glorieta* traffic circles. We turn into the hotel, where the *mozo* lets me out of the car. I'm all the way up in the elevator and into my room before the sick feeling is gone from my gut.

There's no sign Paul has been to his room. I sit in mine and look around. I'm unsettled by the night, by the drugs, by Saturniño Espejo and his cache of ancient, terrifying treasures.

And now I have to deal with other things. It would help if I could remember exactly what happened to me last night. There was a warehouse, I think. Paul and I separated, looking for a way to get in. I was supposed to...I was... dammit, dammit. I have no idea if I can even find that same place again—it's all gone to haze in my brain. Maybe it's the whack on the head that's causing this amnesia.

But if Paul's not here, I really, really need to find him. So how do I start? The question leads to other problems. For example, where is our rental car?

Maybe I should notify the agency that I've lost it. Then too, maybe not. Still, they might be suspicious when I ask to rent another one.

In my current state, this is a serious problem. I rub my eyes and wince.

Anna, there are more rental agencies in the world. All you have to do is find one with a different computer system. Meanwhile, I can start with just a taxi.

Soon I've gotten another car, but I haven't come up with a plan yet. I still intend to look around. It was only yesterday after all, and now I've found vague memories of what we did—landmarks, events. How the warehouse looked from the street.

Urgency is nagging at me like the pain in my head. I know something is seriously wrong. I'm worried about Paul, but I can't justify calling the cops.

Besides, they wouldn't talk to me. I don't have any information, and not enough cash for the bribe it would probably take to make them look at me seriously.

I shouldn't be driving. I'm still feeling sick. Light shears off the pavement and the peeling stucco in hot, bright flares. Traffic is impossible, with crowds of people clogging the narrow streets where I want to drive, spilling off the sidewalks in endless, breaking waves. I'm thinking this area looks familiar, but I'm not sure.

Besides that, it's late afternoon, and I've forgotten to eat. There's a street vendor selling tamales and soft drinks on the next corner. I find a place to park the car, give the woman a handful of pesos.

"*Chica*," she says to me, "where did you lose the handsome *gringo*?"

I nearly choke, half way through one of her tamales.

"Uh. Which one?" I ask.

"The pretty blond one, girl."

That's a clear enough description of Paul. "I'm looking for him now," I admit.

She clicks her tongue at that.

"Looking for him, *chica*?"

"Yes, I'm lost. I was supposed to meet him at the same place as yesterday..."

She turns. "Santiago!" she yells. A brown kid pops up from the sidewalk, weaves through the crowd.

The woman says, "Take this *senorita* back to where we saw her last night." The kid grins, holds out his hand for a dollar bill.

I give him a five. It's cheap at the price.

It's a hole-in-the-wall *cantina*, and the warehouse I'm looking for is right there behind it.

Memory jogs into place. Paul had contacts on the police force that located the kids for us—for only a minimal bribe.

Probably Montoya had paid them off, too, but even cops have to live. Paul and I took what we had, set up to watch and see what they were into. Finally, we followed them here.

And there the memory ends.

I get a beer in the *cantina* and something more substantial to eat—a plate of rice and refried beans. Glancing around, I don't like the looks of the place. It's not somewhere I want to be hanging around after dark. That decided, I pay the waiter and head out down the sidewalk. Then I double back and come up in the alleyway behind the kitchen. If I was here last night—and I'm sure now I was—something happened that left me lying drugged and sick in the road a long way out of town. I'd be stupid to let it happen again.

I loiter out of sight until dusk, then work deeper into the alleyways, headed for the warehouse. The chain link and barbed wire fence rips a hole in my jeans as I go over. I catch a whiff of decay and follow it downwind to a body. It's the night watchman, dumped in the trash. The victim is uniformed, still wearing his gun. I'm not exactly in a condition to be carrying one myself, but here it is—offered in a way I can't refuse. The body's a warning if ever I saw one. Maybe I should stop and call the police now, but I still don't have my phone. I'd have to leave to look for one. I'm really worried about what might have happened to Paul.

I circle the warehouse, looking for a way to get in. There's nothing visible. I'm crazy to be doing this. I'm still feeling nauseous, and my vision fades in and out if I move too fast. But I can't get over the urgency, the idea that Paul's in there somewhere. And that I need to get in there, too. I can't leave him in danger.

Noise from the *cantina* drifts through the night air. Something squeaks and skitters off to the right—maybe a rat. The walls of the building are rusted sheet metal, and likely the roof is, too. In the dark I can't see any windows, but now I vaguely remember them from the daylight—high up, on the second floor. And somewhere, there was a folded fire escape.

It's not long before I've found it. The thing is rickety, rusted out until it's a real hazard. I jump for it, gasp and grunt, then haul myself up. A window at the top of it is already broken. Inside, it's dark as a pit. I get the gun out and wait a while for my eyes to adjust—wait for my breath to slow down and my head to stop spinning. Vague moon shadows resolve into office furniture. A mosaic of bright shards trims the floor. I'm tracking badly. I didn't think to bring what I'd need—like a flashlight. I'll have to be careful not to fall down the stairs.

I start at a movement behind me and lift the gun. The moonlight catches a glint of pale hair.

"Anna?"

I fall against the partition.

"Paul," I whisper. "Dammit."

"Anna, where the hell have you been?"

Right. Now I remember. I was supposed to get some rest, show up for my turn at a stake out this morning—we'd meant to watch for the kids to come around, to make sure this was the place they were conducting their business. Somehow I just never made it back to the hotel.

I close my eyes, feeling Paul suddenly close against me, his breath in my hair, his hand on my face.

"Anna?"

He shakes at me when I don't answer right away.

"Easy," I say. "My head will fall off."

"Are you okay?" he asks.

His fingers stroke through my hair. I jerk my face into his shoulder before he can find the knot over my ear. Pain radiates down my neck at the movement.

"Don't," I say. I open my eyes, try to find the outlines of his face above me. I'm comforted by his warmth, the touch of his hands, the shape of his big shoulders in the darkness above me. I shiver a little, but then it's gone.

"What happened?" he asks.

"Somebody whacked me on the head," I say, and don't go into detail about being drugged—likely most of it was a dream anyhow. I was lucky. I could have ended up in the trash like the watchman.

"Where'd you get the gun?" he asks.

"Guy in the alley," I say. "He's dead."

I ease back away from him, slide the thing behind me and under the waistband of my jeans.

"So what's going on?" I ask. "Have you been out here by yourself since last night?"

"Yeah," he says. "In the general neighborhood, at least. With the car still there, I didn't know where to look for you." His voice intensifies, barely a breath in my ear. "Listen, Anna, it's not drugs the kids are into here. Come on," he says, and pulls at my wrist. "You've got to see this."

We feel our way down the stairs. It's pitch black on the warehouse floor below, dark as a trek through the underworld. Paul has a pencil-thin beam that slashes in front of us intermittently, picks out a pathway through mountainous crates and the dark, oil-scented shapes of machines.

"They're smuggling antiquities," he whispers.

"What? You mean *stolen* antiquities?"

"Yeah," he says. "What else?"

I jerk to a stop.

"Paul..."

"Before we get the hell out of here..."

"I thought we were going to get the Almadera girl out," I say.

"We can't," he says. "We'll have to leave her for the police."

"What about the commissioner?" I ask.

"We can't help it," he says.

"Paul...her dad..."

"We'll have to tell him where she is and let them handle it," he says. "Really, Anna. We can't kidnap her and drag her back home on a plane.

"Look at this," he insists. His shape fumbles at one of the crates. It's open, and he jerks back the packing, triggers the light. The beaten gold rim of an *Indio* mask flares into existence. Paul runs his hand along the edge, his face intent in the golden backwash of light. "Anna," he says, "just think what you could do with just one piece of this haul."

I have to touch it, myself. The gold burns like molten fire in the unsteady glow of his flash. Vertigo breathes on me. A faint red-shift flicks at my vision. I jerk my hand back like it's burnt.

"Paul," I say.

"Yeah."

I can't breathe. "Paul," I whisper, "don't touch it."

"Anna, look," he says, "who really owns this stuff? The Mexican government? What if..."

Seduction whispers at me, and an eerie, rising terror. I turn on Paul suddenly, grab at his wrist.

"For God's sake, Paul, let's get out of here."

"Anna...what..." he begins.

"Now, Paul."

But it's already too late.

"Well, there you are," says a nasal voice. I jerk around as a flash lights above us. Elysia Almadera is standing on the catwalk. She's got a nine-millimeter pistol in her hand, already leveled and ready. It doesn't seem like she's meaning to talk. The hammer cocks back in a terrible slow motion, and then the pistol goes off. Hot wetness spatters my face. My shoulder goes numb, and I rock backward, stagger again as something slaps my cheek. Fire blossoms again, and then I'm falling.

Blackness closes around me, shot with red.

I can't move. I can't do anything but lie there and wait for the woman to shoot me again. Light plays over my closed eyes, dances along the wall. I've got no strength to move, none to object.

"Got them," she says.

Another voice has joined hers then. It argues, accuses. They shout at one another, and then the light's gone away. God, the woman is a psychopath. How did her step-mother not know that?

I suck in a breath, raise one hand to my face. It's wet all down the right side. The air is full of a metallic, coppery scent. My jeans and shirt are soaked, cling to me as I move. Somehow I don't think all the blood is mine.

"Paul?" I say. "Paul?"

There's a dead weight across my thighs. I work my legs out from under him, search for the flash. It's broken, but when I shake it, it flares.

His face is bloody and ashen pale. I can't find a pulse.

I reel there on my knees, lean against the wall. That red haze is in front of my eyes again. But it's not from drugs this time.

I shove to my feet. The gun is still there in my waistband. Then it's somehow in my hand. I'm moving across the floor. Moonlight flares through a window above me, ignites a shadow in my way.

I jerk backward against the wall, but then I recognize the man. I gasp.

"Espejo, what are you doing here?"

"I followed you, Anna Detroyer."

"And brought your personal army along?" My voice is shaking. My shoulder is starting to ache now in fiery, rippling waves, accompaniment to the pain in my cheek. "What do you want?" I pant.

"Only the gold," he says.

"It's yours?" I ask. "Espejo, do you think I had something to do with this?"

I'm shaking all over now. My breath sounds like I've been running, hoarse and rasping in the darkness. Espejo is as still and silent as ever. He's as hard and cold as stone. His voice seems harsh and disembodied, echoing eerily off concrete and steel.

"No," he says. "But I could feel your involvement—your centrality. I knew you would lead me to it. Now there is something else you must do, spirit talker. You are caught in this, and so you must make a decision," he says. "What will you give to safely leave this place? What will you leave and what will you take away with you? The choice lies before you."

I touch the medicine pouch on my chest. How does the man know I'm a spirit talker? My breath hisses out between my teeth.

"Wait," I say. I lurch and reach for him. But it's too late to discuss terms now. He's gone into the gaping cavern of darkness.

So this is a morality play, after all. Choose what you want, Anna Detroyer? What the hell am I supposed to do? This is a complex situation, with lots of people involved. I'm not exactly making all the decisions, and I can barely stand up, much less think straight.

But it's too late to think about it. Guns explode around the corner, the rattle of automatic fire. I flinch and duck. The gold is there behind me. The gun's still in my hand—a hard, angular lump digging into my palm.

I hear running footsteps, echoing, distorted and clattering as they come down the stairs. Voices follow. It's the man and woman I heard before. My lips skin back from my teeth. Red flames sear at my eyes. The scent of blood fills my nostrils.

I know the two of them.

It's the fire escape they want. Espejo and his men will have the other exits sealed. The two could make it to safety, but they won't go for it. First they'll try for the gold.

I back up, fumble for the edge of the crate, slide into inky shadows behind it. Elysia's golden head appears first, a flash in the moonlight. But it's more than just the two of them. They've brought their own dark army to this war. Boots rasp and thud along the concrete floor. Voices pant and whisper, equipment clatters. None of it seems real to me, only the pale blur of Elysia's golden head. She's killed Paul, I think, and now I've got her in my sights. My hand tightens around the pistol grips, slippery with blood. Red mists dance in front of my eyes.

So, Anna Detroyer, what is it you really want? I heave for breath, feel the power fetishes flare on my chest like a ghostly presence. Suddenly I've got control again, and a cold, icy sense of reality jars down. It's not this I want—not revenge.

I shudder and relax, let the gun fall against my thigh. My head drops against the rough wood of the crate.

Then I jerk flat at a spray of automatic fire. Flames spurt in the darkness. Splinters fly. Slugs impact the wall behind me, spang away through the thin metal sheet of the walls. Screams fill the air. Then all of it stutters and dies to silence.

I lie on my belly behind the crates for what seems like forever. There's nothing—no sound. And then that whisper of sense again: Anna, you need to get out of here. I push up out of the shadow and nearly fall over a body.

There's a wild tangle of golden hair, pale arms flung wide—all of it spattered with blood. I stagger and then steady, lean above her. I nearly murdered this woman myself a moment ago, but instead Espejo has done the job for me.

A harsh scuff of boots sounds to my right. Lights flash and shimmer along the walls. On automatic, I pivot and back up, swing my gun around. I don't know what they mean to do—but whatever condition Paul's really in, he's still lying there behind me, and I don't plan to let them touch him.

The troops suddenly realize I'm there. Someone shouts, and their lights snap out. A shot zings above my head, and I duck again, line up my sights on the flash.

"No," says a voice from beside me. I gasp and swivel to cover Espejo. He's materialized from nothingness, standing there right next to Paul. The troops respond, adjusting their positions. I don't care—I've turned my back on them now.

"Get away from him," I say, surprised at my coldness.

Espejo raises his voice then, talking to the invisible army. "Go," he says. "This is of no matter. Bring the trucks."

The shadows clatter and fade from behind us, along with a final shimmer of torchlight. All I have to see by now is the moon, the dim filter of light down the stairs.

I need desperately to lean against a crate, against a wall, anything—but I won't do that just yet. I manage to suck in a breath, twitch to ease the blazing pain in my shoulder.

"What do you want, Espejo?"

His dark head turns away from me, revealing the ancient, elemental profile.

"The gods are an expression of nature," he says. "You can't expect them to be kind—only reasonable."

He takes a step, looks over the bloody carnage—at the girl, down at Paul—surveying them without expression, only the cold, impassive cruelty that's native to his face. I feel a chill run up my spine, a whisper of eternal cold.

"Is that what the mirror tells you?"

"It reveals the dark shadows of the soul," he says. "That which gives mortals knowledge, and the means to make a choice." His obsidian eyes slide back to me then, and the moonlight casts pale bars across the dark mask of his face. "Spirit talker, I see that you've made your choice," he says.

I close my eyes. "Is he alive?" I ask.

"As you want," he says. He spreads his hands.

Espejo moves away. I keep the gun aimed dead at his heart, take his place above Paul and feel for a pulse. The bastard wasn't lying. I can feel a pulse-beat this time, clear and strong under my fingertips.

Relieved, I glance down for a second. When I look up again, Espejo is gone, faded into the dark shadows of the underworld.

I don't care.

He's left me Paul, alive and breathing.

Chapter 3

DEATH IN NAIROBI

I'm investigating luggage theft for Lufthansa this week, playing bait, and in a brief swing through Europe and the Mediterranean my luggage has been stolen twenty-seven times. In eleven cases, the thieves were airline employees. Eight of the other bandits were professional types—doctors, lawyers, businessmen. Somehow I'm not surprised by the stats.

The luggage tour has veered south, worked its way through Egypt and Tanzania, and now we're going to wind it up in Nairobi. For the fourth time, I'm standing in line at Jomo Kenyatta International Airport for a visa stamp. My dark skin blends in with the crowd, even if my face doesn't quite fit. I shift from one foot to the other, search visibly through my purse. I jiggle the lure, set it down and move a few steps away. The lure is an expensive-looking piece of luggage I've been towing behind me, and I'm much better dressed than I normally would be on my pittance of a salary—courtesy of Lufthansa—like maybe I'd have high-priced jewelry in the bag. Within seconds, a man excuses himself through the line, headed for the restrooms on the other side of the terminal. As he goes by me, he snaps at the hook. Security nets him within a few yards, and he leaps and thrashes like any fish, tries to run. The waiting line flinches, startled and ready to duck, but nobody gives up their spot. The immigration guy hardly looks up.

The commotion dies down, and I step out of the queue like I'm headed to get my bag back. Actually, we're going to call it a wrap, and I'm set up for a meeting with the Lufthansa agent in his office. He's tall and polite and offers to help me with local arrangements, but I've already got things set up with my friend Sylvia. Before I fly back to Miami, I'm going take a few days off to see some of the countryside here.

I head back to the claim area for my real bag then, a duffel that's quite a bit scruffier than the decoy and completely unlikely to get stolen. On the other side of the gates, I run smack into Sylvia.

"Anna!" she shrieks and grabs me in a hug, duffel and all. "Did you bring Paul?"

I manage to get my breath.

"God. No," I croak.

"But I thought..." Then she catches my expression. "Oh, Anna, what...?"

I don't really want to talk about it. He's been drifting even farther away from me since our recent job in Mexico—like something happened inside him when he was almost killed. I'd wondered if the dangers of the job were suddenly getting to him, but instead it almost seemed to be me. Did he think he owed me his life, maybe? Was that what suddenly made him uncomfortable around me?

"Somebody's got to watch the shop." I shrug and dredge up a crooked grin.

It's glossed over the awkwardness, and Sylvia gallops ahead. "Well, is this all your luggage? God, Anna," she says, "but you look great. It's been such a long time . . ."

Jomo Kenyatta International Airport is eleven minutes from downtown, per the travel guide. My impression of the city is bright flashes: mosques, bazaars, and curio shops flashing by the car windows, a tangle of streets, all brash with noise and color. A few years ago, people were still killed by lions in the streets of Nairobi, but now the old colonial core is surrounded by high-rise office blocks and modern apartment towers. I get a glimpse of slums around the outskirts, tin-roofed shanty towns that house the migrant unemployed. Still, overall, my impression is that the place is thriving.

Sylvia is, too. She's a golden blonde, seared by the tropics and noticeably ripened since Miami Dade Junior College— how many years ago, now? She went on for a master's degree and now she's in love with an older man, from her letters, a wildlife researcher that she's anxious for me to meet.

"Wendall's going to wait for us at Abdul-al's," she says. I've got no idea where that is, but it's okay with me. She accelerates like a NASCAR driver, then slams her foot down on the brake. We lurch to a stop, cut off by a mass of cyclists. "I'd hoped he could take you out to the research camp," she says, frowning pensively and biting her lip, "but now . . ."

Whatever that thought is, she's forgotten it in a second and accelerates into traffic again. She chatters on about local sights as I nod and smile, clutching the car seat in terror.

I briefly relax as we stop at her apartment to ditch the duffel. But then we're off to see Abdul-al's and her darling sweetie, Wendall.

Abdul-al's appears to be a restaurant and bar jammed in behind an old market. There's a flight of steps down, beaded curtains, an impression of alcoves for dining, and a mahogany bar. It's dark and cool inside, quiet as a sigh after the garish-bright glare of equatorial streets. The waiters slip by on soundless feet, and someone who must be Abdul-al himself greets us, a pale shade in white Muslim robes and a cap.

"Ah, Ms. Westlake." He has a soft voice, a welcoming smile in a dark, bristly beard. "The gentlemen are waiting."

Gentlemen?

Sylvia is fast. She's had to arrange this little addendum while I was making my pit stop at her apartment.

"Shut up," she says, catching my eye. I decide to take it in the spirit it's offered.

Wendall doesn't look like a handsome, darling sweetie to me—but of course that's all a matter of taste. He's a smallish man with a sunburnt dome and tufts of hair like pampas grass sprouting above both ears. He smiles at me distantly and forgets completely to shake hands.

The other guy does better. He's movie star-ish and maybe thirty-five: light-brown hair, aviator glasses, and heavy, muscular arms. He reminds me of Paul—but then, that's my taste showing. Sylvia would know what type I go for.

"I'm Carson Stern," he says, standing and extending a friendly hand. "I work with Dr. Wendall Holmes Harriman, and I'm"—he glances at Wendall, apparently to see if he's noticed the "Holmes" part—"extremely flattered to be associated with someone who is so noted at the famous Serengeti Research Institute."

"Huh?" I say. "I mean, what for?"

"In his research on lions, of course."

"Oh. Uh . . ."

We sit down. Wendall stares into the middle distance. Stern is teasing both of us, but his grin quickly dies. He's distracted, too. Actually, when I notice it, they all look pretty grim.

They order Bloody Marys, Nile perch, and fried bread. It sounds good to me, so I follow suit. Then I plan to relax and follow the conversation as the first round of drinks starts to have its effect. There isn't any conversation.

"What's wrong?" I ask, finally.

They've forgotten I'm along. Sylvia actually starts. It's Carson who explains.

"Someone was killed last night out in the bush," he says, "apparently by a lion."

That's why, I assume, my trip out to Wendall's camp may be off.

"Oh?" It seems a safe comment.

"This is disgraceful," fumes Wendall. He flaps his napkin, repositions it in his lap. "I have been barred from all activities until the problem is solved."

"Oh," I say again. "Ah. That's too bad." I'm wondering if somehow I could get another drink. "How is a problem like that usually solved?"

"Well," says Sylvia. Her eyes skate sideways at Wendall. "If it is a lion, they'll probably find it and shoot it eventually."

It's my turn to blink, just as the waiter arrives with the dinner tray. He's obviously responded to my wish.

"Shoot it?" I say. "Is that politically correct?" I shove my glass at the waiter, who nods curtly as he drops off my plate. He swivels and disappears into the bead-laced dimness.

"It may not be a lion," says Carson.

"Oh?" Now I am curious, and I study their expressions, looking for a clue.

"The victim wasn't exactly politically correct," he goes on. "He was a safari guide, in the old sense of the term. Snows of Kilimanjaro. Stuff like that."

"I must be jet-lagged," I admit. "I thought all safaris were photo ops these days. Endangered species and such?"

Sylvia snorts. At first I think she's choked on the perch, but it's just a comment.

"You can still buy a white rhino," she says, "if you're rich enough. Lions go a dime a dozen."

"Oh." I feel naive, but I've caught the general drift. "So the guy was an asshole, and it's likely he was murdered?"

"The police are looking for an old native from one of the farms," says Carson, "who's supposed to have threatened the man earlier in the week . . ."

The waiter arrives with my second Bloody Mary, and Sylvia's fork clanks suddenly against her plate.

"Anna!" she exclaims, throwing up her hands. "What an idea!"

"Huh?" At first I think she's talking about the Bloody Mary.

"I'd totally forgotten you're a PI!"

Wendall blinks, coming back a bit from the distance. Carson falls back in his chair, looking shocked. "Not Ms. Agatha Christie?"

I give him a withering glance. There are times and places for a sense of humor.

"I'm on vacation," I say. "I just want to see a little scenery."

"Ha," says Sylvia. She subsides, finds her fork. "Visits to the research camp will be strictly limited until this is over." She gives me a seductive smile, spears her fish. "Unless someone can solve the crime, of course."

I try the withering glance on her, but it bounces off.

"It's a ridiculous idea," I say. "I don't speak the language. I don't know my way around."

"Wendall can get you an escort from the staff."

"The police will throw me out of the country."

"Joseph Gatora is just the man," says Sylvia. "Don't you think so, Carson? He's a smooth operator, knows the countryside . . ."

I frown at her. I can see she's got it all planned. It's blackmail to get her darling sweetie back to work, and there goes my holiday out the door.

But maybe I can just stir around a little and pretend to investigate. I could see the countryside just as well that way and keep the peace with Sylvia, too.

"Okay." I sigh. "I'll think about it. Just tell me a few of the details."

Over the Turkish coffee, I've got the rest of it, and I don't like the facts. I'm reminded that this is a foreign country. Outside of this circle of faces is a different world—a native culture—and what I said about the police is likely dead on.

The deceased was Bryant Garr, a definite Hemingway type, heavy drinker—arrogant, racist, misogynist—you name it. He must have annoyed everyone in Nairobi at one time or another, blacks and whites alike, and his affronts didn't stop at the city limits, either.

He committed regular scandals with bored socialites from the local estates, and the squabble that was supposed to have killed him was with an elderly man from somewhere north of the city. Something over killing the wildlife, or messing with the man's grandson, or both. Sylvia's not completely sure.

Garr was found in the hills, clawed to ribbons, disemboweled, and what looked like lion tracks were easily visible around the body, overlaid by other prints. So why didn't the authorities think it was really a lion?

Africa, the "Dark Continent," was a hotbed of cults not that many years ago. The British colonials made a sincere effort to stamp out the various quasi-religious rites because they promoted organization in the native societies—and not only that, but disrespect for white claims on the best farmland. One of the most stubborn cults used forged-iron claws and carved-wooden sandals to obscure the evidence of their terrorism. The "lion-man" cult disappeared without leaving any trace of what its other functions might have been, but the police thought the old man might have had the requisite implements hidden away somewhere. They couldn't ask him about it in person because the old guy had hobbled off into the bush, taking his grandson with him.

"It's tantamount to admitting guilt," says Carson, waiting while the waiter fills his coffee cup. The pot is Arab-style, brass and long-handled, and it glitters darkly in the room's obscurity.

"No, it's not." Sylvia's hair stirs against her shoulders, dark gold as the brass. "Of course he'd be scared to death," she says. "He threatened Garr right out in front of a whole crowd of people, and those claws aren't so hard to come by. Even the Serengeti Institute has a set. I've seen them in the display case."

"Oh really," says Carson, noncommittal.

"Don't they, Wendall?" she asks, turning to him.

"Eh?" says Wendall, looking up from his coffee.

The evening flickers out, and morning comes too soon for me. Sylvia routs me out of a warm bed in her apartment at seven.

"Joseph's going to be here at nine," she says. "Do you want something to eat?"

"God," I say, burrowing under the pillow. I've never exactly been a morning type. "Can't we just forget all this?" I ask.

"I thought you wanted to see Kenya," she says.

"Maybe we could do some shopping later."

"You can't disappoint Joseph. I told him you'd offered to pay him."

"What?" I lurch upright. "Pay?"

"Ha, ha," she says. "That got you up, didn't it?"

It turns out that Wendall is going to pay, for Joseph's time and mine, too. Sylvia's a great operator. Fortified by two cups of coffee and a fat sweet roll, I follow Sylvia down to meet Joseph at nine and to start the investigation, whatever it's going to be.

Surprisingly, Carson is there too, turned out in a smart white hunter outfit. "Hello," he says, with an engaging smile. "I hope you don't mind if I come along."

Joseph is sturdy and athletic looking, attractive but old enough to seem grizzled, which probably means he's a grandfather, at least. He's wearing a loose chambray shirt and dark shorts and shakes hands with a definite reserve.

The truck is a Jeep Cherokee painted with vivid stripes, and I wonder if that's for visibility, maybe to keep errant safaris from shooting at us by mistake. Joseph takes the driver's seat, and we head off through the warren of streets, encounter farmland quite suddenly.

Carson goes into a canned tour guide routine, and when I ask a few questions, he starts to tell me about the people and the countryside. It's interesting. To this point, I have had nil education on African history.

"These are mostly Kikuyu who live in this area," he says, "and they're farmers. The Masai and some other herders live to the south and west, over near the Serengeti."

He points out that we're headed into the Great Rift Valley where hominid hunters constitute the fastest growing population segment.

"They're looking for the Gumba," Joseph says, "the little people who were here in the earliest times. They disappeared underground and never came out."

Carson frowns at the interruption. I give Joseph a sidelong glance and find his face is completely deadpan. The man's sharp. He's got Carson's number already—and likely mine, as well.

The farm plots march up the hills, some with new tin-roofed buildings and wire fencing, and others with round thatched roofs and stick fences that look more traditional and picturesque. Beyond the hills, the mountains of the Rift walls loom sheer and distant through the morning haze.

The Kikuyu were always a progressive people, Carson explains, generally interested in new methods and advantages, and after the first colonial contacts, they quickly adapted to British ways. The Europeans actually held them in contempt for their friendly attitudes—which was a mistake. The result was the Mau Mau wars of the 1950s when that cult conducted a bloody campaign of assassination and sabotage from camps hidden out in the local mountains. The British responded with executions and torture, and most of the Kikuyu people were imprisoned. Thirty-two white settlers and thirteen thousand Kikuyu died before the rebellion finally broke the British rule and Kenya found its way to independence. Then the Kikuyu got their land back. Lately, they've made the leap to professional positions: doctors, lawyers, financiers . . .

. . . and under their administration, Kenya is doing just fine now, thank you.

Joseph doesn't come right out and say that, but I've got a handle on his attitudes now; I can feel what's behind his stoic reserve. The wars left hard feelings that still haven't gone away, and the natives might just as soon be free of Westerners, except they need the investment capital.

The tension between the men leaves me pissed off. I'm supposed to be on vacation here, and I don't like being in this cross fire. I appreciate the history, but Carson has been an asshole in the way he has related it. Whatever, it's a relief when the tea plantation finally heaves into view.

We're about fifty miles from Nairobi now, on the southern fringe of Aberdare National Park, where Garr was found dead. Carson has reverted to tour guide mode and left off with the history. Apparently, it's served his purpose for now.

The fields are green and waist high to workers with baskets strapped to their backs. Beyond a screen of trees, I can see the plantation housing, neat rows of whitewashed huts facing the road. We stop at one of the fields. Joseph calls out a question and gets an answer, after which we drive on. We're looking for the old man's daughter.

"Dede Njere is at least ninety," Joseph comments, pulling into the access road. "He would make a very mangy lion."

The daughter's gone to visit relatives in a village somewhere off in the hills, but we find a neighbor who's willing to talk. She doesn't look so young herself and neither does her husband. He's toothless, dressed in shorts and a faded shirt, and she's outfitted in a Grateful Dead T-shirt and a native wrap. The visit takes a while, as I gather Joseph has to go through formalities before we can ask any questions: inquiries as to their health and that of their families, etc., at great length.

Finally, he turns to me and asks, "What would you like to know, Ms. Detroyer?"

"Um," I say, trying to get together a train of thought. "Where was Mr. Njere the night of Mr. Garr's death?"

He asks and they answer.

"Out prowling the bush, they think. The old man comes and goes as he wants, and his daughter has no control of him. They are pleased that Garr is dead."

"No alibi," says Carson.

"Shut up," I tell him, without even looking. "Do they know where the old man is now?"

The woman shrugs.

"*Dorobo*," Joseph interprets. "By this, they mean 'wild,' that he has gone to the bush to stay and taken the boy with him."

They've answered these questions before, and it's the same answers I've been told, but now the difference is, I get to watch their faces as they talk.

"Why did he take the boy?" I ask.

"Because the boy is like him."

"Oh?" It's not what I'd expected to hear. "And how is that?"

"Of the old way," they say, and with that I catch the mismatch of assumptions, the sham of their ragtag Western clothes. I have my granddad's talents as a spirit talker, and I see realities other people don't see.

I take a breath. "Ask them about the iron claws and carved sandals," I tell Joseph, and they laugh.

Damn.

"Does Njere have relatives anywhere else?" I ask.

The woman thinks. "In the village where his daughter has gone. A cousin in Nairobi."

"What's the boy like?"

"A good boy, but like his grandfather."

"Would Njere have killed the safari guide?"

"If he wanted to," they say.

I'm grappling with ephemera. The two of them look simple and solid, but they're elusive, slipping out of my grasp like a fog. Joseph sees it, but Carson only looks sullen and miffed.

"Can we find the daughter?" I ask, turning to Joseph.

"Perhaps," he says. "We have to go to Limuru anyway. It's near the park, and the men who found the body are from there, too."

We head into terrain that's volcanic and rough, north of the prime farmland and so relatively unpopulated. The truck raises a wake of ochre dust that settles on the forested veldt behind us. I'm glued to the window now, watching for wildlife in the scrub—it's mostly birds and antelope in the daytime, but still exotic to me. Once, I see a pack of hyenas. The vista looks almost familiar now, thorn trees and yellowed grass right out of National Geographic.

"Like it?" Carson asks. He's apparently recovered from his snit.

"Sure," I say. And then the track runs out, like we'll have to walk the rest of the way. I wonder if hyenas will bite. I'm afraid the answer is yes.

It's a rough climb up an animal trail to the first trace of civilization, which is a partially harvested field. The village is just beyond, a dirt track through a clutter of family compounds, and we immediately attract a crowd. It turns out no one's here that we've come to see. Njere's daughter is already headed home, and the men are all gone hunting. Everyone's excited but polite, and Joseph cuts a deal for us. I'll stay and rest in the village while he and Carson go out to see if the hunters are headed back this way.

I'm not sure that it's fine with me, especially as the plan seems to irritate Carson. Still, it seems to please our hosts, so I gather I've been placed in the traditional female role. What the hell? I don't mind—it would be about the same thing in a Seminole village.

As soon as the guys are gone, I'm offered lunch. The women and kids are shy and curious. Soon they're asking questions in broken English. Lunch seems to be mush and greens, bland but not inedible. I have no instructions about what's safe from Joseph, so I go ahead and eat.

Questions eventually get to my love life, and when they find I'm unmarried, I'm shuffled off to someone who can help. It's a middle-aged man sitting in a hut that smells ancient as the land. When my eyes adjust, I see that there's a grass mat on the ground, a couple of cartons against the wall and hay-scented herbs in the rafters. One of the girls has come to interpret, and she tells me to leave my shoes at the door. At the old man's invitation, I sit on one of the mats.

"Daughter," he says, "do you want a love charm?"

"Will it really change the man?" I ask.

He smiles faintly. "No," he says. He's thin, dressed in a knit polo and skirt, and his earlobes are stretched and bound into knots with thick silver rings.

"Then I'll pass," I say.

"You are wise," he says. "What is it you want then?"

"I want to know who killed Bryant Garr."

"The hyenas feasted on his entrails," he says, and looks pleased with the fact. By now I'm not surprised.

"Well, yes," I say. "But do you know who did it?"

He reaches behind him for implements, shakes cowrie shells out of a gourd and studies the patterns they make in the dirt.

"It was not Njere," he says.

"Then who?"

"The shells point to Nairobi," he says. "You will find the killer there."

"Can you tell me how?"

"Wait and he will come," he says. "His fear will bring him to you."

That's all he has to say on the matter.

"Is Njere a lion-man?" I ask.

The girl looks immediately spooked at that, but she translates it for me anyway.

The old man studies my face. "It was said that he is," he answers.

I sort through the grammar, and then I want a second opinion on the definition.

"If that were true," I say, "what would it mean?"

"That he could command lions, and perhaps to become one."

I've got a shiver now. The veil of rationalism seems very thin in this hut, out in this wilderness, just now.

"Do you think he could command lions now?" I ask.

"Oh, no," he says, waving a hand. "His lions are all dead. The Christians killed them many years ago."

Well, damn.

The crime scene is anticlimactic. The grass is torn up, but the remains are gone. The Nairobi police have already searched the area and found nothing at all.

Joseph and Carson seem to have declared a cease-fire on the way back home, and for that I'm thankful. We retrace our way through the green farms beneath mountains floating on the blue clouds of sunset. Nairobi glows ahead of us like a pocket of stars, resolves finally into last night's maze. I've traveled too far, too fast, and now all I want to do is sleep. We climb down from the truck and dust off our clothes.

"Would you like to go out to dinner?" asks Carson.

I study his face, the pale hair and blue eyes, the set of his shoulders. Suddenly, I'm very much aware of Joseph standing behind me.

"No thanks," I say. "I'm really tired tonight."

Tossing in bed later on, I wonder if I was wrong in my choices throughout the day. Maybe I should have taken that love charm after all. Paul seems to have no use for me at all these days, and I can't even think about another man, regardless of the movie star looks.

Sylvia wakes me at six thirty in the morning. If I remember correctly, it's Saturday. The woman must jump up at the crack of dawn every day.

"Well," she says brightly, once I'm upright, "how did it go?"

"It didn't," I grumble. And then, after a cup of coffee, I add, "But it was interesting anyway."

I have to take some gifts home for my cousins' kids, so Sylvia has shopping planned for today. About midmorning, we plunge on foot into the maze near Abdul-al's. It's a bright swirl of carved figurines and patterned fabrics, crude baskets and brown pottery jars. The air is heavy with spice and food scents and boisterous with shouted price reductions, just for us.

We eat dinner at Abdul-al's again and head for home as the city dims, puts on evening like a mask.

There's a shadow waiting by the apartment door.

Sylvia starts. "My God," she says, "Joseph, what are you doing here?"

"I have found the cousin," he says.

I thought I'd finished with all that yesterday.

Joseph's brought his own truck this time, and Sylvia swears she'd come along except that she's got to meet Wendall at eight for some lecture. I climb into the Jeep beside Joseph all by myself. After a while, I don't like the look of the streets.

"Where are we going?" I ask.

"Kibera," he says.

The word is a challenge. I study him sideways, see he's waiting for a reply.

"Fine with me," I say. "But you're in charge of safety. Okay?"

His chuckle cuts through the dusk like a growl.

Kibera is a slum, and it stinks. Open sewers, I think, testing the wind—or maybe it's none at all. The roads are dirt and too narrow for a truck; we have to abandon it early on. A yelling tribe of kids offers to watch it for us, but Joseph hires a scar-faced thug instead.

The whores that work the backstreets are blatantly sexual. One of them tries to pull Joseph in through a doorway. There's a shouting match, and I wonder if I should act possessive, but Joseph seems to do all right by himself. We make another turn into red dirt alleyways lined with shacks built of piled debris. Mostly naked children play in the dirt.

Finally, we arrive at something that looks like legitimate apartments, a building five spalling stories high, decorated with dank strings of hanging laundry. The stairs smell like piss, and cockroach bodies crunch underfoot. In the gloom of the fourth-floor hallway, something larger darts by us—a rat, I figure. Joseph pounds on a rickety door.

The man who answers is short and ugly, dressed in dirty shorts. Behind him, three women are sitting in a circle, cooking over a brazier. Half a dozen children stare at us with curious eyes.

The cousin seems evasive, producing a monologue that's truly amazing, even though I can't understand a word of it. The women stare and scowl.

"Now what?" I ask, as the door slams behind us.

"The neighbors," says Joseph. He's got a good head for detective work. He gives the woman who answers the first knock a coin, and she opens the door up wide as her gap-toothed smile. She doesn't like her neighbors much.

Musa has too many wives and can't support any of them, she says. Yes, he's had visitors from the country, just this week, an old man and a boy, but they didn't stay for very long. Maybe Muthoni downstairs could tell us where they went. She knows everybody's business, whatever you want to know.

Muthoni isn't home. She's gone to the bar to find her husband, who usually spends his whole week's pay on beer. She wants some money herself this week. Her oldest daughter says we can come back later on.

"Now what?" I ask Joseph. It's full dusk now, shadows closing down on us. Music drifts in the air, the sounds of distant carousing. The smell of cook fires wafts through the alleyways.

"We should try again tomorrow," says Joseph. "It's too dangerous to be here now."

We start the trek back to the car. There are no streetlights here, only the distant music, and stark, moonlit shadows flare on the walls. Soon I have icy fingers on my neck. I turn, staring behind us through the gloom. I start as a rat squeaks, reach out to catch Joseph by the arm.

He gasps as my nails dig into his wrist.

Suddenly, the world has changed. I don't know what it is, maybe a sixth sense developed from years of experience—or maybe the insights of a spirit talker. It's the sharpening of my ears that catches the faint shift of a heavy body behind me, the faintest rasp of breath from the shadows. Now I've caught the glimmer of something that looks like eyes. Likely it's the rat—but maybe not. Who else? The scar-faced thug? Friends of the rejected whore?

I'm pumped with adrenalin, and now I think Joseph feels something, too. I motion for a split, head off noisily down the alleyway. He stays behind, hidden in an alcove. When I hear a commotion, I wheel and dash to help, but there's no need.

The boy's wearing traditional African garb, which is to say, nothing much—only a beaded G-string and a blanket. He's like an animal, twisting under Joseph's weight, lithe and sleek, with delicate features, hollow cheekbones, and a mouth that looks bee stung.

Joseph plants a knee on the kid's back and twists his hands up to loop them together with a leather thong. But before he does that, he pries off a silver bracelet. The boy says something in a peremptory tone, and Joseph comes right back at him. He sticks the bracelet in his shirt pocket, but somehow he doesn't look comfortable with what he's done.

"What is it?" I ask.

"A *bolniga*. I have pulled the cub's teeth," he says, showing his own. "At least as much as I can."

I let out my breath, decide not to ask what the hell he's talking about.

The boy looks to be about sixteen. The sleekness comes from the good jobs his parents have at the tea farm.

"Kamau," says Joseph, "where is your grandfather?"

The kid hisses something, likely curses. Joseph shakes him.

"Don't," I say.

Maybe it's good I do; the old man is standing there now, slid out of the shadows behind us like a phantom. He motions. Joseph tugs the thong loose, and the boy twists to his feet, fades into an alleyway. Somehow I don't think he's gone very far.

"What is it you want of me?" asks Njere in a voice as old as the valley walls.

"Just to talk," I say.

Joseph must be right about his age. The old man is shriveled as a dried plum and snowy-haired, nearly blind. Propped on a carved wooden stick, he looks completely incapable of killing anyone as young and strong as Garr was supposed to be—still there are ways, I suppose.

"You are not the police?" he asks.

"No," I say.

He shifts his weight on the stick. "Then why do you want to talk to me?" he asks.

"The . . . uh, investigation is stopping people who want to work," I say.

He considers, likely wondering if I'm for real.

Joseph puts in his two cents worth then—dialect I can't follow, and the old guy looks at me again and nods like it could make sense after all.

"I did not kill Bryant Garr," he says. "But of course I had thought of it. I was tracking him, and I saw the man who did it . . ." He has his mouth open to go on, but then his milky eyes blink, fasten behind me.

I jerk sideways. I'm half expecting this will be the boy, but somehow I know it's not. There's a thump and a grunt to my right, and Joseph falls. Light flares, blinding, into my face.

If Njere were any younger, he'd probably have run, but instead he's maintaining his dignity. He grips his stick, peers into the glare with narrowed eyes—the same as me.

"Well, sweetheart," says a voice I recognize. "Somehow I thought you'd find him for me."

"Carson?" I gasp, trying to block the light with one hand so I can see him. "What the hell are you doing here?" Like it's not obvious. His hazy shadow has a gun in its hand.

"I'll have to kill you all," he says, "so no one else will know. The setting's perfect—the slum, the riffraff. Thank you, dear . . ." It's that damn sense of humor again—an appreciation for irony.

"You killed Garr?" I ask. I'm stalling, trying to decide what the hell to do about this. Dive for the alley mouth? Then he'll get the old man—and Joseph too, lying unconscious at his feet.

I want my gun, but I've left it at home. I could never carry it here.

"I had to," Carson explains. "Garr killed my lions, half the pride I was studying. My research was ruined."

"You got the claws out of the case at the Institute?"

"Of course," he says, "I . . ."

The old man dodges suddenly sideways. Stern jerks, lines up to fire at him. Too late. A heavy shadow leaps, and he goes down, screaming. The gun slides. I grab for it and roll, come up behind Joseph with the pistol aimed and ready.

For a second, I freeze. It's a lion, and a young one. The body is supple and taut. A fine, wispy mane clothes the shoulders in a halo of light. The animal crouches over the body, eyeing me balefully, its tail twitching. It's watchful, green-eyed and ghostly in the wash of the fallen torch.

I blink, gasping for breath. This is a modern city. There are no lions in the streets of Nairobi. Still my brain is working. Slowly it processes, decides, and then I know who I'm dealing with. I raise the gun and click on the safety.

The moonlight flickers briefly. A cloud crosses the moon's face, and then it's gone. The alley is empty, except for me, a definite corpse, and a man's dark, stocky body stretched on the ground beside me.

"Ouch," says Joseph, stirring faintly. "What happened?" He sits up, feels along the back of his head. "Are you okay, Ms. Detroyer?"

"Yeah," I say. I stand and shove the gun in my pants, lean to help him up. My hands are shaking.

He looks at Carson's body. "What happened?" he asks.

"Don't ask," I say. "Joseph, get us the hell out of here. I think we've earned our pay

Chapter 4

SPIRIT WITCH

All the way from O'Hare we've been flying over snowfields, white anvils banked against the sky, with hills and moonscape valleys yawning below. Now we've sailed out of cloud country and into the sun, and we're flying over a collage of mottled earth and deep blue sky, embellished in unlikely palettes of peach, tarnished copper and gold.

I'm looking at layered realities. That's the ground below us, the southern expanse of the Everglades with Miami off to the east. Coming down, I could see the straight line of the Tamiami Trail cutting through the broad empty sweep, and beyond that, the half-moon of Florida Bay framed by the Keys. Now we're too close to the ground for an overview, and all I can see is color and texture, like a painted canvas of superimposed sky, stippled by mud flats and colored by mineral tints below the water line. There's no sign of any grass, even, this far south.

Then suddenly there's development, and the hard concrete of the runway jolting up through the seats. The plane engines roar, decelerating, and we're down. It's been a hard trip, and a harder trial. I had to testify as a witness to a money-laundering scheme Paul and I stumbled onto last year, but now I'm home, and hoping Paul will be at the airport to meet me.

He's not at the gate.

Dammit. You'd think after all these years I'd be used to this, but I'm not. There's been no sign in the fifteen years we've been partners—and actually evidence to the contrary—but somehow I still expect him to notice I'm alive.

Irritated, I make my way on down to baggage claim, and waiting for my bag to wend its way through the machinery, I give the office a call. It's the voicemail that answers, and I sigh, key in the code to check for messages. There are two hang-ups, a drunk wanting to make hotel reservations, and then a message from Gloria.

"Listen Anna," she says. "I need to talk to you. Give me a call when you get in."

That's all. I'll have to catch the shuttle home.

My bag comes out, freshly dented, and I make for the exit. Halfway there, I'm halted by my name, broadcast to the world.

"Anna Detroyer," the P.A. blares, "please meet your party at the information desk."

I stand there and listen to it play again, wondering what the hell kind of emergency this is. There's nothing to do but head that way and find out.

"Hi," the kid says. "I'm Joel Angstrom."

I'm floored. I stand there with my mouth open.

"You're Anna Detroyer?" he says. "You look just like my dad described."

Fortyish and graying? His resemblance to Paul is jolting.

"I'll take your bag," he says. He has a beguiling smile, but I slide it away from him.

"Give me a minute," I say. "Just where the hell did you come from?"

He looks at me.

"Well, I guess this is Miami," he says.

"I can do without the crime stats," I say. "It's not what I mean."

"Washington State," he says then. His shoulders twitch, not quite a shrug, but he stays civil. "I'm here for the summer, headed back to college in the fall."

Somewhere in the back of my mind, all this time, I've known Paul had an ex and a kid out west. But I'd thought the kid was six or so. Time flies. Damn. Fifteen years of it.

"Dad had to go to Jacksonville for a few days," he's saying. "So I'm at the house by myself. I just thought you'd like a ride home." He looks uncertain, like maybe he's done something wrong. It makes me feel like a heel.

I shove the bag at him with my foot.

"Sorry, kid," I say. "You just took me by surprise."

Going outside is like walking into a sauna, and the sun hits us like a fist.

The boy's got Paul's SUV. He tosses the bag into the back and actually gets the door for me—first class—his mama's taught him manners. It takes me by surprise again, and suddenly I wish I had on something more professional than faded jeans and old athletic shoes. Paul is tending to suits these days.

We're headed down the exit ramp then, and Joel says, "Which way?"

My apartment's not far away, and he hauls the bag up to the door for me.

"Come in for a beer?" I ask.

"Not right now," he says, giving me that blinding grin again. "I've got a date for lunch."

That's no surprise. I didn't have anything decent anyway.

The apartment is stale and empty, and it's getting harder for me to do anything about it these days. I've got most of the day left and not much to unpack, so I decide to see what Gloria wants before I start. Gloria's an old friend and a cop, and from her tone on the machine, I expect she wants to call in a favor.

I call and key in her extension number. It rings once and she's got it.

"Lisowski," she says, and pops her gum.

"It's Anna."

"Where the hell have you been?" she asks, like I've been delinquent.

"Chicago," I answer. "What do you need, Gloria?"

"Lunch at Vinnie's," she says. "Half an hour."

Summer in Miami is always scorching, but now we're deep in a year-long drought. Life's at its lowest ebb. The rich folks have cleared out for cooler climes, and nobody's left but us baked working types, plus a few misguided tourists. Europe will close down about September and the Florida economy will pick up from the tourist trade, but meanwhile, the place is a pressure cooker ready to blow, tempers constantly at boiling because of the heat.

I head down the stairs to my car, feeling a shimmer off the concrete steps. They're hot enough to fry eggs just after noon, and not something you'd want to walk on barefoot, not even to run down to the pool.

My car's parked in the sun and blazing hot. I can't touch the steering wheel, so I sit for a minute with the AC blowing before I put it into gear, wondering what Gloria's got going that she can't handle herself.

Vinnie's is a hole-in-the-wall Italian place, tucked up against the police station downtown, which is built like a tiled fortress. It looms at the edge of Overtown without much luck at intimidation. I park on NW Second and walk around the corner to the restaurant. I'm early. There's no sign of Gloria yet, so I order a beer and kick back to relax. I'm wondering now what the hell Paul's doing in Jacksonville. He'd gotten worse lately, damn secretive, and I hardly even run into him at the office. There was a time when we actually worked together…

"Hey," says Gloria, dropping into the other side of the booth.

We both went to Miami Dade Junior College years ago. She's five-eleven and sturdy, frosted hair, on the edge of matronly after four kids. She worked a beat for most of her career, but a couple of years ago she made detective, and now she's out of those tight uniforms that never seem to be cut for a woman and into plain clothes. She looks a lot more relaxed.

"Want a beer?" I ask.

"I'm watching my weight," she says. "How come you never gain anything?"

"I'm too busy."

"Well, dammit, so am I," she says. She pops her gum and waves at Vinnie. She chews gum all the time. It keeps her from smoking.

I order baked ziti and she gets a salad and crackers.

"What's on your mind?" I ask.

"Something weird," she says. "There's a broad stealing babies."

"That's weird?"

"That part's not," she says, "but the description is." She jams her gum into a paper napkin. "She's tried three times now in different places around Miami, but the moms have been quicker. Had one tug-of-war over a stroller, but that's the closest she's come."

"So what's the description?"

"Dark woman, broad face, pile of beads, multi-color cape and a long skirt." She breaks a cracker with an audible snap. "What does that sound like?"

It sounds like a Seminole or Miccosukee Indian, except they don't dress that way anymore.

"Escapee from a festival?" I ask. It's my best guess.

"I dunno," she says. She pours enough dressing on her salad to make it the caloric equivalent of my ziti. "The major sent some guys out to tribal headquarters, but they didn't get shit. It could get to be an incident, and it's been dumped in my lap."

Well, now I know what the problem is. The reservations are actually in Broward County, not Dade, and they're supposed to be sovereign. The tribal councils don't like Miami cops tracking around on their land. Gloria probably remembers I helped the police out on something like this once before.

"You've still got cousins up in Big Cypress, haven't you?" she asks.

"Yeah," I say.

"Got time to go visit?"

"I'll see what I can find out," I say. "Have you got any parents I can talk to first?"

"Sure. Your turn on the check," she says, stuffing in a fresh wad of Juicy Fruit. "Want some gum?"

Two of the victims' families are tourists and bolted north already, but one family is resident. The address is Liberty City, near the airport. Given that, I'm not surprised to find the mother is black.

The yard is untidy, with broken toys and sand spurs bristling between islands of brown grass. The house is concrete block, blistered and peeling, with torn wire hanging from a rickety screen door. I rap on the bare wood, and in a minute the woman comes to the door. She has a sweat sheen on her skin and a baby on her hip.

"Yeah?" She looks at me like I'm selling insurance.

I show her my P.I.'s license, while the baby stares and sucks his fingers. He's beautiful, blond and green-eyed, with freckles dotting a mocha skin.

"I'm helping the police," I say. "Finding out who tried to snatch your baby."

"I never heard of nothin' like that," she says.

It's doubtful she's going to let me in. She's already reaching to slam the solid door inside the screen.

"Was the woman an Indian?" I ask quickly.

It catches her attention. "Yeah," she says, grudgingly. "It look like it."

"Why did you think so?"

"Them clothes. An' that hair do."

"What kind of hair do?"

"Pin up over somethin' in front so it look like a hat brim. The witch was old, white-headed. She wasn't goin' to get my Cecil away from me, though."

I figure not. She looks ferocious.

"Where were you when this happened?" I ask.

"Park out on the Trail." She bounces the baby, rolls her head in a westerly direction.

I have to think about it. "Tamiami Park?"

"Yeah," she says. "School trip to the art museum. My oldest, she be watchin' Cecil, and I hear her scream. Get there just in time."

"Where did the woman go?"

"It look like she disappear into thin air. Musta come from there, too. Nobody seen her before she grab Cecil."

I need to talk to Gloria again. I head back to the office, rummage through the desk drawers for a dog-eared map of the city.

"Lisowski," she says, and the gum cracks.

"Where did these baby snatches happen, Gloria?"

They're all on the west side. That's Miccosukee territory, not Seminole. So at least now I know who to ask.

There's a message from Joel on the voicemail.

"Want to go to dinner?" he asks. "I hate to eat by myself. Give me a call at the house."

What the hell, I think. Why not? I've got nothing else to do.

The South Beach area has blossomed recently into Art Deco and blazing neon night spots, to meet the expectations of tourists who watch too much TV. I don't go so far as to dress up like it's a date. Probably everybody will think I'm his mother—but I do shower and change out of the jeans and into a pair of linen slacks and a green silk blouse.

"I just wanted to talk," Joel says, steering Paul's SUV across the causeway. Ahead of us Miami Beach shimmers in the dark reflecting pool of Biscayne Bay. "I've heard so much about you and about the P.I. business."

"Who from?" I ask.

"From Dad, of course."

I stare sideways at his profile, wondering if he's for real. Irritation crowds up, but I bite my tongue.

"Tell me about Washington State," I say, and glare into the stream of headlights climbing the bridge to meet us.

We have dinner at one of the refurbished Art Deco hotels, listen to a jazz band for a while in the steamy atmosphere by the pool.

"Want to walk on the beach?" he asks.

Finally we're in a place that's comfortable. I take off my shoes, sift the coarse sand grains between my toes. There's a brisk wind blowing off the ocean that snarls my hair, whips it across my face hard enough to sting. Joel's shirt snaps like a flag. Phosphorescence rolls up the beach, fired by the hotel lights behind us. A gull shrieks in the dark overhead.

"Are you in love with my dad?" Joel asks.

"What gives you that idea?"

"There's something wrong," he says, facing me. "I thought that might be it."

"Are you the hell looking for a mother?" I shout at him.

The surf hisses. Lights blaze to the east of us, a cruise ship headed for the Bahamas. Joel is a pale shadow of his dad, but not so tall. In the shadowy dusk of the hotel lights, I can see his nose is peeling, already fried by the Florida sun.

"I've got a mother," he says.

I step around him abruptly, headed on up the beach.

"Anna," he says, catching up. "Wait. I didn't mean to snoop..."

"Get the hell out of here," I say.

"Okay," he says, reasonably. "How are you going to get home?"

"I'll take a taxi."

He ignores it.

"What are you doing tomorrow?" he asks, after a brisk quarter mile of wind, surf and silence.

"Working," I say.

"Can I come along?" he asks.

"What the hell for?"

"I might want to learn the business," he says. "What are you investigating?"

"Baby snatches," I say. "Do you like babies?"

"I don't care what you're doing," he says.

"Well, I don't need you tagging along."

He's right that something's wrong. Later, lying by myself in bed, watching car lights careen across the walls, I wonder what the hell Paul is up to, after all these years. It makes me mad, not knowing enough to guess.

By morning I'm feeling like a heel again. After all, what goes on between Paul and me isn't the kid's fault. I'm planning to head out to the Miccosukee camps today, and it won't hurt me to have a little company on the drive. There'll be plenty for him to look at while I ask around. By ten o'clock I've talked myself into it.

I call and apologize, swing by Paul's house to pick him up, and we head out the Tamiami Trail. Joel's quiet, but I'm not surprised. I'd be pissed-off, too.

The Trail is quaint near the Miami downtown, with a distinct Spanish flavor, but further out the strip starts to run down, and prostitutes strut blatantly along the street corners. Traffic thins out finally, and grass starts to crowd the tarmac, interspersed with cattails, both of them sere and yellowed by the drought. The terrain starts to look mucky—like you wouldn't want to run off the road by mistake.

This is Seminole country—actually they're recent migrants to Florida. When Columbus first showed up off the coast with his development plans, Florida was populated by other tribes. Early fatalities left a void for refugees to haul-ass into, and it wasn't long before they did—mostly Creeks, forced south along with runaway slaves. After years of war, the migrants were shoved into the Everglades at the very tip of Florida, and then the U.S. declared that a national park and told them they'd have to move.

Now days the Seminole Wars continue, but they've mutated into political and economic warfare. The tribes have built casinos, and now they can afford to hire high-priced lawyers to do their fighting for them. They sue at the drop of a hat, which, of course, is why Gloria has called yours truly.

"What's that?" asks Joel, sitting up straight in the seat.

It's a monstrous alligator in the road. I slow down in case he decides to snap at the car. They've been known to crunch up whole fenders.

When I tell Joel that, he laughs, suddenly pleased with the trip. He rolls down the window to watch the thing disappear into the wet grass prairie behind us.

"Is that a fire?" he asks, pointing to smoke ahead.

"Controlled burn," I say, eyeing the smudge. "It clears out the saw grass and non-native plants so new growth can come in."

"Oh," he says, studying the cloud.

We're getting close to our destination now. The Seminoles live mostly north of Miami, and they're pretty cosmopolitan. You're more likely to see satellite dishes and RV's at the reservation in Hollywood than wood fires, but the Miccosukees out west on the Tamiami Trail are downright reactionary. A bunch of them still ignore the U.S. government's claim to the Everglades, live in illegal squatter's camps and eat off the land. The tribe does have a headquarters and runs a commercial village and cultural center for tourists. Lately they're busy enough that they've had to add Spanish to the English on their signs.

The village has grown from a couple of temporary thatched *chikees* and a small crafts store to a booming business, including a restaurant, an amphitheater, a gift shop, air boat rides, and various culture and crafts displays. On festival days you have to fight your way in, but the place looks completely dead today. It's too hot for tourists, maybe. There are only a few dusty cars parked in the dirt by the info center.

"Want some lunch?" asks Joel, looking hopefully at the restaurant.

"Later," I say. "I want to find out who's here first."

He sneaks a sigh, but he doesn't complain, and follows me across the road to where we have to pay for admission.

Joel is immediately distracted by the gift shop, which suits me fine. I really don't want him along while I'm trying to work. We set up a time to meet, and he wanders off to look at the leather goods and hand-sewn jackets by himself.

I check out the shop and the open pole structures of the *chikee* huts beyond it, finally work my way through the compound and back as far as the museum. Jimmy Bowlegs and his brother Tommy are working there today, fitting new pressure-treated lumber into a rotted section of boardwalk.

"Hello, Anna," Jimmy says, and goes on working like I'm not there.

"How've you been, Jimmy?"

Jimmy is a member of the tribal council, and likely to know what's going on, if anybody does. The two men look comfortable, half-naked in cut-offs and no shirts. The muscles ripple across their shoulders, glossy and dark in the sun.

"I'm really busy," Jimmy says. "We've got a lot to do on this today."

It looks like they're almost done.

"How's Edna?"

"Fine," he says. "You know how it goes. We've got to get these repairs done before the rainy season sets in."

There's not a cloud in the sky. It's as dry as it gets in the Everglades, just now. By the end of last month, it should have been raining every day, but sometimes it just doesn't. The water flow is disrupted by development and farming, and the results have ruined the local ecology. What he says could make sense, but instead it sounds like a brush-off— Native Americans are notoriously indirect. I decide to get right to the point.

"Had any Miami cops out to see you just lately?"

Tommy's black eyes slide over in an oblique glance, but Jimmy just keeps on working.

"Can't say as I've talked to any," he says.

"Nothing about a woman trying to steal babies over in Miami?"

"Anna," he says, "you know I can't keep up with everything that goes on out here."

"I'd imagine gossip gets around," I say.

"I guess it does," he says.

"I guess if this is an internal problem, you'll take care of it?"

"We do try to keep on good terms with the Miami police," he says, "but you know I can't tell people what to do."

"How about a few suggestions on likely penalties?"

"If I talk to anybody who knows about it," he says, "But like I said, I've been really busy lately. Not much time to talk."

He's never looked up. We've come full circle now. I've said about as much as I'm able to. The Miccosukee are matrilineal, regardless of the U.S. fixation on dad's surname. It's always worked out fine, kept the paternity suits to zero, but it means I've got no real family within the tribes that I can make claims on. My grandma was Black Seminole, which mean I am, too, regardless that my grandpa was full Seminole and my dad half white and half Miccosukee. There was a time when Black Seminoles were part of the tribe, but they got dis-enrolled a while back when tribal membership got to be a benefit. Discrimination might figure into that some, but it was mostly about money, I'd guess. Whatever, it means I'll always be an outsider with no real place in the tribal structure. Jimmy may pass along what I've told him, and he may not. He means what he says about not telling his neighbors what to do.

I'm tired of standing out in the heat, so I say "so long" and head off to look for Joel, only to find he's discovered the alligator wrestling. It's not traditionally a Native American sport, something they've set up for tourists. It's scary and dangerous, even if they do make it look easy. Of course Joel is wild about it, fills me in over 'gator tail, chili and fry bread for lunch.

I'm not real pleased by my conversation with Jimmy, but it's hard to resist Joel's enthusiasm for life. As we head back to Miami, I'm seeing the country suddenly brighter and fresher through his eyes, from the massive osprey nest in the pines ahead to the snowy glide of egret wings disappearing into the river of grass to the south. On the horizon an island of cypress blooms from the marsh, a delicate tracery against the sky. It's a shame everything looks so dead, just now. The Everglades are fading—and this year, maybe a little more than most.

It would be nice if the trip took care of things, but it hasn't. My phone rings at six a.m. It's the middle of the night as far as I'm concerned.

"Goddammit," Gloria yells, "Anna, are you awake?"

I've knocked my phone to the floor, feel for it off the side of the bed. "Um?" I say, and find I'm holding it upside down against my ear. I can hear Gloria, anyway.

The woman got her kid this time, just before daybreak, in the parking lot at Lakes Country Club. I swear and lurch into the kitchen to make the strongest coffee I can stand.

Out on the Trail, Jimmy Bowlegs isn't even pretending to work today, just standing alongside the alligator pens, watching them stir as the heat starts to shimmer off the limestone rock lining the pool. I stick my hands in my pockets, kick the concrete wall beside him.

"I was expecting you," he says.

"Jimmy, this is serious," I insist. "I've got to have that baby back, or you'll have federal agents crawling all over the reservation by tomorrow."

"I'll have to ask around," he says, staring at the alligators. I curse to myself. There's nothing I can do about it, so I get into my blazing hot car and head back to Miami.

I put in a hard afternoon at the office studying a child custody case that's going to court midweek, and about six o'clock the hall door rattles. It's Joel.

"What are you doing here?" I ask, locking the door again behind him.

"How's the baby case going?" He moves a stack of paperwork from my extra chair, looks around for another spot and finally drops it on the floor so he can sit down. "I saw it on the news."

"It's not going," I say. "It's a police problem, or maybe the FBI. I can't get involved."

"Why did we go visit the Indian village, then?"

"A favor," I say.

He stares at traffic out the window. "Want to go to dinner again?"

"I can't," I say, sounding like Jimmy Bowlegs, only worse. "I've got too much work to do."

"Okay," Joel says. He's just too damn amenable.

"Look," I say, and then the office phone rings.

I snatch at it. "Hello!"

It's Jimmy.

"Dammit," I snarl. "I've been waiting long enough."

"I've got something," he says. "Can you take a ride up into the 'Glades tonight?"

"What's going on, Jimmy?"

"It's medicine stuff," he says. "I don't know."

"Okay." I sigh. "Where do I meet you?"

Of course, Joel wants to go along, and I don't have time to argue now. It's dusk by the time we get out to the village again.

Jimmy has got somebody with him. The old man's name is Coffee Billy, and he's the closest the Miccosukee have to a medicine man. They've lost so much of their culture that they can't do it the old way anymore, but still they give it a try. In the lights from the car the old man has got skin like leather and white hair.

The grass is peeping with frogs. Somewhere off in the distance a bull 'gator roars.

"Got your bug repellent?" asks Jimmy, liberally spraying his clothes. He's got a head for necessities. "Let's get going."

I'd thought we'd take the tour boat, but Jimmy has brought his own airboat, instead. It's lighter and higher, the Cadillac engine and propeller enclosed by a steel cage in the back, with the driver's seat bolted up high in front of it. The bottom of the boat is flat and armored. We don't even need water to run.

"What's this?" asks Joel.

"An airboat," I say.

"I'm going, too," he says.

"No you're not," I insist. "You're here to back us up. If we don't come back by midnight..."

"Edna knows where we're going," says Jimmy. "Let him come along."

"Dammit," I say, glaring, but I'm already undermined. Jimmy doesn't think I should tell other people what to do, either. Or maybe he thinks we'll wreck the boat, and he needs another strong back to haul it upright again. It's an idea. Coffee Billy and I won't be much help.

I let Joel sit in the second seat below the driver so he can see, and huddle alongside the old man myself, well back of the squarish prow.

Jimmy fires up the engine, and immediately we're deaf. Thunder rolls across the marsh. We slide off the trailer and down the sandy bank into the water, ease slowly past the restaurant and out toward Miami again. Once we're in the clear, Jimmy guns the engine, and then we're skimming the reeds and pools, light as a gallinule.

It's completely dark now, and invisible saw grass whips the prow, showering us with trash. Jimmy turns on his jacklights, but they're nearly useless. The stars seem fiercer now.

If I was with anyone but Jimmy, I'd be worried about our speed. Instead, I've got other concerns. I ride for a while in silence, and then I lean over closer to Coffee Billy.

"Mind telling me what we're getting into?" I yell.

He stares into the darkness. "The woman you ask of is the spirit of renewal," he says. "She seeks for a rebirth."

"Ha!" I say, "Is this some damned mid-life crisis?"

He shrugs and wipes his nose. "Take it however you want."

After a while I decide I'd better apologize for the disrespect. I should know better, but somehow I've been off my game just lately. I rub at my face.

"I'm sorry. I didn't mean to piss you off," I say. "I'd just rather have something more practical to go on."

He's quiet for a long time, still huffy, I figure, but then he surprises me. He shrugs again, squints into the lights of the boat. "Daughter," he says, "you can't always have what you want."

"That's no news to me," I say.

"You're a spirit talker, aren't you?" he asks.

"Yeah," I say. I might as well admit it.

"Then you know about these things," he goes on. "Developers don't understand this land. They put in drainage canals and concrete to change what was here, but they don't really kill it. Those ancient things stay there right underneath, and when the developers are looking the other way, they start to wake up again."

Being a spirit talker isn't something I normally talk about—I'm wondering how he knows. Still, maybe Coffee Billy can recognize a kindred talent. I'm betting he's not along just for the ride.

I'm getting a chill from the wind, muggy as it is, and what he says sounds like layered realities again, like looking at the marsh from miles above.

"Unseen things lie all around us," he insists. "The land is dying, and now there are ghosts rising from the River of Grass."

He means the Everglades. I can believe it. Our lights seem very feeble in the emptiness. They catch the fiery sparks of eyes, and once the spectral shade of a white-tailed deer. Further in we'll find the Florida panther, mutated and poisoned by mercury—population: two hundred. Or maybe some dead wood storks.

We're running now through patches of flying mist. After a while we leave the open water and turn toward a cypress strand. Jimmy slows the boat. Columns of cypress loom on either side of us, buttresses crowding the slough. Bromeliads and orchids hang in the shadows overhead, festooned like bright-jeweled webs. Monstrous spiders scuttle away to safety in the moon flowers, and a ripple cuts the dark water ahead, an ominous snout with golden eyes and a massive, threshing tail.

Beyond the slough, we skim another flat of prairie, six inches of water smothered in grass, and aim for the dark shape of a slash pine hammock ahead. This is an island in the swamp, high and solid, overgrown with brush. Jimmy cuts the engine and drifts in to the shore.

Now the hush is deafening. Mist flows over the island like a sluggish river, eddies around masses of choking saw palmetto and matted fern. Fallen pine snags lie twisted and rotting, bound with briar and slimed with ancient, hoary lichen. Disturbed by the wake, a glitter of cottonmouth slides into the water, flicks away in a poisonous swirl.

I hope Joel knows enough to avoid the snakes. I've figured we're headed to some isolated camp, and I must be right. I wonder how far we are from Miami now.

We climb out of the aluminum hull, wade bravely into the weeds. Mosquitoes descend in a cloud. Too late, I'm worrying about red bugs and deer ticks in the grass. The bug repellent might not be enough to fend them off.

Jimmy materializes from the cloaking mist, a dark, stocky shape in boots and jeans.

"Wait here a minute," he says.

It seems there's to be a ceremony. Coffee Billy produces a rattle made of turtle shell, tosses powder in different directions and starts to chant. The mosquitoes are put off by the repellent and they're not biting, but still they bat against my eyes, buzz inside my ears. Joel chokes. Apparently he's swallowed one.

Coffee Billy finally leads off, a flashlight in one hand and the rattle in the other. Now and then he shakes the rattle, chants prayers to the wind. A briar tears through my hair, rakes my cheek. We force our way through the palmetto, and I'm worrying about rattlesnakes now.

"Where are we going?" I whisper to Jimmy.

The question is too late. We're already there.

The place is a ruin, a ghost camp of rotting *chikees* and fallen thatch, the house timbers leaning under the weight of must and age. Odd garbage middens lie about in the weeds, pale shells of rusted-out buckets, tools like skeletons decaying to ash. Eyes catch the light. An animal hisses, a startling sound in the waiting, eerie hush. It's only a raccoon, faintly visible, lashing its tail back and forth as it heads away from us.

A faint breeze stirs, swirls the mist. I catch the smell of smoke. Would that be from the controlled burn?

No. It's from right here.

Jimmy Bowlegs and Coffee Billy slide from the brush into the clearing, alert and careful of the shadows.

"Anna?" Joel whispers, uncertain.

"Let's go," I say, and move to follow them.

We're all silent and watchful now, padding through the ruins. Storage sheds form the outside ring of huts, and the sleep *chikees* are next inside. Shreds of torn netting hang from the rafters, billowing and ghostly in a vagrant draft.

The smoke comes from the cook shack, a faint miasma of wood ash and fry bread floating in the air. Embers glow like shells in the sand. We assemble at the blackened logs, but there's nothing here to see.

There's only silence, except for a light drip of moisture. Then a faint wail cuts the air.

I jerk around, trying to judge direction.

"There," Jimmy whispers, pointing to the rightmost shed.

The baby has heard our voices. He slides down from the half-ruined floor. He's blond, maybe three or four, dressed in a dirty shirt and light blue shorts. He stares, not sure what to make of us, and then as I step forward and call to him, he takes a tentative step.

There's a hag between us.

She forms from the fog, a ghostly ectoplasm as sheer as the billowing shreds of net. Then solid, ugly and real, she hobbles forward, coming between us and the child.

"Stop," she says. "You cannot have him."

It's Muskogean. I can't speak the language at all, but somehow I understand what she says anyway. She's ancient, wrinkled and bent. With the elaborate coif, dressed in the rainbow patterns that cost so dear in the crafts stores now, she looks like something that's walked out of the past.

"Witch," says Coffee Billy. "Give us the child."

She's not paying attention. Her eyes have shifted, and she's looking at Joel now. Her voice murmurs gently.

I'm slow on the uptake. The boy is mesmerized, moving toward her before I realize it. Too late I see the resemblance between him and the child. He's young enough that she's called to him.

"Joel!" I hiss, and lurch forward, but Jimmy has got me by the arm.

"Don't," he whispers.

"The hell," I say, and I yank lose from his grip. "That woman…"

He snatches at me again. "Let me get the baby," he says.

I see what he means to do. I jerk to a halt while he circles. I shiver, but then he's got the toddler safe in his arms.

"Spirit talker, call your friend back now," says Coffee Billy. "Then I will take care of the witch."

I'm glad to have him to back me up. I step forward. "Joel!"

He starts slightly, dazed, still standing in the filmy glow of the woman's arms. For a second I'm terrified, not sure he's going to hear me.

"Joel!" I say again, with all the sharp authority I can muster. "Come here to me."

He moves this time, steps back slightly away from her. "Joel!"

The woman moves to follow, drifting along. Coffee Billy scoops up fire with the remains of a bucket, steps between the two of them and hurls the coals at her face.

The woman shrieks, swirls away into darkness with the rush of flame. Sparks lodge in the dry thatch behind her, smolder and catch in the wind. Joel is standing in front of me now, outlined in a lurid glare.

"Are you all right?" I ask him. I've got one hand wound in the fabric of his shirt, just in case.

He presses his hands against his eyes.

"What happened?" he says.

Coffee Billy is shaking me by the arm. "We've got to get to the boat." Another *chikee* is burning.

"Let's go, Joel."

Dry as tinder, the grass explodes into flame.

We run, fighting our way through the undergrowth, half-blind and choking. Seared by the flash and roar behind us, somehow we get back to the marsh. We're too far east—but Jimmy knows the way. We splash through the water, and he dumps the baby in the boat, scales the rungs to his seat. The engine fires, adding its thunder to the roar of the flames.

We're clear of the worst smoke then, coughing, our eyes smarting—and into the open air. Behind us the island is a flaming inferno, sparks raging in gusts of superheated storm, rocketing upward in the draft.

The boat glides away over the water, leaving the conflagration behind. At a distance, it still towers over us, flaming like the very gates of hell, reflecting in the pools like we're running over a lake of fire.

The child in my arms wipes his eyes, stirs to look around at the craft.

"Is this a boat?" he asks.

The fire flashes along the water, blazing through the dry, sere grass. It's a cleansing that far outshines the stars. The spirit has her renewal. The flames won't hurt the slash pines or the palmettos; they're adapted. The animals take cover in deeper water. Within a week, fresh growth will riot on the island and wild masses of flowers will grace the marsh.

And I think I've been blindsided by some kind of renewal, too—something I didn't expect. With luck, maybe this feeling will last me for a while.

We're on our way back in, and there's a different thunder. I look up.

Above us it's starting to rain.

Chapter 5

SNOWBIRDS

I'm sitting at the front desk trying to demolish the mountain of unfiled case notes when the office door opens and an old man hobbles in, pushing a walker. He stops in front of the desk.

"Are you the receptionist?" he grates. He's got a raspy voice and a heavy accent—it sounds German, which doesn't make him any easier to understand. Another guy works in behind him and shuts the door. He's not much younger, but he does look spryer.

"No," I say. I give them both a onceover and stuff the folder I've been working on back into a drawer. I shove back my chair and stand up. "I'm Anna Detroyer."

"Oh." The first guy blinks and jerks his head toward the door. "Uh. That Detroyer?"

"Yes," I say. "That's right."

The sign reads, "Detroyer and Angstrom, Private Investigators."

He shifts his feet. "Is...?"

"Mr. Angstrom's isn't available," I say flatly, and don't go into any details about why. "Come back to my office," I say, and lead the way. "It's more comfortable than standing out here."

It's a little better than a cubbyhole and a lot neater now that I've gotten the pile of paperwork out front where visitors can see it right away—no waiting. The two of them hobble after me, scuffing painfully over the stained terrazzo floor.

"Sit down," I say, "Mr..."

"Bragi," he says grudgingly.

I assume that's acknowledgment of my fitness to work on his problem. Regardless of whether he likes my gender or my face, I'm still the best option for a certain kind of case.

"Thrazi," says the other one.

He helps Bragi slide into one of the worn chairs—they look like brothers, or cousins, maybe. Thrazi parks the walker off to one side, and then eases himself down, too.

"How can I help you, Mr. Bragi," I say. The two of them glance at each other. Thrazi nods almost imperceptibly.

"My wife has disappeared," Bragi says, turning to me. "I want you to find her. She's a young woman—beautiful, blond."

He hands me a photo. Sitting in my office, he looks like he's a hundred if he's a day, with lines etched deep in his face like crevasses in an arctic landscape, and hair like frost. His eyes are sea blue, but it's an iceberg color, not the bright indigo of the Gulf Stream that surges off the Florida coast. The woman in the photo looks about twenty, and he's right—she's young and radiant enough to make me feel every gray hair I've got. In the picture she's wearing white, a draped tunic of some sort, and carrying a basket of apples.

The photo was taken somewhere else, an orchard maybe, up north.

"Miami is your winter home?" I ask, glancing up.

"Yes," he says. He clears his throat. "I own a condo on the beach."

Snowbirds. They migrate to Miami every year, clutter the beach with wrinkled, pale bodies. Nobody cares; they're rich.

"Is that where your wife disappeared?" I ask. "The beach?"

"Yes," he says. "I'm a writer—a poet, actually. I was working and I noticed it was getting late, past dinnertime, and she hadn't called me to eat. The maid couldn't find her. She was gone."

"She disappeared right from the condo." I ask. "She didn't go out shopping, or anything?"

"From the condo," he says. "She just walked out."

"Did she receive any phone calls before she left?" I ask.

"I don't know."

He frowns. He was working, after all.

"Did you notify the police?" I ask.

"They seem to think she left of her own accord." He sounds stuffy now, like he doesn't think much of the police.

"Any ransom notes?"

"None."

My innate crap detector has gone off. Something's wrong with this, I think, something they're not telling me. I study the two of them sitting there, but I can't see what it is. And I've got no grounds to refuse, however I cut it. I need the money.

"Mr. Bragi," I say finally, wanting to clear things up, "I can take the case, check around some. But if she doesn't want to be found, I can't do much about it."

Bragi frowns like a winter landscape, and I think I've hit on the problem, but his friend Thrazi interrupts.

"Of course," he says smoothly. "We understand. If that's the case, Bragi just wants to know where she is, and that she's all right."

He's less of an iceberg, but he rings false, too, not quite reassuring. I still can't give them a clear reason to refuse, much as I want to.

"What's the maid's name?" I ask.

Bragi has to think about it, as if he's deciding how much information he can give me.

"Delores Cardozo," he says.

"All right," I say grudgingly. I hand him my generic contract. Bragi signs and pays the retainer in cash, big bills. I write him a receipt for it, and the two of them climb painfully up out of the chairs, unpark the walker. It's an ordeal for Bragi even to make the door, and I wonder how they got in here from the street. I look again at the pile of cash and the girl in the photo, and think about how old he is. It's none of my business, though.

The phone rings. It's Paul Angstrom, the other half of the sign. The way my personal life is tangled up, I've got no room to be smug about the Bragis.

"Anna?" he says.

"Get lost," I say. "I don't need you cluttering up my life."

I hang up before he can say anything else. The phone rings again, but I ignore it. If it's a client, the voicemail will catch it. I just sit studying the photo, wondering where she would go, and if she had a lover. That's a definite possibility, little as I like to categorize the young, beautiful wives of old decrepit men. I decide to give Gloria a call, my friend who works on the police force.

"Hi, Anna," she says. "What do you want?"

"Can't a girl call to be sociable?"

"Not you," she says, and I can hear her gum pop even over the phone. "You're always working."

She sounds pissed, and the gum is catching hell. I sigh, thinking I deserve this.

"Okay," I say, "You're right. Guy named Bragi. Lost his wife. Did you work it?"

"Nah," she says, "but as usual, Gloria will see what she can find out for you."

"Thanks," I say, wincing at her tone. "Tell Eddie hello for me." She and I are old friends, went to school together. Eddie's her husband of the moment, father of two of her kids.

"Tell him yourself," she says. "It's been a long time since you've been to the house."

Neglected friendships come back to haunt you. I'd better make the time. I'd meant to drive up to Hollywood Friday night to visit my Aunt Patti—it's been a while since I've seen her—but I can do it Saturday, instead.

"Okay," I say. "Do you want to take the kids to a movie Friday night?"

"It's a date," she says. "I'll call back when I've got the info for you."

I get my keys out then, ready to head to the beach and see what I can find out.

It's early October in Miami and last week it was just under ninety degrees, with humidity about that, too. It doesn't matter so much on the beach, with a wind to blow the heat away. The sun glares off the pavement, and you only get rare glimpses of ocean now and then through the high-rise development. This week it's slightly cooler and rainy, but it's still humid as hell.

I'd thought the address Bragi gave was in the exclusive section, and I'm right. The place is a tasteful flamingo-pink fortress with palm trees and coral bougainvillea spilling over the wall. There's a gate that locks, plus a security guard to make sure it does, every time. It's not likely his wife was kidnapped by somebody she didn't know, then.

I don't try to get in. I just had to verify the place. I want to talk to the maid instead, who's at her address back across the causeway in picturesque Little Havana. My ratty compact car is laboring as I ride over, arcing above the showy, white luxury boats dancing on whitecaps in the bay. In contrast, I've been nursing the car along, hoping it will last till December so I won't need air conditioning for a month or two and I can roll the windows down. I've been wishing I could afford new transportation—but I won't buy anything. I've got payments to make now that are important to my pride.

Little Havana is all concrete block and red tile roofs packed into a tight development just off I95. I cruise up and down a few minutes looking for the address, then park in the drive and climb out to knock on the door.

It's opened by a short, plump Cubana with curly hair who must be Delores herself. I can hear kids screaming in the background.

"Mrs. Cardozo?"

"Yes?" she says, looking wary and drying her hands on a towel. She's a young woman and I expect the kids are hers.

"I'm Anna Detroyer, a private investigator. You work for the Bragis, don't you? I wonder if I could ask you a few questions about Mrs. Bragi's disappearance."

"Ah? Like that Magnum, P.I. on television?" she asks.

It's an old show, but still playing in reruns. I grit my teeth. "Not quite, but that's the general idea."

She studies my license with her brown eyes, frowning, and then she makes up her mind.

"Alright. Come in," she says, standing back so I can get through the door.

The house is typical of the neighborhood, hastily thrown up when the city first ballooned to take in the surge of refugees back in the nineteen-sixties. Back then, the governor sued the Feds to pay for the overflow. This house is well taken care of, a transplant right out of old Havana with banana trees nodding in the windows and a brand new flowered sofa in the living room.

Delores breaks into Spanish, sending the kids into the bedroom to play so we can sit on the sofa.

"*Vamos!*" she says to a little one who wants to clutch her knees. Once he's gone with the others, she turns back to me, "Would you like some coffee?"

I accept. It turns out to be heavy and black, but I like it that way. I sit on the couch and get into the questions. I can do it in Spanish, which is always a help in Miami. Mrs. Cardozo must have been born here, but she's still *Cubana* to the core. That doesn't wear off—not here.

"Those Bragis," she says, sounding like she's heard the questions one too many times before. "They're causing me so much trouble." She slaps the dishtowel across her knees.

"When did you first realize Mrs. Bragi was gone?" I ask.

"About seven last Tuesday," she says. "She had a headache earlier and lay down for a while, but I went to ask what to fix for dessert, and she was gone."

"Did she receive any phone calls?"

"No," she said. "I always answer the phone when I'm there. I was busy making dinner, broiled salmon and asparagus that night, but I'd have heard it, anyway."

"Mrs. Cardozo, do you know if Mrs. Bragi had any lovers?"

She looks scandalized, so I know the answer is a gossip sheet before she even answers.

"A different one for every month!" She inclines forward. "That woman! And that Bragi, he sent me home the minute he knew she was gone—just when I needed the work. I can't afford to sit here and wonder if Jorge's pay is going to cover all the bills we've got..."

"Mrs. Cardozo," I interrupt. "He sent you home?"

"So I won't know about his business," she says, tight-lipped, falling back against the cushions.

"I don't understand," I say. "As old as he is, I'd have thought he'd need more help—not less."

She looks at me in complete puzzlement. "Old?" she says. "Mr. Bragi's not old."

It's a total breakdown in communication that I can't explain—assuming that really was Bragi in my office, and not his grandad. It's one more thing about this case that annoys me, like I don't know half of what's going on.

The car is steamy inside now from sitting in the sun, intermittent as it is today. I call the office voicemail on my phone to check for messages. Gloria has checked in already, and I give her a quick call.

"Scuttlebutt is," Gloria says, "she took off with one of her boyfriends." Traffic rumbles behind me, drowning her out.

"Verified, or just opinion?" I yell.

"Opinion," says Gloria. "Don't yell. I can hear you."

Well. That's why Bragi didn't look like he had much confidence in the police. He figured he was being blown off, and he was.

It sounds right to me, too, considering how impregnable the condo looks. I hang up and sit in the car, thinking about it. Assuming the police opinion is justified, I can figure: a) Bragi doesn't want to believe it himself, b) he wants her back to salve his pride or c) he wants her back to beat hell out of her. There are some other possibilities too, but those are enough to begin with. I study the photograph in the orchard again, and she looks so sweet and innocent that I decide maybe she was kidnapped by one of said boyfriends against her will. Maybe Bragi is the one that's justified, after all. I'll just have to keep looking.

Paul has a message for me on the voicemail, too, but I ignore that. I decide to head out to the beach again, to check out the vicinity of the crime—or whatever—a little more thoroughly.

I get caught in a rain shower going back over the causeway and the wipers thrash wildly for a few seconds while the downpour is at maximum. It's gone by the time I park on the strip, but now the air feels like a Chinese laundry. I hike up and down in the haze, showing the picture at the office supply and the post office (Yeah, I see that fox all the time, but not this week. Split somewhere?) and at the coffee shop down the street (Buys donuts and coffee and flirts with Cal over there. Bitch never gains any weight.)

Nobody has seen her in a week, though. I'm about ready to give up this angle, so I shell out two dollars and ninety-nine cents to the woman for the donut and coffee special. I don't gain weight, either—too poor, maybe. But Cal's not my style. I lean on the counter, trying to think where else to look. Beachside? The condo has a private area cordoned off, and she might have gone for a swim. Except Delores thinks she left in the clothes she was wearing.

When I'm done at the diner, I've OD'ed on caffeine and sugar both. I leave a dollar tip and stand outside under the awning, all but jittery, to check out the status of the storm front. It's pouring in North Miami now. A homeless type steps out of the alleyway.

"Spare change?" he says, and I jump.

The city tries to obscure this little problem, tries to evict it from under overpasses and out of parks. It's an eyesore unsuitable for the upscale tourists. There was another discussion last year about making the homeless buy licenses to panhandle. Looking at this guy, I figure he not the type who could afford one, so I dig in my pocket for another dollar and pull out the photo, too.

"Ever see this woman?" I ask, out of pure habit.

"Yeah. Last Tuesday," he says. "Thanks a lot."

"Wait," I yell. He's turning away, but I've got him by the sleeve.

He looks at me like I'm crazy. He's got long, greasy, gray-streaked hair and an unkempt beard and a backpack that must hold everything he owns. Probably he's been camping out in the alley.

"Where did you see her?" I ask.

I let go of him and he eases back, leans against the stucco of the donut shop, watching me warily in case I do something else weird. He's younger than I first thought, maybe a serviceman laid off from some job up north. Like most people, I hadn't really looked at him before.

"Up the street," he says, nodding at the flamingo pink spire.

"What was she doing?"

He looks me up and down. "Have you got a right to ask questions, lady?"

I get out my license and tell him the bare bones of the story: the woman missing, her husband worried. He studies the license, then the photo again.

"She's a beautiful woman," he says. "I noticed that face. She got in the car with a redhead. I noticed him, too. Pale complexion, dark shirt and jeans. The car was a gunmetal Porche, and they drove off north up A1A. That's all I can say about it."

"Hey," I say. "Is this your local address?" It's the best break I've had all week. I dig out the twenty I keep for emergencies and hand it to him.

He grins and makes the bill disappear. "Yeah," he says. "If you need a witness, I'm Clarence Bow."

I head right back to the office and call Gloria to ask if there's an R.K.C. on a redhead with a silver Porche. Once I've done that, I need to check in with Bragi to let him know I've made some progress.

There's dead air on the line.

"Hello?"

Then he says flatly, "Thank you, Ms. Detroyer. That information will be adequate. You've been very efficient."

I'm taken by surprise. "What do you mean?" I blurt out.

"I won't be needing your services any longer," he says.

"What the hell..." But that's not good customer relations. I cut it off right away and start a ten-count but don't make it.

"If you're concerned you won't receive your full fee..." he begins.

"I'll send you a bill," I say, and hang up the phone.

Not good customer relations at all. The message light on the office phone is blinking and it's an Angstrom, but not Paul this time. It's Joel, the other half of my personal problem.

"Listen, Anna," he says on the voicemail—sounding completely sincere. "I'm sorry. Can we talk?"

I'm sorry too, kid. I decide to get drunk, but I can't do it after all that caffeine. I sit in the Katze Klub drinking and scowling, and after a while I know why it is Bragi has cut me off so fast. It's like Delores says, he doesn't want anyone messing in his business. Bragi knows who the redhead is.

It's not a good thought. I remember Bragi might want his wife back just to beat hell out of her. It happens all the time. Husband kills wife and lover. I wouldn't put it past the man, with those iceberg eyes. Or maybe she'll do him, old as he is.

I think about calling Gloria again, but it won't make any difference. The police have to have a crime to act on—they're not much on prevention—especially the Miami police. These guys are overworked with what's already happened. If there's going to be any prevention, I'll have to do it myself.

Maybe I'm still pissed off, or drunk, after all. Whatever, I walk out of that perfectly comfortable bar and head for the beach again in the misty haze of late afternoon, ready to stake out the flamingo tower.

It doesn't pay off until well after dark. I'm tired and starved and thinking better of it by then, parked in a side street with binoculars so I can check the cars going out the gate. About ten I catch a flash of snowy hair, and I see it's Bragi and his friend Thrazi leaving in a wine-colored Mercedes.

I start my car and pull into their wake, well back in the stream of headlights. They head north and west, going at a fast clip for such old guys, and end up in the bad section of town north of Little Havana.

It looks like a small warehouse, run down, with rusty metal siding that flaps in the wind and boarded up windows. I've got a chill now from that cold front coming in, and look for my jacket. I don't like the looks of the place, so I dig in the glove compartment for my .38 and slide it into my jacket pocket.

The place is dark and quiet, and tatters of trash blow in the weeds. The Mercedes has disappeared into a fenced lot, and likely they've gone in a side door that I can't get to from here. I fade into the alley, looking for a place to peer inside. Torn clouds race across the moon, trailing incipient tornadoes. The air feels electric with the storm. The wind gusts and drops, and something runs across my foot in the dark. I stifle a yell, but it's only a crab, a pale phantom feeling its way along the wet tarmac, looking for the sea.

Back of the place, the boards have rotted off a window and the latch has rusted through. I'm ready to try breaking and entering. I'm over the line now, but this could be important, so I pry the window up with my handy pocketknife and work my way inside.

I'm in a dark corner under the stairs, and I ghost around, locate voices in an office to one side of the littered floor. It's more than just the two I tracked in, and the voices are loud and angry. They sound occupied, so I edge up to the shaft of light and peer inside from behind the door. There are five of them, old as sin, and they've got the redhead tied to a chair.

I see right away what Clarence Bow meant—he's striking. He's got sharp features and elegant bones, looking near the woman's age—about twenty. His hair is a lustrous red that burns against bone white skin, touched with flame in the yellow light. His eyes look to be dark, not the iceberg blue of the rest of the family, and right now he's got blood on his face. But he's not taking the abuse easily. He looks stubborn and ready to spit.

What the hell have I gotten into? Some kind of Mafia affair?—Get the hell out now, Anna.

But I don't like the looks of what's going on, five to one. Plus some of the old guys look grim, regardless of their age. I twitch, fidgety and tense. I'll need a distraction if I'm going to do something about this and keep my nose clean with Gloria, too. What? Dammit, think Anna!

I've got a plan in a minute, collect an armload of scrap and set up behind the door. I played softball back in the dim past and I've still got some arm, so I use it to lob chunks at the walls. The first two or three could have been the storm, but the full barrage catches their attention. I'm afraid they'll leave somebody in the room, but I've caught them by surprise. They all trample out to check the doors, or more likely the expensive cars parked outside in the lot.

I slide into the light and use my pocketknife again. The redhead flashes me a hot look, but he doesn't ask any questions. We're across the floor and out the window then, and into the cold, stormy night outside.

"Thanks," he says in a muffled voice. He's got a slight accent, too. He starts to take off, but I've got my gun out now.

"Hold it, mister." I'm standing well away from him—he looks dangerous, the way he moves. He swings around again, sizing me up. "I want some answers for my trouble," I say.

"The hell with you," he says.

"My car's over there," I say, motioning with my head—not with the gun. "Get going."

The car is safe where I left it, and I toss him the keys. "You drive." When the neighborhood drops behind us, I settle against the door, ready to watch his face.

"Where's the woman?" I ask him.

He flashes me a look, and even in the dark I can see his eyes are strange. He pulls a hanky out of his pocket and starts to dab at his lip.

"Who're you?" he asks, and he sounds snotty and arrogant.

"Private detective," I say, unruffled.

"You work for them?" He spits it out like a rank taste in his mouth, jerks his head back the way we've come.

"Not now," I say, staying cool. "I'm just interested in what's happened to the girl."

He stops for a red light, looks me over again. He's seeing a dark woman, fortyish, but still tough and capable. I don't give a damn what he thinks.

"It's none of your business," he says.

"I've just made it my business," I say. "I'll help you if I can, kid. The man wants his wife back."

"I'm not a kid," he says. His eyes are definitely strange, with a flare in them like embers in the dark.

"Don't snap at me," I say. "I did you a favor."

"Why the hell should I care?" he says, heating up.

"You want to go back to those guys? You're welcome," I say, and lean over him to shove open the car door. "Get out of my car."

"Wait," he says then, and he doesn't move.

I sit there waiting.

"You're in trouble," I say. "Take the help while it's available."

"I don't have her," he says finally.

"Where is she?"

"I set it up for somebody else."

"That was real smart," I say, and he flares.

"You don't know anything about it."

"You want to tell me?" I ask.

"No."

"Then I'd recommend you think of a way to get her back," I say. "And fast. It'll get those guys off your back, at least."

"Shit," he says, sullen, and his eyes flash at me again.

"The light's changed," I say.

He jams down the accelerator and the engine coughs. We chug to the beach in stony silence—except for him muttering curses at my car. I remember he drives a silver Porche.

"Are you going to tell the police?" he asks finally, as we stop at another light.

"Not if you'll do something about it," I say.

"I can't," he says.

"Why not?"

"All right," he says then, sweetly. "I'll think about it."

I can read him now. The man's a shark, but he's got charm.

"Damn you," I say. "Where do you want to get out?"

He shoots me a scalding look. "Hell. Anywhere."

"Pull into that parking lot."

It's a finance company, beachside, and closed for the night. Traffic streams by us on A1A. Waves beyond the buildings crash on the sand, storm-driven, audible even from here with the windows cracked. A flock of gulls squats on the pavement, facing into the wind. I fish a business card out of my pocket. I still haven't put the gun away.

"Call me if you're ever serious," I say.

He glares at me.

"Out," I say.

I slide over as he shuts the door and put the car into gear. Then I hear chaos erupt behind me—a crack of exploding wings. I turn to look, and the gulls have scattered. It's a fish hawk that's disturbed them, a pale shadow of an osprey that's airborne and headed south. And dammit—there's no sign of the guy anywhere around in the wind-blown night.

Spirit talker, I think, you've done it again. That was something more than a man that was sitting in my car, talking to me like he was ordinary and sane. The Native American shape-changer is called a skin walker, but this didn't have the right feel for that. Something about the fire in him suggests I should be careful about what I'm getting into.

There's a message from Gloria on the voicemail.

"Anna," it says, "how do you come up with these guys?"

Tell me about it.

I sigh.

"Anna?" says Joel's message. "I didn't want to talk this way, but I will if I have to. Dad didn't treat you very well—I know that. But I didn't know what he was doing. Honest. I swear..." He sounds sincere as hell. Dammit, again.

How old do you have to get before you stop doing stupid things? Not 'til well after forty, I guess. My own private soap? I spent fifteen years working with Paul Angstrom and he completely shut me out, but his son was something else. Paul aimed the kid at me, and while I was occupied with that, the bastard tried to sell the business out from under me. I sued to stop it, and now the payments I stretch to make every month are to him, for his share of Detroyer and Angstrom. I trusted both of them, and where did it get me? The business is mine now, but it was a hell of a jolt.

My character judgment has gone completely awry. Now I've likely made a mistake with this redhead, too, that Gloria says has more aliases than a movie star. I'm getting into trouble here.

Bragi calls the first thing in the morning and accuses me of the business the night before, but I deny it. Then I brood in the office, screwing with a divorce case that's due for court next week while rain whips at the windows. The storm front has stalled, run into warm air coming up through the Florida straits. It will pour for the rest of the day, at least.

The phone rings late, just as I'm rummaging for my umbrella to leave. I debate letting the voicemail catch it, but another case or two would help with the bills. I answer it myself.

"Detroyer," he says. "I've decided you're right."

I don't recognize the voice at first, juggle the phone. "Huh?" I say, but then I catch the accent, the biting tone.

"Do you know who Bragi's wife is?" he says.

"Huh?" I say again—I'm not exactly brilliant tonight.

"Are you following me?" he asks.

"Yeah," I say, tracking now, "but I still don't know who she is."

"This is going to be a damn lot of trouble." He sounds spiteful.

"So?" I say. "It's not something I did." Coming right back at him—human or no.

He laughs.

"Call Bragi," he says, "and tell him I'm bringing her in tonight. But I'll need help. The guy that's got her...I can't do it by myself."

"Will he help you?" I ask.

"He'd better, if he wants her back. One a.m., Ms. Detroyer. On the beach."

I'm holding a dial tone then. He's gone.

"Dammit."

I strain my brain, but I still can't figure what's going on. Not understanding it leaves my stomach tight and queasy. Finally I just call Bragi.

"What?" he says. "What?" It's like he's getting Alzheimer's now. Or maybe he's deaf. His friend Thrazi comes on the line, and I tell the story to him.

"Thank you, Ms. Detroyer," he says, and hangs up the phone.

"Dammit," I repeat. I'm worried about the woman, so I decide to crash the party again.

All that fancy condo security is great, but it has a weak point that makes it essentially useless. You can't fence out the tide. It won't be easy swimming the ocean in this storm, but I've done worse. I have an old wet suit in the closet that we used on a job years ago, and I'm just sorry Paul won't be there to back me up this time. That's too much baggage. The water will be treacherous, and I think of calling Gloria, but it's too much baggage again. Still, I feel obligated, and I'm going to do it, dangerous or not.

I'm in the wetsuit and out on the public beach north of the condo by midnight—that had to be where he meant. It's quit raining except for a fine mist that blurs the skyline, and the surf is pounding like a hammer. The waves are sienna with sand clawed up from the bottom, and the rip will be vicious. I mean to stay out of the water as much as I can. The suit is for emergencies, and to keep me warm, and my gun relatively dry. I start hiking, and the foam hisses and spits, phosphorescent, lashing at my legs. The wind howls and gnashes its teeth.

Glare from downtown lightens the sky, searchlights from the airport playing like UFO's on the fog. I make good progress, counting the condos, not sure I'll recognize the right one from the beach. I do, and I slide up out of the water just inside the chain link barrier. Now what?

I don't have to worry about it. A patrol picks me up right away. I think at first it's security, but it's Thrazi and one of his buddies I didn't hang around to meet last night, a tough-looking bastard with just one eye.

"Who's this?" he asks Thrazi, as I stand there with my hands up and lights glaring in my face. I'm wondering what they've done with the hired condo guards.

"Detroyer," says Thrazi. "She's Bragi's detective."

"Who invited her?"

"Don't ask me," Thrazi says, and shrugs defensively.

"Take her up and lock her in," One-eye orders, like he's the general in charge.

It's okay with me. They've not found my gun.

We turn and start hiking.

"Are you guys family?" I ask Thrazi. I'm still sure they're Mafia or something.

"Aesir," he says shortly. The answer is nearly obscured by the surf, and it rings a bell somewhere, but I can't place it. We just make it past the high tide mark and there's a shout from below.

I swing around, and Thrazi does, too.

A reception committee has assembled out of the dark, phantoms just back of the phosphorescence, and at first I can't locate what they're pointing at. I'm confused, expecting a boat. All I can see is a couple of birds.

In this storm?

One of them is the osprey I saw last night. And the other is a dark, massive eagle.

It's deadly flying in that wind, worse than swimming the surf. And this is a battle.

Blood stains the hawk's feathers, and it's laboring. The eagle shrieks and strikes, plummeting like a deadly spear, talons extended. The osprey evades, swoops, tumbles sideways. They lock together, the eagle screaming in rage, and they flail and fall in the surf.

Everybody runs. Including me.

The eagle is wet and furious, still shrieking, but the osprey's gone. In its place a ripped, bloody fish thrashes into the waves and disappears.

I'm stunned, but the old guys aren't. They grab at the clawing, biting eagle, helpless to fly with its wet feathers.

Finally it changes, too, becomes a giant with shaggy hair, and lies cursing and exhausted on the wet sand with six or eight of them sitting on top.

"Where the hell..." begins One-eye. He's looking for the fish.

It's me that finds it. It looks like a salmon, belly up, floating in the surf. Stranded in the storm wrack, it flops over and then it's a man with a bloody shoulder, wet and gasping for breath.

"Are you all right?" I ask, falling to my knees beside him.

But the others aren't so concerned. One-eye prods the guy with his foot.

"Where is she?"

The redhead sits up then and holds out his hand, opens it to show a dark mussel shell. He tosses that into the air and it falls and becomes a woman, young and radiant and dressed all in white. She's got the apple basket with her still.

She laughs, sweet as all of daylight, and turns. "Thank you, Loki," she says. "I didn't like the place where I was."

And then I know who they all are. She's Idun, famous for the golden apples of youth, and while she was gone, they've all gotten old. We get all kinds in Miami, retirees from all over the world, but Norse legends are a little much.

My bonus is an apple. It sits on my desk looking like a golden delicious—but it's a long way from that. Soon I'm going bite into it.

It's going to be funny as hell to be twenty again.

Chapter 6

SOULS

I come in the door just in time to catch the office phone. "Detroyer," I say, expecting it'll be Craig Noe.

It's Joel Angstrom instead.

"Wait," he says. "Don't hang up, Anna. It's business."

"I'm expecting a call."

"I'm in trouble," he says.

"Call your dad."

"I can't," he says. "He's out of town."

So what am I now? A surrogate mom?

"Listen, Joel," I say, clearly and distinctly. "I don't want to get involved with either one of you right now. You'll have to find somebody else to help you out."

"Anna..." he insists.

There's a desperate note in his voice. I hold the phone above the cradle for a minute, trying to analyze it. Then I heave out a sigh, shift one hip onto the desk and the phone back to my ear. Why me?

"What's wrong, Joel?"

"I…" he says, and breaks it off. "Anna, could we meet somewhere for lunch?"

"Tell me first what's going on."

He thinks about it.

"Some guy is following me," he says. It's hardly loud enough for me to hear over the phone.

"Do you know who?"

"Yeah," he says. "He's a black guy. I think his name's Macoute."

"What's he following you for?" I ask.

"That's what I need to know. It's like…"

"Like what?" I prompt. "Like he's in love with you or something?"

"Anna," he says, "don't laugh. That happens sometimes. Usually I just say 'no thanks' and that's it. But this time…I mean…it's like he's…well…stalking me, or something."

Well, I'm not surprised that guys hit on him, too. Joel's a sharp-looking kid. But I don't like the sound of this stalking. Maybe he's got reason to be upset.

"There's no reason for him to follow you?"

"None I know of."

"Okay," I say. "Vinnie's at one o'clock."

There is a message from Craig on the phone. "Anna," he says. "I can't help you out this week end. I've got this dive job down in the Bahamas. I hope next week is okay? Let me know. I'm gone."

Well, there goes a good job down the toilet. The clients are offering a big pay-off, but they need the work done right now. As in pronto—this week end. I tap my nails on the desk, sit there listening to the growl of traffic past the office windows. It's already Friday. I ought to be calling dive shops to see if I can get another backup for the weekend, but instead I'm thinking about Joel Angstrom.

I've not seen the kid for a while. He transferred to college at Florida International in the fall, and I met some of his friends before his dad and I had our falling-out. I'm not a P.I. for nothing, and I've got plenty of time before one o'clock.

I take a chance and riffle through the phone book, luck out on the second call.

"Teresa?" I say. "Have you seen Joel Angstrom lately?"

"Who is this?" she says.

"Anna Detroyer," I say. "I'm a friend of his dad's."

She thinks about it. "I've not seen him," she says. "Try Audrie Benoit."

"Is she in the book?"

"No," she says. "Got a pencil?"

I try the number and voicemail answers. But I've got one myself; I can't complain. Maybe she'll call back before noon.

"This is..." I start, and then the phone clicks.

"'Alo," it says. The woman has got something of an accent.

"...Anna Detroyer," I finish up. "Can I talk to you about Joel Angstrom?"

She has to think about it, too. "Wha' for?" she says.

"I'm a friend of the family."

"Okay," she says finally. "Wha' you want to know?"

"I'd rather talk in person. Have you got time for coffee?" I ask.

The north campus of Florida International is up Biscayne Boulevard in the same general direction as Vinnie's. It's late winter in Miami and shirtsleeve weather today. Sun glints off the water in brief, bright flares. Then I make a turn into the developments and it's gone.

I know when I see the girl she's Haitian. We're in a hole-in-the wall coffee shop near the campus. I order mine heavy and black, sit down opposite her in a booth. She's gorgeous, creamy pale, pouting lips, a svelte figure in designer jeans and a flame silk shirt. There's a slight kink to her shoulder-length hair and a slight spread to her nose—the only indications of black ancestry—and you have to look hard to see that. The accent is the tip-off: high class French Creole. Her family's not off some refugee raft.

"Teresa said I should call you," I say. "What's Joel up to these days?"

"You begin to wonder?" she asks.

"Yeah."

"That boy, he run with a bad crowd these days. Maybe soon he drop out of school."

I have to set my teeth. "What's the problem, Ms. Benoit?"

"I don' know him that well," she says. "We go out, maybe one time, maybe two. Then I think maybe he's not so good for me, after all."

I have to wince at that, and the girl catches it. Her cool eyes flick up at my face, slide away. She's not drinking her coffee, just stirring it, watching the swirls with frowning concentration. Maybe she thinks I'm not so good for her, either.

"I talk to you because I like Joel," she says. "I think he is..." She doesn't finish.

"In bad trouble?"

"*Oui*," she says, and frowns harder. "If not already, then soon."

Damn.

"Do you know the people he's hanging around with?" I ask.

"Some of them," she says.

"He says a guy's following him. Somebody named Macoute."

I jump as her spoon clatters down.

"I have to go," she says, and reaches for her bag.

"Wait a minute." I grab after her, catch a handful of flame-red silk. "Who is this guy?"

"Let go of me," she says.

Her face has blanched enough for me to see freckles across her nose. Her eyes are suddenly as green and vivid as a cat's. I realize what she's said, look down, let go of her. She throws a five dollar bill on the table and jerks out of the seat. Bells clatter as the door slams behind her.

I've lost my taste for coffee. Maybe I should go down the street to the Club Bar instead.

Headed back south again, I roll down the windows to let the heat out of the car and click on the radio. Planning on that dive job, I've been watching a cold front roll down through Georgia, hoping it'll get past us in time to leave good weather for the week end. The radio tells me it's stalled now over North Florida, promises it will stay there. I don't need any more complications to my life.

By the time I get to Vinnie's, I'm totally pissed off. Joel is already there, sitting in one of the booths that line the back wall. I have to look twice to realize it's him. His hair is shaggy and unkempt. It looks like he's lost weight, and he's dressed in rags of faded jeans and an old flannel shirt.

He's still got grace to spare, stands up when he notices I'm there. I slide into the seat across from him and drop my elbows on the Formica shine.

He doesn't look good close up, either. There are years more in his eyes.

"Are you on drugs?" I ask.

He gives me a look that's almost venomous, glances away.

"No," he says.

I reach out and catch his chin, pull his head around so I can see his eyes. The pupils aren't dilated. He flushes when he realizes what I'm doing, reaches up and knocks my hand away.

"Anna..."

"Sorry, kid." I look at the menu. "What do you want for lunch?"

He orders spaghetti and I get ravioli. The waitress brings us salads.

"You look different," he says. "Younger."

"You look different, too. Older. It's been a long six months."

"I didn't have anything to do with it," he says.

"Yes, you did." Then I catch his expression. I have to look away myself, study the plastic grapes on an overworked trellis nearby. "Maybe you just didn't know it, kid."

He sighs, rubs both hands over his face, digs the heels into his eyes. "All right," he says. "We can leave it at that."

"Are you okay, Joel?"

"Yeah," he says. He drops his hands, but he still won't look at me. He starts to pick at his salad.

"So what can I do for you?" I ask.

"I told this guy I had a steady girlfriend, but he didn't believe me. Let me hang around with you for a while, sleep on your couch for a couple of nights."

"You really think I'm going to do that?"

He won't look at me.

"Why not talk to your dad about it?" I ask.

"I've not seen him in a while."

He catches me staring, glances away again.

"Where are you staying?" I ask.

"An apartment."

He starts visibly as the waitress shows with our orders. Joel's not eaten his salad, so she leaves it, takes my plate away. He doesn't seem to notice the spaghetti.

"Eat your lunch," I say.

He looks at the plate. "I'm not hungry," he says. He shoves the dish suddenly, jerks sideways out of the booth.

"Joel." I know better than to grab at him.

He stops, shifts his feet. "Yeah," he says.

I'm looking at his back, but at least he's not running away from me.

"Sit down."

His shoulders twitch, but he does it.

It's the innocence that's gone out of his eyes. He's not the same sweet kid I met last year. His face is leaner and harder, the bones standing out clear and sharp, heavily shadowed by dark smudges beneath his eyes. All of the sudden he looks less like Paul and more like somebody I don't know very well at all. I want to ask him how it is between him and Paul, but I can't find the words. It's clear he's always idolized his dad, and now…Well, I've had that same feeling.

"Can you drive a boat?" I ask.

He blinks. "Huh?"

"You know. Those things that run along the water. People use them to…"

"Anna," he says. "I'm serious."

"So am I," I say and reach across the table for his plate. "If you're not going to eat your spaghetti, can I have it?"

He gets possessive. "I'll eat it." He finds his fork, pokes at a meatball.

"So, can you drive a boat?" I ask.

His eyes flash up at me. "Yeah," he says. "What about it?"

"I need some help for the week end. I have a job with heirs looking for missing papers. They're supposed to be off the Keys in a sunken yacht."

"You do salvage work?" he asks.

"Not usually." I shrug. "I've got a friend that passed the job along to me. She's going to rent me her boat, but I can't go out by myself—it's too dangerous. I'll need at least one other person to back me up."

"I'm not a diver," he says.

"I can do that part," I say. "I just need someone to run the boat."

"All week end?" he says.

"No," I say. "We'd be back Sunday noon at the latest. We'll have to get an early start, so you can sleep at my place tonight. All right?"

"Okay," he says, and frowns. He pokes at another meatball.

The kid just knocks me over with his enthusiasm. I sigh, search around in my wallet for money to pay the check.

"I've got arrangements to make," I say. "I'll see you tonight. Nine o'clock at my apartment. Okay?"

He nods.

Back at my office, I call Geraldine about the boat. Also, I need to know who this guy is that's after Joel. I tap my nails on the desk again and decide to call Gloria, my best buddy down at the police station. Maybe she can get me the goods on him.

Her voicemail answers.

"Hi, Gloria," I say to it. "It's Anna. You got anything on a guy named Macoute? Black, maybe Haitian, ugly type? I'll be gone on a job for the week end, but give me a call. Thanks."

I drop the phone back on the hook. I need to get my air tanks filled now, and all my gear down to the boat by tomorrow.

By nine thirty I've decided Joel's not going to show. Damn the kid. This could be some kind of joke—or worse. In a contest between Paul and me, there's no real doubt in my mind which way the kid would swing. Maybe they're up to something again. Maybe I've rented the boat and gone to all this work just to be stood up at the docks out of pure vindictiveness.

But then, I don't like the way Joel looks right now— the hard, haunted quality around his eyes, the set to his jaw. The kid's at risk somehow. Maybe I should worry about him instead.

Welcome to mom-hood, Anna.

The doorbell rings at ten thirty.

He leans over the rail in a graceful curve to check out the parking lot below. Then he turns back to me, drops one shoulder against the stucco wall. With me standing on the step, we're eye to eye now.

"I forgot to ask," he says. "Did you have something planned for tonight?"

"I rented a movie," I say.

For the first time I see the ghost of last year's grin on his face. He glances out over the clattering fronds of palm trees that circle the pool. "Was I supposed to bring popcorn?"

"You missed the whole damn thing." I'm not going to point out it's not a date. Damn kid. I move back so he can get in the door.

I sleep restlessly, thrash when the alarm goes off. I feel around for it, and then remember I left it across the room. Joel is still face down on the couch. He starts violently as I rumple his hair.

"God," he says. "It's still dark."

"It will be until seven o'clock. Want some espresso?" I ask.

I check the weather report one last time and it sounds fine. The cold front is dissipating in front of a warm air mass pushing up from the Caribbean.

"Let's go," I say, and drop the cups into the sink.

Joel wrinkles his nose when he sees the boat.

"What is this thing?" he asks.

"A workboat," I say. "It works better than it looks." I start handing him gear to load onboard. "It belongs to some friends of mine in the salvage business, but the guy had a heart attack last month and they're up in New York. They may have to sell it now."

Geraldine and Flynn started out with just a hull and modified it themselves. It's thirty-five feet with big engines under the deck, extra gas tanks, a watertight cabin—the thing could capsize and still float just fine. A dive platform opens out right to the waterline in back. Inside the cabin there's a cramped head and a tiny galley. A couple of bunks are packed into the empty space up under the bow.

I nod at the pilot's seat. "Go ahead."

It takes Joel a couple of tries to start it. He flips on the instruments like he knows what he's doing, backs it out of the slip.

"Okay?" I ask.

"Yeah." He's frowning. "It's just bigger than I'm used to."

The diesels provide a solid, dependable pulse as we head on out through the port. The docks are eerie and deserted this time of morning. Reflections shimmer on the water. Out in front of us, the big cruise ships are outlined with lights like Christmas, and the air has a faint stink of oil, along with the salt smell of the sea.

We follow the channel markers and the jetties out through the glimmering, chilly darkness, turn south. The sun comes up red through a drifting, bloody haze.

"Uh-oh," I say, watching it. "I don't like that."

"What?" asks Joel.

"The sky."

I try the weather service again, but it just gives me the same report: Front breaking up. Warm and sunny today and tomorrow. It's the usual optimism, mandated by the tourist trade. Florida never has foul weather unless evacuation is imminent.

Watching Joel run the controls makes me feel better about what I've done. I've taken a serious chance in asking him along as a single tender, little as I know about his skills. But he does fine with the boat. He understands what I'm talking about when I show him where we're going, sets the heading, turns on the autopilot. Then he takes a look around the boat for himself.

"Did they build this themselves?" he asks.

"Yeah," I say. "What do you think?"

He shrugs, "So far, so good," and gives me a grin.

Joel has come alive in the sun, and his eyes flash like rays off the water. He takes off his shoes and shirt, and beads of spray catch on his brown skin, scatter the light in bright flares. The wind whips his hair around his face. He sits on the deck to stare at the wake, and I watch the long curve of his back, the flex of his shoulders as he adjusts to the swell. I have to look away—damn the kid. This doesn't feel like motherhood. He turns his head to follow a dolphin's splash, and I notice his nose is already red. I dig in my gear for the sunblock.

"What have we got to eat?" he asks.

By afternoon I'm watching the weather again, but south of us this time. I give up on listening to the radio and check the barometer instead. In another hour we'll have the Keys off to starboard, and Joel starts monitoring our position on the GPS. The wind drops and the air feels close and muggy. When I check the barometer again, it's falling.

"Damn," I say.

We're there now. We've found the Coast Guard marker. But the barometer is dropping like a rock. A squall line dances along the horizon. I decide the weather service doesn't know jack about predicting the weather. I'd bet my ass there's a tropical depression forming in that warm air mass—and here we are right beneath it.

It's too early in the season for that, but then, shit happens.

We've come a long way, and it's all wasted if we head back now. Plus, we'll still be caught by the storm. If I put off the dive until this blows over, it'll be too late—Murphy's laws set the odds. The wreck's not that far down, and the dive shouldn't take me that long. I need the money bad. I'm going to gamble I can beat it.

"What are you doing?" asks Joel.

"Going down," I say.

"Is that safe?" he asks.

"No," I say, "but then, neither is running home through a tropical depression. One hour shouldn't make that much difference."

The air may feel heavy and close, but the ocean is at its coldest this time of the year, the currents carrying northern arctic waters barely heated by a quick churn through the tropics. I've brought a wet suit for insulation and get suited up in a hurry—all the time keeping one eye on the sky.

The squalls seem to be keeping their distance. The swell is running six or eight feet, but that's not bad. We drop the buoy and the dive flag. I shrug on the tanks, check my regulator and mask.

"Stay close," I tell Joel, and roll backward into the water.

Green depths close over my head, a hiss of fine bubbles rising. Sun flows down from above like a watercolor wash. Flickers of silver glance away from me, fish startled by my sudden arrival. I turn and orient downward, start the descent with a resolute kick.

The yacht is in about a hundred feet of water. I can get down to it quick, but coming back up will be slow because of the time I'll need for decompression. Make it fifteen minutes on the bottom, max—about an hour for the total dive.

If this were a bigger wreck, I'd worry about making the dive by myself. But this is only a luxury yacht lying below me—twenty-five feet, with a minimal cabin to get trapped inside of. In a few seconds more, I locate a pale smudge on the bottom with the beam of my light. It shimmers like the ghost of a yacht. The water is indigo around me, shading to black. The silence is deafening, punctuated by the periodic rise of CO2.

The pale smudge differentiates into a solid boat shape. The *Seduction* is lying over on her port side, the sharp point of her keel extended like a stiff phallus—an incongruous appendage for a female boat. Closer, I can see the tangle of lines and deck chairs still bound to her rails, the sail lying snugged along the boom. The stern end looks dark, vaguely charred from an engine fire. The damage doesn't look to have reached the cabin though, where I can expect to find the papers I want.

I work my way in through the cabin door, locate the safe where they're supposed to be. They're not there. Geraldine has given me the combination along with the job, and it works like it's supposed to. There's a few thousand dollars there in packs of hundreds, but no watertight package of documents. I stick the money into the net bag fastened to my waist. Maybe it'll help if I can't find the papers, but somehow I doubt it. Anybody who would own a yacht like this won't miss a few thousand bucks.

I'm starting to feel the cold. The mixture of helium and air that I'm breathing is safe, but it can increase the effects of hypothermia. I shudder and flash my beam around the cabin again. If the papers aren't in the safe, then where else could they be? There aren't that many options, but it'll take a while to sort through them. My time estimate for the dive is way too short. I start a systematic ransack, and find—nothing at all.

I am seriously annoyed. Maybe granny hid them under a loose deck board, but I can't take the whole damn yacht apart on this one trip. If the family wants to pursue this, they'll have to get the hulk raised and towed into Miami. I slide out of the cabin and start my ascent.

Thirty feet and wait, then twenty, then ten. I can already tell at twenty feet that something's wrong up above. The blue glow I left is deadened to an ominous gray. At ten feet I can feel the turbulence. I've been down a lot longer than I expected. The decompression is interminable; the wait for daylight and clear air is a worrisome, fretful pain in my stomach.

I rise into a raging storm. My head breaks the surface a few feet from the marker, and lightning splits the sky, a slash that leaves me half blind. Thunder crashes down, and rain hammers across the water. I gasp for air around the regulator, search the thrashing waves.

There's no boat.

I push down a surge of panic, ride the swell up. It's rising twenty-five feet by now, if it's an inch. Visibility is near zero. It's dark from the storm, getting late—too near the winter dusk. Rain shrouds the sky, fractures the waves with sparks of impact. Dammit. Dammit. If the boat were anywhere close I'd see the running lights. I slide down the swell to forever, fumble for my light in the trough. As the swell rises again I turn it on and flash the light in a signal, searching the sea for something, anything. Rain slashes across the light beam so it refracts and scatters. Lightning blasts it to nothingness.

What the hell has happened to Joel? He's supposed to be here. I'm gasping, floundering. I can't stay afloat in seas like this. I've tried to signal and that's all I can do for now. I grip the regulator in my teeth and duck back under the waves.

That cuts off the immediate fury. It's quieter here, calmer. I'll use up less energy. At first I can hear the hiss of rain along the surface, the crack of muffled thunder. Further down there's only the tug of turbulence again. Panicked and breathing hard, I try to relax—I'm still using air too fast. This is hard work. It's too dark, too close—I can't stay here forever. I haven't enough air.

The gage falls too fast. Fifteen minutes and I have to go back up. The rain is still there waiting for me, the flailing storm, the bucking, heaving whitecaps. I'm an insignificant speck in the iron-gray sea, lost and forgotten—hanging above an infinite pit of empty darkness and numbing cold.

Hypothermia is creeping up on me. I'm out of air, and the tanks are dead weight now—I'll have to let them go. I've swallowed way too much water. I can't fight this any longer—can't kick—can't breathe.

Still there's nothing out there. And then there is something, a shadow looming through the wind and rain.

Thank God. It's the boat.

I fumble at my belt with numb fingers, flash my light at it. The shadow seems to slow, turns slightly to port. The dive platform swings past the buoy and I reach for it. I've got no energy left, and I miss. A wave closes over my head and I swallow water as I go down. God, this is so hard. I want to relax and drift, fall down slowly through the indigo depths, and never worry about anything again.

I'm going to drown with the boat right there within reach. I rouse and manage a feeble kick, break the surface again, and then he's got me. I have a vague notion of being dragged up over the platform edge, then a shift through the air and the deck comes up hard under my back. The rain is slashing right into my face now.

"Anna?" he yells at me. "Anna!"

There's a white haze in front of my eyes that's more than the rain, and for a second it's all I can see. Joel shakes me. When I don't respond, I feel his fingers on my jaw. He's forcing my teeth apart. He holds my nose, and then his mouth closes down over mine.

I have just enough presence of mind left to know what he's doing. I turn my head to the side, pull away from his hand.

"No," I cough. "'M okay."

I don't know if he's heard me above the wind, but he's felt the movement. His arms slide under me again, and then the rain is gone out of my face.

There's deck plate against my back again. The noise level has gone down, and there's wan, greenish light from the instruments above me. I can feel the boat roll like crazy. Joel has got a towel, wiping off my face. Then he's tugging at the zipper to my wetsuit, jerking the rubber down over my shoulders. I'm not wearing anything underneath, but I'm so far gone I don't care.

Once he's got me stripped and rubbed down, he throws a blanket over me, wraps me up in it and drops me on one of the bunks. I'm starting to shiver by then, big shudders that rack my body from head to toe. My teeth sound like castanets. Joel's gone somewhere, and then he's back.

"Anna?" he says, and he's got something in his hand. It's a hot cup that smells like coffee. "Here," he says.

It's laced with bourbon, and I choke, get it down. I'm still shaking like I'll never stop. What I can feel of me is like ice. My hands are still numb, and I slide down into the bedclothes, fold them inside the blanket against my ribs.

"God. 'M ff...freezing," I say.

It must be hardly coherent through the clattering of my teeth, but then there's movement above me in the glow of the lights—Joel stripping out of his shirt. He slides into the bunk behind me, tugs another blanket over us. I can feel the pressure of his body where he hugs me against him, but not a degree of warmth. It's like I'm made of ice.

"Joel. The boat..." I say, and I feel his hand slide over my wet hair. He whispers into my ear.

"Shh," he says. "It's okay. I closed the hatch. The autopilot's doing the work."

He's right. The ship is rolling like hell, but it's not wallowing in every trough. We're making headway. For a long time I can't relax for the shuddering, but then suddenly I do.

I've been asleep. I don't know for how long. Joel is asleep behind me, still wrapped around me under the blankets. I can tell he's used to sleeping with a woman by the way his arm curls over me and up between my breasts. His breathing is deep and regular, and I can feel him clear and sharp through a thin layer of fabric between us.

The storm seems to have died down outside the cabin. The rain has nearly stopped, and the boat's not rolling so bad now, but still I'm sick. Likely it's the salt water I swallowed.

When I move, Joel tightens around me.

"Let go," I say. "I've got to throw up."

He moves his arm and rolls backward. I make it to the head and unload my stomach, splash some fresh water over my face to clean it up. I look like hell in the mirror, gray as death. I wrap the blanket tighter around me and snap the light off before I step back out into the cabin.

I go sit back on the bunk and run one hand through my hair. Joel's heating up the coffee again.

"Never mind," I say, and heave up to get the bourbon and the cup.

"Do you think you ought to drink that straight?" he asks as I splash out a hefty dose.

I down it and cough, wipe my mouth and splash out another one, carry it back to my spot on the bunk. Joel's leaning against the pilot's seat now with his arms folded. He's a vague, pale shape in the lights, dressed only in brief dark underwear.

"Thanks for coming back for me," I say. The bourbon feels like fire in my stomach. My tone isn't quite friendly.

I can see it go over his face. "Anna..." He uncrosses his arms, ducks to sit on the end of the bunk opposite me. "Let's talk."

"What about?" I ask.

"Did you really think I'd leave you?"

I have to look away from his eyes.

"We lost the anchor," he says, "and I didn't realize it until I'd drifted way the hell off. I had to make half a dozen passes to find you."

"I didn't get the papers," I say.

"Why not?"

I take a breath. "They weren't in the safe. Weren't in the cabin anywhere that I could see. Maybe that was the real reason for that fire in the engines." I shrug, hug the blanket around me. "Whatever, it's up to the family."

"Bad luck," he says.

"Well, it happens." I shrug. "At least they'll know there's a problem. Maybe they'll hire me to follow up."

I unscrew the bottle cap, spill out more bourbon into my cup. The stuff tastes like crap.

"You shouldn't drink all that," he says.

"I feel like getting totally crocked."

"What for?" he asks. "The wasted trip?"

"Yeah," I say. "And partly it's a general comment on my life to this point."

I catch the anger in his eyes before he can look away to hide it.

"I really didn't know Dad meant to rip you off," he says.

"I know. You said that."

"Then can you let it go, Anna?" He looks down at his hands. "If it makes any difference," he says. "Dad and I had a big fight about it."

That snags at my attention.

"We've been out of touch," he says. "Last night I tried to call him. When he wasn't there I left a message I was going out on a job with you."

So they're not getting along? It's hell of an insight into what's going on here. And how Joel might be using me. I inspect the idea, and I don't much like the way it feels.

"Your dad's going to be pissed."

"I don't give a damn what Dad thinks," he insists. "I make my own decisions."

"Don't lie to me," I say. "I don't believe that."

There's another flash of anger in his eyes. "You've had enough," he says. He shifts position, reaches for the bottle. I splash another shot into the cup, let him have it.

"So what do you really want from me, Joel?"

In answer he leans over and kisses me hard on the mouth. It's a complete surprise.

For a long moment I stare at him from a two-inch distance, and then I manage to get my breath.

"I am not even going to ask about your motivations for doing that," I say.

I've realized my own lust, of course, partly the cause of my troubles last year—and I still have plenty of bitterness wound up inside me. The kid reminds me so much of Paul, and he's got that long, taut, muscular body that's so alive that I can't keep my eyes off of him. But the psychology of this is just too complicated.

He inclines away from me, stows the bottle.

"Why not?" He sounds stubborn, and he's not talking about the motivations.

"I'm a lot older than you are."

"So what?" he asks.

"Who's seducing who here?"

"Who cares?"

I close my eyes and notice I've got no resistance. It's too late. He's so close to me I can feel the heat off him. I've slept against him already, felt the hard lines of his belly and thighs against my back, the tightening of his hand between my breasts when I tried to move.

"I'm not exactly sober, you know."

"I said you shouldn't drink so much," he says.

"God, Joel," I say, and I draw a long, shuddering breath. "You are over eighteen, aren't you?"

"Twenty," he says. "You're safe."

His mouth clings this time, works across my cheekbone. He breathes into my ear, a breath as quick and unsteady as my own. Then he slides a tentative hand inside the blanket still wrapped around my shoulders.

That's enough. The blanket falls away. I roll him backward and come up sitting astride him. He lies there for a brief pause. "Does this mean 'yes'?" he asks.

It's a good match. He's quick, but so am I.

He's young, and after a few minutes he's ready to do it again, but slower this time. God, it's so sweet. Later, lying there beside him and easing down into sleep, I like the way he holds on to me. I'd like to think this wasn't all just a line of BS.

I wake up the next time to clearer light and a dull headache. It's morning, a gray daylight outside. The cabin is gloomy as hell and boat is still pitching, but the rain seems to have stopped. A warm body stirs behind me. I roll over and verify who I'm sleeping with, and then I bury my face in the pillow and groan.

"God," I say, "this trip has been a complete disaster."

"That bad?" Joel asks. He tries to sound hurt, but he can't. He looks smug.

"You son-of-a-bitch."

He laughs, then slides over to wrap around me.

"Just a minute," I say.

I get up and go to the head, then check our position, alter the speed and heading so we might get home sometime today. And then I sit in the pilot's chair to think about things in the cold light of morning. What the hell was I thinking, to get myself drunk like that? As if I can blame drunkenness for what I've done.

Considering it doesn't do any good. My mind just drifts, and thinking about Joel lying back there in the bunk starts that lance of pleasure up again.

I think I'd better not inquire too much into my own motivations here. People have just so much capacity for truth.

Hell. Maybe life is what you make of it after all.

It's four o'clock Sunday by the time we get back to Miami, a rough trip all the way through the wind and heavy seas. The ugly old boat has proved her worth—there are no complaints from her—not even a creak. Twice more we run through heavy storm and rain, but nothing so bad as last night. The jetties rise out of the chop, and we follow the channel markers back through the port, tie up at the dock. It's nearly dark by the time we get the gear off-loaded and into my car—lots later than I'd meant to be home.

Joel falls back in the seat as I start the engine. I turn on the wipers and the radio. The weather service has noticed it's raining.

Joel runs one hand through his hair. "God, I'm exhausted," he says.

"I don't know why," I say, "you've slept most of the day."

He gives me a quick grin, checks for music on the radio.

The rain has stopped by the time we turn into the parking lot at my apartment. We load up with gear, haul most of it up the steps in one trip.

"I'll get the rest," Joel says. He drops his load on the living room floor and heads back toward the stairs.

It's a while before I realize he's been gone too long.

I check over the railing, can't see him out by the car. Then I remember what he's been worrying about.

"Joel?" I call.

There's no answer. There's nothing on the stairs. Nothing out in the parking lot. Dammit. Where else? Maybe the pool.

The pool is behind my apartment building. There's a sidewalk, grass, a chain link enclosure off to my left. Wet darkens the parking lot, rises in a faint, drifting mist. Wind and shadows tear at the clouds, mutating the familiar landscape into something eerie, threatening and strange.

I hear the voices first. And then I see something on the lawn, a hulking figure, half-distorted by darkness and a shapeless, flapping shirt. He's got something slung over his shoulder that gives him a hunch-backed, monstrous shape. Closer, there's a stench on the wind that turns my stomach, a reek of death and corruption that emanates from the shape. The thing on his back is a basket, misshapen and crusted with filth. The guy has got Joel cornered against the fence.

The kid looks frozen and desperate, spread against the woven wire.

"Joel!"

I sprint into the shadowy space between them.

"Keep away from him," I say to the ugly hulk. "He's mine."

The thing looms, towering over me, but somehow I still can't see him. He's made of darkness and the daunting stink of the grave. Black shards that might be eyes glitter at me from between wild dreadlocks and a wind-blown, flying beard. The creature grows and swells, casts a shadow that's big as all of night.

My knees are shaking, but the bastard doesn't know that. I grit my teeth and stand my ground. I know if I give back an inch, he'll take us both.

"*Mon amour...*" The creature sighs, spreads its arms with a lust that buffets like the wind. He clenches and unclenches his hands, reaching for me—for Joel. "*Mon cher...*"

"No," I say.

There's nowhere to go. We're trapped against the fence, caught in the creature's dark umbra. I can feel the cold of his breath. I'm sinking, frozen, helpless, sliding into darkness. Behind me, I feel Joel gasp and shudder.

I have to find strength from somewhere to fight this. I raise one hand, clutch at the medicine bag under my shirt. Sparks flare like embers against my skin. I gasp in a breath, feel a new strength in my knees. We're standing in a halo of light, an island in the storm. The wind rushes in at us, an electric swirl that lifts my hair, prickles along the bare skin of my arms.

"*Mon cher...*"

There's a flash so bright it burns my retinas. A hammer comes down like the world ending. When I open my eyes, I'm lying on the concrete deck, surrounded by trash, the reek of burning cloth.

"Anna?" says Joel.

He gets to his feet, drags me up. He pulls me backward, heading toward the apartment building. I struggle weakly. The thing has to be after us…

The wind gusts, the shadows shift…there's nothing there at all.

"God, Joel," I say. "What happened?"

"Lightning," he says against my ear. "We nearly got hit by a lightning strike."

I'm shaking in his arms. Did it hit the fence? The water? I don't know. Whatever, we seem to be alive and unburnt.

"Let's get upstairs," I say.

I slam the door and lock it behind us, peer out the windows. There's only empty, windblown darkness behind the blinds, the distant clatter of palms. Joel looks pale and sick. He falls on the couch, slides down and kicks off his shoes. I turn and search his face as he lies there.

"Joel," I say. "Are you alright?"

"Yeah," he says. "Just exhausted."

"You're sure?"

"Yeah," he says.

"Then you might as well sleep in the bed."

He only lies still, closes his eyes. He sighs, and then somehow he looks at peace.

"Okay," he says.

He goes to sleep right there. I throw a blanket over him, pace back and forth. Everything seems quiet outside— there's no rain, just the wind. Finally I relax some, get out a beer and check the messages on my voicemail. There's one from Paul wanting to know where the hell we are, and then there's the one from Gloria that I was expecting to find. She sounds worried.

"Your Macoute must be some kind of a haint," she says. "Watch out for him, Anna. He's got no record, but the Haitians around here are all scared stiff of him. They call him the soul-stealer—some foolishness like that. Let me know if you need any help. Okay?"

Well, maybe not. I reach up to touch the medicine pouch against my chest, feeling the faint tingle of power still alive in the talismans. Maybe I've defeated the haint all by myself. We'll just give it a while and we'll see.

Chapter 7

THE STALKER

One unsurprising fact about living in Miami is that we get a lot of international visitors. Miami is the fourth largest urban area in the US, and the population inflates and deflates on an annual cycle depending on how cold it is everywhere else. The climate is always warm, the beaches are clean and the natives are friendly. Because of these attractions, the city gets a lot of business. It's considered a center for finance, entertainment and international trade. Of course, there's a certain amount of trouble that's imported, too.

The entertainment and trade seem to be what the Traegers are here from Australia about. I'm ignoring the insistent flashing light that says I've got voicemail and trying to be patient while Alyssa Traeger gives me a list of her concerns.

"My husband Jerry is in Miami to work on a film," she says. "He's producing and directing both, and he is sooo overworked. The crew got here about a month ago. They started shooting last week."

I try moving her along.

"And you think someone is stalking you?"

She's brunette, a pretty woman with a heart-shaped face, designer haircut and light make-up. She's dressed casually in a summer sun-dress that shows off a pink sunburn. Standing, we were nearly eye-to-eye. She has an ugly, visible bruise on the left side of her throat that looks like a hickey.

"What?" she says.

"A stalker?"

"Oh," she says. "Yes…"

"Why do you think so?"

She closes her eyes, reaches up absently to touch the bruise.

"Shadows move," she says. "I just have this feeling that… that dire things are happening. It's nothing I can put my finger on." She drops her hand, opens her eyes. "It's really unsettling," she says.

"How long has this been going on?" I ask.

"Since before we left Australia," she says.

"That long?" I ask. "So you think someone has followed you here?"

"Yes," she says.

She frowns then, stares out the window. On the street outside my office, traffic flows by in a continuous snarl, emitting white noise. Alyssa cocks her head, as if she's totally lost her train of thought.

"Mrs. Traeger?"

Her eyes come back to me. "What?"

"You were telling me about a stalker?"

"Oh, yes," she says. "I'll be honest, Ms. Detroyer, I'm talking to you because I heard you...I mean, I think there might be *galka*...sorcery involved."

Finally she's gotten to the issue.

That's getting to be my reputation. Anna Detroyer, ready to take on all your supernatural woes. I do seem to get a lot of those kinds of cases, where the trail leads off into uncertain and ambiguous directions. Maybe I've got the reputation because I persist where other P.I.s would give it up. Or maybe my Native American heritage gives me vision where others would just see murk—the spirit talker seeing clearly. Whatever, here's another of the same.

"Why do you think so, Ms. Traeger?"

She blinks at me. "Oh," she says. "I've got something..."

She reaches into her bag, pulls out a serrated spike that looks like bone, holds it out.

I take it, turn it over in my hands. It's about five inches long, familiar, of course, though most people wouldn't be able to identify it like this—unattached from the original owner. I have a scar on my ankle from an encounter with a live version a few years back. I was sick for a week from the venom.

"This is a sting ray spine?" I ask.

"Yes," she says. "It was on my doorstep yesterday morning."

I'm not sure what the symbolism is, but given her concerns, the meaning is fairly clear.

"It's associated with sorcery?" I ask.

"Yes," she says. "In Australia it is."

"Why would a *galka* sorcerer be interested in you?" I ask.

Something flickers in her eyes.

"I haven't the faintest idea," she says. "I'm…I'm just concerned about my family. I need to do something about this."

"Have you contacted the police?"

"They just laughed," she says.

Of course. That would be their standard response to complaints about sorcery.

I'm not happy about that flicker in her eyes. She's not telling me everything. If I had good sense, I'd tell her she needs to take care of things herself, but maybe it's not something she's completely in control of. She's not tracking well. Drugs? Alcohol? I can't tell what it is, but I need the work. I'll take a chance on her, but I'll need to hedge my bets, too.

"Mrs. Traeger," I say. "I'll see what I can do for you, but I'll need a fairly sizable retainer up front."

She lets her breath out in relief.

"Thank you, Ms. Detroyer," she says. "Just find out who's behind it." She opens her purse, starts writing me a check. She tightens her lips. "We have Aboriginals on the crew," she says. "You should check them out first."

"Do you think one of them is responsible?" I ask.

"Who else would it be?" she says. "They're…savages."

I have a kneejerk urge to toss the check back at her, to make a stand on that—but I still need the money. I can't afford to be picky, and it's not just her. I'd hate to be responsible if she's right her family is in danger. I take a deep breath, run a ten count.

"Where is your husband shooting the film?" I ask.

It's on the beach.

I should check my voicemail, but I decide to head out to the film shoot instead.

Miami Beach has gotten to be fairly well known over the years because of TV show reruns like *Miami Vice* and *CSI Miami.* It's got a lot of local color and enough glitz and mansions to give it a movie-star glamour. Still, that's not my life. The AC in my little car is still struggling, hardly able to keep up with the humidity as summer approaches. In the shimmer of heat waves off the pavement, I can see trouble looming that has nothing to do with Alyssa Traeger and her *galka*-infused sting ray spine. It's my personal life that's gone out of control.

I find where the crew is shooting easily enough. There's a roped off area of the beach beyond the high rise hotels and condos where they've set up for a scene. The sand here is raked and pristine. Beyond, the blue of the Atlantic is sunlit and sparkling. A small clutch of tourists is watching, and I join them to have a look.

A man rubs sunscreen on a woman's back. They kiss passionately, run into the waves. Traeger cuts. It looks like the crew changes the camera angles slightly. They rake the sand. Then they repeat the same thing over again. And again. Traeger looks to be a Type A personality. He's impatient and irritable.

After a while they take a break, apparently for lunch. The cast and crew make a general movement toward a large canopy set up a little further down the beach.

There's a skinny blonde gal with a clipboard who seems to be in charge. I work my way over to where she's standing.

"Ma'am," I say. "I'm Anna Detroyer, a P.I. that Mr. Traeger's wife has hired. I wonder if I could talk to him for a moment?"

She looks at me. My scruffy jeans and baseball cap don't make a big impression, maybe, but they do help me blend into the background.

"A P.I.?" she repeats. "Have you got a license?"

"Yep," I say.

I get it out and show it to her. She inspects it carefully, and I get the impression she's something of a stickler about details.

"Alright," she says. "I'll see if he's got a moment."

It seems he does. I duck under the rope and head over to where he's collapsed into a folding chair under the canopy. Close up, he looks overheated. Sweat stands out on his forehead, and he's clearly in need of another glass of ice water—or two. His skin has a bright pink tinge, even though he's been wearing a hat.

"Mr. Traeger?" I say.

He looks up. Brown hair, brown eyes, heavy eyebrows. He blinks like he's come back from somewhere else.

"Do I know you?" he asks.

I decide to be direct. After all, Alyssa Traeger was.

"Anna Detroyer," I say. "I'm a P.I. Your wife has hired me to investigate possible sorcery on the set."

At that, he flushes a deeper red.

"I told her to leave it," he says. "We've got enough problems with the film without her manufacturing tales about sorcery."

"Then let's say she has some concerns about safety," I suggest. "This could be just an ordinary stalker with unknown intent."

He rubs at his face. The blonde woman stops by and drops off a paper-wrapped hoagie.

"Alright," he says.

He starts to unwrap the paper. I pull up another convenient chair, take a seat.

"So what's been going on?" I ask.

"Nothing I'm too worried about," he says. "There's been some bad luck on the set, equipment breaking, minor accidents—nobody really hurt."

"She did mention stalking," I say. "What was that about?"

"She thinks someone has been hanging around our house," he says. "Last weekend she took the children out to the zoo. She thought someone was following them."

"Children?" I ask.

"We have two," he says. "They're adopted—Aboriginals, five and seven."

"And then the sting ray spine?" I ask.

"Yes," he says. "I'm sure that was some kind of joke. Everybody on the set thinks Alyssa is crazy."

I glance around. Word must have spread about what I'm doing here. The cast and crew are carefully looking somewhere else. It's likely they think I'm crazy, too.

"You have no idea who might be behind the stalking?" I ask.

"None," he says.

"Do you mind if I talk to some of the crew?" I ask.

"Go ahead," he says. "Maybe it will make Alyssa happy."

"Thanks," I say.

Lunch appears to have been catered. Trays of sandwiches and chips, veggies and fruit are spread on a long table under the canopy. A bin of iced drinks sits at either end. A stiff breeze is blowing in from the ocean. It snaps the trailing edge of the canopy, tugs at my hair.

Most of the crew seems to be standard, white-bread Australian types. They're chatting, laughing at jokes. There are three that look exotic, though—two men and a woman. They have the black hair and coffee skin tone that likely indicates Aboriginal blood. I decide to start with the blonde in charge with the clipboard. Her name turns out to be Peggy Alburton.

"Ms. Alburton," I say, "have you seen any signs of a stalker around the set?"

"Nothing," she says. "There are always a lot of people hanging around to watch, but there's been nothing suspicious."

"Sorcery?"

"Nobody casting spells."

"Alright," I say. "Thanks."

Eventually I get around to the Aboriginal types. The first man's name is Walter Johnson. He's very light-skinned and has green eyes.

"As much as I'd like to believe the myths of the Dreamtime," he says, "there's no such thing as sorcery. If someone is threatening Traeger, then he should call the police."

"I don't think there have been any threats that could be identified as such," I say. "Mrs. Traeger is just worried."

"Is it about the children?" he asks.

"What do you mean?" I ask.

"Nothing," he says.

He shrugs, looks away. The surf breaks on the shore, highlights his silence. At a little distance, someone is windsurfing on the waves, the white and gold sail bounding through the blue water. Further down the beach, children are running and screaming.

"Do you…" I start.

"Nothing," he breaks in.

His face has closed down. I need to let it go.

"Thank you," I say.

I try another couple of the regular crew and then I tackle the other Aboriginal man. His complexion is darker. He's tall and long-legged, sitting a little apart from the others, watching the flock of gulls shrieking and trolling for sandwich scraps.

"I'm Anna Detroyer," I say. "Got a minute?"

He looks at me. Australia's Aborigines have come from Africa through India and Asia and stayed isolated on their own continent for thousands of years. They're one of the oldest strains of human beings on the planet. The mixed, exotic heritage shows in their faces—the lines, the arrangement.

"Sure," he says. "I'm Johnny Branch."

"*Galka?*" he says when I ask. "I don't know anything much about it. It's practiced by a lot of people in the Outback, of course, but you'd have to ask someone else about it. Maybe Walter or Izzy."

"I understand that the Traegers' children are Aboriginals," I say. "Would there be any connection there?"

"I don't know," he says.

I can tell from his eyes that there is. I watch the gulls for a moment.

"How do they come to have Aboriginal children?" I ask.

His dark eyes skate over, slide away.

"There's an adoption program in Australia," he says.

"An adoption program?"

"Yeah," he says.

I try to work through that. His meaning isn't immediately clear, but I'm worried that he will shut down the way Walter did. I can come back to it later.

"Have you seen any signs of a stalker?" I ask.

"No," he says. "At least, not on the set. They might be having trouble at their house."

"Okay, thanks," I say.

The woman is the darkest of the three, possibly full-blood Aboriginal. Like Johnny, she's standing a little apart, drinking a soda and watching the line of surf break on the white sand of the beach. Her eyes are large and wide-set and her nose and mouth are broad. She's about six inches taller than I am, dressed in jeans and a white polo. She looks tough and athletic.

She also looks very sullen. The three of them know they're being profiled. I'm sorry about it—but I need the information.

"Are you Izzy?" I ask. "I'm Anna Detroyer."

She looks me over.

"Yes, I'm Izzy Walker," she says.

"Ms. Walker," I say, "I'm a P.I. investigating for Ms. Traeger. Have you seen anyone who might be suspicious around the shoot?"

"No," she says. "Just the usual tourists. We don't have any stars big enough to attract a real nutcase."

"Have you noticed any signs of sorcery?"

Her eyes flicker over at me.

"Sorcery?" she says. "I suppose you mean *galka*?"

"Yes," I say.

"No," she says. "I really don't know much about it, though. You'd need to ask Walter or John. I'm sure they'd know way more about it than I would."

I've heard that twice now, which makes it suspicious. It sounds like a redirection of bad energy. I know something about the way sorcery works. Properly done, no one will see the witchcraft, only the results. The sting ray spine was a calling card to make sure the Traegers knew they were a target.

"Would you know of any connection to the Traegers' children?"

Her dark eyes flicker again.

"What about the children?" she asks.

I can tell she's not going to give me any information. At least not in this environment. Peggy Alburton is already calling an end to the lunch break, so I'm out of time. I'll have to come back to these questions later.

"Thank you," I say.

I didn't really expect to get much information from this tactic. I've let everyone know I'm on the job, and I have gotten a little to start with. First, it's more likely I'll see the stalker hanging around the Traegers' house than at the film shoot. Second, it's likely the children are involved in some way. And third, two out of the three Aboriginals know something about *galka*—at least enough to turn away bad energy.

When I get back to the car, I call Alyssa. "Mrs. Traeger," I say, "I wonder if I could come out to your house?"

"What for?" she asks.

"I'd just like to look around," I say. "I may want to set up a stakeout tonight to watch for your stalker."

"Alright," she says. "I have to pick up the children from school, but if you'd like to come around two o'clock?"

My phone has a load of messages, but I resolutely stick it in my pocket. I'm not going to deal with that now.

I get lunch and then head out to the Traegers' address in Miami Shores. It's a gated waterfront community and a nice area, if not five-star quality. There's a neighborhood watch that should keep it safe from random thugs. That's not what I'm worrying about, though. The biggest concern is that someone might be stalking Alyssa or the children for kidnapping and ransom purposes. Or, maybe just the kidnapping part. I need to find out what's going on.

I do a drive-by of the house. It's a Spanish-style, gold stucco with a red tile roof, two stories. The house sits on a corner lot with a landscaped, perfectly manicured lawn. Clusters of elephant ear and ginger run riot under the palms. Something that looks like a fig tree crowds the security fence in back. The whole thing is tasteful, well-maintained. Regardless that Izzy didn't think they had much in the way of star attraction for the film, the Traegers must have a decent housing budget.

I park my ratty Chevette in the curved driveway, ring the bell at the front door. Alyssa answers it.

"Ms. Detroyer," she says. "Come in."

The house is as manicured as the lawn. The entryway arches above me, lit by clearstory windows above. The living area is open and spacious. Out the French doors in back, I can see a patio and reflections from a pool. The children are sitting on a rug in front of the fireplace, playing with an assortment of plastic trucks and dolls. They have the faces of full-blooded Aboriginals.

"Lindsey, Arthur, say hello to Miss Anna," says Alyssa.

"Hello, Miss Anna," they say in a chorus.

Arthur is the oldest. He stands up, holds out his truck.

"Look," he says. "There's a man inside here who drives the truck."

I bend over, inspect the details.

"I can see that," I say. "What's his name?"

"It's William," says Lindsey. "This is my doll, Martha."

They seem to be bright, well-behaved children. I look around the house. The French doors to the patio don't look very solid, but there's a six-foot privacy fence behind the pool. Outside, I can see foliage hanging over the slats. The gate to the back yard has a latch inside, but there's no hasp for a padlock.

"Thanks for the look-around," I tell Alyssa. "I think you should get a padlock installed on your back yard gate and cut back some of the trees. I'll get here about nine—see if anything happens during the night."

She frowns, hugs her shoulders. She looks out of it again today. Still, her pupils aren't dilated and I can't smell alcohol on her breath. Maybe it's the worry that's getting to her—or maybe it's just the sunburn.

"Thank you," she says. "That will make me feel a lot better."

I'm not sure what time shooting on the film will wrap for the day, but I'm back out on the beach fairly quickly and blended into the crowd of beach-goers. It looks like Walter is the script supervisor, and Johnny and Izzy work on the sound crew. The two of them spend the afternoon minding mics and booms. It's about four when Traeger calls a halt, and they help with breaking down and stowing the equipment in the trucks.

I have a choice now about who to follow. From the faint drift of conversation that's crossed the beach sands to me, it seems like most of the crew is headed to the Trap Bar to relax a little before dinner. Traeger isn't going along. He looks exhausted and sunburnt, gets in a car and disappears. I decide to keep an eye on Izzy and John.

They stop in the shade of one of the trucks, strike up a tense conversation. I can see it in the flash of their eyes, the sharp movements of their hands.

"Izzy! John!" calls Walter. "Are you going to the Trap?"

They give it up.

"Sure," calls John. "Be there in a minute, Walt."

I'm wondering if the conversation was about me. Whatever, I could stand to relax a bit at the Trap, myself.

It's a sports bar, and the walls are lined with TVs in constant, flickering motion. At this hour, it's packed and noisy with laughter and conversation. I've done the official questioning about Alyssa's stalker. This kind of mingling will be more relaxed, should give me different results.

I wait a while and look to see how the groups settle out. Unsurprisingly, Izzy, Walt and John don't seem to mix well with the others. More of a surprise, the female star takes a seat at the bar by herself. I ease my way around, manage to work in next to her.

"What'll you have?" asks the bartender.

"*Dos Equis*," I say. I've picked up a taste for Mexican beer just lately.

When the beer comes, I look over at the woman. She beautiful in that sort of perfect, movie star way—a blonde with sea-blue eyes and pouty, swollen lips. She's slender and big-busted, long-legged, draped on the stool like she's in a scene out of *Casablanca*.

"Aren't you…"

"Mercy Alliston," she says. "You're that detective who was at the shoot this afternoon, aren't you?

"Yep," I say. "Still hanging around."

I try out the beer. As I expected, it's perfect after the hot day outside.

"How's the film going?" I ask.

"It's the pits," she says.

I look over at her.

"Oh?"

"I wish I'd never gotten involved in this."

"What's the problem?" I ask.

"Traeger," she says. "The man is a complete bastard. And that wife of his…"

"A dictator?" I ask.

"Casting couch mentality," she says. "Among other offensive attitudes. Plus, his wife is totally jealous."

"Oh," I say.

It's a useful addition to my store of information on the case. I look around the bar, wondering how many of the other women he might have hit on. Some of them might consider sorcery to get back at him, but *galka* would be unusual from a white-bread Australian. The Aboriginals are still the most likely candidates. The three of them are watching me, their eyes dark and suspicious as they sit in the back of the club.

By dusk, I'm out in Miami Shores again, staking out the house. The night is long and boring. The shadows are just shadows. The gate to the back yard stays closed. I doze a little toward dawn, wake at the first faint lightening of the sky. I put the car into gear, head off to my apartment. There's a message taped to the door that says, "Meet me at Vinnie's 12:00 J." It's big and bold, written in black marker—impossible to miss.

I pull it down, drop it on the dining table as I go through the kitchen. I catch a couple of hours of sleep, then shower and head down to the office. There's a note taped to the office door that says, "Vinnie's 12:00 J."

I tug the paper down and drop it into the trash can inside my office. Then I sit down and put my feet up on the desk. The problem with this Traeger job is that I'm a long way from Australia. I really don't know anything much about the policies or the politics about adoption, either one—much less about *galka*. I do know someone who might, though.

Her name is Amanda Watkins and she teaches anthropology at Miami Dade College. I did some work for a friend of hers a couple of years back. I'm lucky this morning, get her on the phone at the first try.

"I've got a free hour at ten," she says. "We can have coffee then."

Ten o'clock isn't that far off. The college is a little east of Overtown. I head that way, manage to find a parking spot about a quarter 'til.

Amanda is a heavy-set red-head. She's solid and freckled, and always in a good humor. I knock on her office door, and she holds out her hand.

"Anna Detroyer. Sure, I remember you," she says. "Let's sit in the lounge. It's much more comfortable than here."

It's a faculty lounge around the corner. There's a small kitchenette and some Formica dining tables. The windows overlook a lawn and sidewalk, with a clutter of construction machinery outside. There are doughnuts and coffee on the counter.

"My husband is from Australia," she says. "You're right that I spend a lot of time there."

"I need to know about *galka*," I say.

"In general," she says, "the term applies to sorcery or witchcraft. It has to do with spirits or people who will cause intentional harm. There are specialized practitioners in the Outback who have training and powers to access the realm of the dead for very dark purposes, but there are also methods that anyone can use. These usually involve taking items of clothing, locks of hair—that kind of thing—and then chanting or making images to bring about harm."

"Would there be any way to identify who's behind the witchcraft?"

"You're asking about a hit-man?" she asks.

"I'm sorry?"

"A *galka* sorcerer?"

"Sure," I say. "Is that what it's called?"

"Yes," she says. "I don't think there would be any sign of who the sorcerer was. Still, if the Traegers are targets, then there must be a reason."

"That's my next question," I say. "They've adopted two Aboriginal children."

"Oh," she says.

Her face has closed down. I'm getting used to this now.

"Am I right that this could be part of the problem?" I ask.

She sighs, lays down her half-eaten doughnut. She looks out the window, where a backhoe is destroying the lawn. In the silence that follows, I can hear the rhythmic whine of the machinery.

"It likely is," she says finally.

"Why?" I ask.

She frowns, nudges the doughnut with one thumb.

"The Australian government has a policy of assimilation," she says.

"Okay," I say. "And how does that work?"

"The Aboriginals have a very different culture, and they have been slow to embrace Western thought and Western ideas, so they've not assimilated in the way the government would like. One of the tools of the policy is adoptions. Children's Services declares the Aboriginal mothers unfit, and then the children are taken into the foster care system and adopted out to white parents who will raise the children within the typical Western culture. They are then encouraged to marry white partners."

"Oh," I say. "Isn't that…"

She looks at my expression. From my Native American side, I understand about cultural pressures, and how this can affect an aboriginal population.

"Um, yes," she says. "It is something of a controversial policy. You can imagine that it's not very popular among the Aboriginals."

She checks the time. "I've got class in a few minutes," she says.

"Right," I say. I push back from the table. "Thank you, Amanda. You've been very helpful."

"Any time," she says. Then she pauses. "Sorcery, it's…be careful, Anna."

Her eyes seem very dark.

"Thanks," I say. "I'll try."

After she's gone, I stand at the window for a while and watch the backhoe bite off grass. It's getting close to eleven now, and I'll have to decide what to do about lunch at Vinnie's.

It's Joel, of course. I'm a little bit late, and I see him as soon as I come in the door. He's lounging in a booth, the long, graceful curves of his tee shirt and jeans arranged against the wallpaper, his ankles crossed. He looks good, the problems from earlier this year all blown away. He's got his arms folded and he's staring into space, waiting patiently.

When I stop at the table, he pushes up straight.

"Hey, Anna," he says. "I didn't know if you'd come."

I drop into the other side of the booth before he can get up.

"I got the message," I say. "Was that you on the phone, too?"

We're interrupted by the waiter. I order spaghetti and Joel gets cannelloni. We fold up the menus, let the waiter carry them away.

"The texts are from me," he says, "but you've likely got voicemail from dad."

I look at him.

"Why would Paul Angstrom be calling me?" I ask.

"I told him we were sleeping together," he says.

I roll my eyes.

"Look, Joel," I say. "I'm all for openness, but in this case a little discretion might be…"

He shoves back his blond curls, props his chin on one hand.

"Don't you think it's something he needs to know?" he asks.

"It's none of his business what I do," I say.

"Well, I wanted him to know," he says.

I consider that.

"So you've got an agenda?" I ask.

"Doesn't everyone?"

At that point the waiter drops off our salads. Joel looks stubborn and unrelenting. I sigh.

"How's school?" I ask.

"Fine," he says. He munches on salad greens. "I'm just taking a couple of courses this spring. That's something else I wanted to talk to you about, though."

"School?"

"Yeah," he says. "I'm signed up for the exchange program this fall. I'll be going to school in Germany."

So, the kid's stirred up a hornet's nest here and now he's going to skip town? I'm wondering about that agenda again. It wasn't Anna that seduced Joel, after all. This is looking more and more like something he's got going on with his dad.

"I'll be in Dusseldorf for a couple of semesters," he says.

"Are you that fluent in German?" I ask.

"Good enough," he says. "If I'm going to major in International Relations, then I need some experience in European politics."

It seems like he's really excited about it. When the check comes, I reach for my wallet.

"I'll get it," he says. He reaches out, snags the check.

"How's the balance on your student loan?" I ask.

"Not bad," he says.

He leans across and kisses me then. His mouth clings, drifts toward my ear.

"I'll miss you this fall," he says. "Can you come to visit?"

I let out a shaky breath.

"Send me a post card," I say.

After he's gone, I go sit in the car and check the messages in my voicemail. Paul is really pissed off, I can tell. I don't really have to call him back, though. I'm thinking he needs a while to cool off.

I sit there for another minute, and then I decide I need to talk to Alyssa about her children. Amanda gave me the broader picture, but someone closer to the case will need to fill in the details. I start the car and head over to the house again.

I'm earlier than yesterday, and the kids are still at school. She answers the door in another sundress, and I'm thinking the sunburn looks worse. She seems feverish today, her eyes dull and her lips dry and cracked.

"Are you alright?" I ask.

"Sure," she says. "I just overdid it a little at the beach. Come in, Ms. Detroyer. Could I get you a drink?"

She already has one for herself. It looks like lemonade.

"Just a beer," I say. "If you've got it."

"Sure," she says.

"I need to know about the kids," I say, once we're settled by the pool. "Did they come to you from a foster program?"

"Yes," she said. "That's standard practice for adoptions."

"Their parents are still alive?"

"I don't really know," she says.

"Do you know who the parents are?" I ask.

"Not really," she said. "The agency handled everything for us."

She's got that flicker in her eyes again, and I think she's lying to me. This has got to be the source of her trouble.

"Mrs. Traeger," I say. "I can't do much about a problem that's been imported like this from Australia. I think you should contact the adoption agency and find out the details on the adoptions. If there's an issue there, then you have something to take to the police."

"They're my children," she says. "I'm not going to give them up."

"Mrs. Traeger," I say, "if you think you're being targeted by a *galka* hit-man, the children are a likely cause. If you'll give me the name of the agency, then I'll try to check for you."

"I'm not going to do that," she says. "You've got to help us."

Her chin is trembling like she's about to cry, but she won't budge. I sigh.

"Alright, Mrs. Traeger," I say. "I'll do what I can."

That leaves me with the stakeout again. Maybe the sorcerer will put in an appearance tonight so I can catch him or her in action and be done with it.

I head back to the beach to see how the film shoot is going. They've moved on to another scene today. Mercy and her leading man come out of the water, flop onto a blanket in the sand. They argue, and he gets up and strides away down the beach. They repeat this with slight variations. About four the light is changing and Traeger wraps. They start to pack up for the day.

They're headed to the Trap again. I get a seat at the bar by myself and watch the crew come in. Traeger isn't with them today, either. They cluster up about the same way they did yesterday evening. I'm nursing a beer and sifting my way through the information I've collected so far, trying to narrow down the possibilities. I study the faces, watch people relate. I decide Izzy is my gal.

She's sitting with Johnny tonight. After a while he gets up, heads for the loo. It's my opportunity to talk privately.

"Hi, Ms. Walker," I say. "Could I join you for a moment?"

She looks up at me. I study her face in the light from the window and then I'm sure. The children look like her.

"John's sitting there," she says. "He'll be right back."

That means I'll have to be more direct.

"Are those your children?" I ask.

She stares at me, and then her face flushes darker.

"No," she says. "I don't know what you're talking about."

I drop into the empty chair, lean on my elbows.

"Look, Ms. Walker," I say. "I checked into adoptions in Australia, and you have my sympathy, but if there's any sorcery going on, it needs to stop. Now."

She stares at me again. It looks like she's really thinking about it this time. She tightens her lips.

"Ms. Detroyer," she says finally. "Why are you saying this to me?"

"I'm thinking you're responsible," I say. "If you're planning anything, you should give up the idea."

"I'm not planning anything," she says. "Why do you think so?"

"The Traegers are sick," I say.

I'm not even sure of that until I say it. It's something in the way they look—the reddish skin, the dull eyes, the difficulty they have in tracking. There's another feel about them, too—as if they're half gone into the spirit world already, even though they're clearly still alive and breathing.

"What do you mean?' she asks.

"They've got something worse than sunburn," I say. "That lost, feverish look in their eyes? Isn't that from sorcery?"

She blinks, studies my face. For a second I think she's going to talk about it. She opens her mouth, but nothing comes out. She closes it again.

"Some people make their own problems," she says.

John is headed back this way. I shove backward against the chair.

"Thanks," I say. "I'll be at their house all night if you have any second thoughts."

By nine o'clock I'm at the Traegers'. The light fades gradually from dusk into an indigo darkness. A wind off the ocean rattles the fronds of the palm trees growing around the house, nods the head of bromeliads. Now and then a car passes, headed for an address somewhere else. The street lighting is subdued but good enough for what I need to see. The corner lot makes it easy to monitor the grounds from my car, and I've parked at a diagonal across the street so I can see both the front door and the gate to the back yard.

I'm watching the house, but I'm thinking about other things, mostly Paul and Joel Angstrom. It's strange how things never seem to work out for me. Now I've got two of them to deal with—and worse, I've got emotional chaos going on. I was furious with Paul for the way he acted, so what am I doing now? Sleeping with Joel out of revenge? Is this affair something I can justify in any way?

The kid seems to be great for me. So why am I feeling guilty?

It's a long night. The moon rises about two, a bright quarter crescent. It lightens the yard, deepens the shadows under the palms. First light is about five a.m. I left about this time yesterday morning, but I've got nowhere to rush off to, so I continue to sit there. A light goes on inside the house about 5:15. The children wouldn't get up until later for school, so likely one of the adults is an early riser. The upstairs light goes out and a few minutes later the outside light comes on downstairs. I can't really see the back of the house from here, but I catch the reflection off the pool—a shimmer of luminescence on the dusky trees and dark-slatted fence. At the same time, I see shadows move on the lawn.

A shiver runs down my spine. It's eerie, the shimmer and simultaneous drift of shadows, like they're connected in an invisible way. I find I'm holding my breath—ease it out. I shift into action, reach over to the seat and slide my .38 out of its padded case. I flip off the light switch, ease the car door open carefully and slip out.

Maybe I should call and get the police out here, but I've not really seen anything yet. Just the lights on in the house and the shadows. I'm not even sure what I saw—I could have been dozing, dreaming. I need to see something solid before I make a call—a person that I can identify to the dispatcher.

If it's something else, the police won't be able to help me.

The eastern sky is dusky pale now, easing the shadows. The world is still in twilight, the colors greyed and misty. As I dart across the street, the air feels moist and unearthly, like I've dropped into Dreamtime, somehow—into the primordial prehistory of creation. I work my way across the lawn, keep a careful watch. I think I see a shadow flow over the gate. The hinges creak faintly; the latch rattles.

There's no sound from the other side, nothing of shoes hitting the pavement, no cry or challenge from whichever of the Traegers is on the patio. I pick up my pace to a jog on the heavy turf—surer of what I've seen this time. At the gate, I stretch and reach over, feel for the latch. Alyssa hasn't installed a padlock yet; I can unlatch it from the outside.

The latch clicks; the gate swings open.

The thing looks like a goblin. It's got red skin and a head that's too big for its body. Instead of normal hands and feet, it's got sucker mouths at the end of its limbs. Alyssa is in her nightgown, stretched out on the flagstones of the patio. The creature is lying on her like a lover, sucking out her blood.

I dart through the gate, lift the gun. Someone hits me from behind, shoves the gun down. We fall into the grass. This isn't the best procedure for gun safety.

I start to say this.

"Lie still!" Izzy hisses.

The goblin has noticed us. The ugly head shifts, turns our way. The little eyes are searching. It lets go of the woman's throat, shambles in our direction. The patio lights play along its scarlet skin. Alyssa Traeger doesn't move—she lies there and stares into the dusky sky like she's gone somewhere else.

"Play dead," whispers Izzy.

She's lying on me, hissing into my ear. I want to struggle. I want to thrash and shove her off and get away from the horrible thing that's after us. I want to fire my gun into it until it stops slobbering and wheezing and drops to the ground.

"You can't kill it," says Izzy. "Play dead and it will leave us alone."

I lie there shuddering under her. The thing slobbers up, snuffles around us wetly. Izzy is as still as death, and I try to follow her lead. She seems to be right. After a while the thing leaves us alone, shambles back toward the patio.

Izzy moves then, rolls off me.

"Can we get into the house?" she asks. "I've got to get the kids out."

I push up to my feet.

"What about the Traegers?" I ask.

"They're already dead," she says. "We've got to get the kids."

She grabs hold of my shirt, drags me around the corner of the house. We're out of sight of the goblin now. I try to get control of my breathing.

"Wait," I say. "What is that thing?"

"It is Yara-ma-yha-who," she says, "a creature of the Dreamtime. It will consume them, turn them into others of its kind."

"Isn't there anything we can do?" I ask.

"It's too late," she says. "They brought the creature with them. It was already too late when they got here from Australia."

It sounds like I'm going to lose my client.

"I'm sure you know there are different levels of reality," she says.

It's my gift to see them. Whether it's because I'm a spirit talker or because of the potency of my grandfather's medicine bag, I'm not sure. I touch it now, where it lies against my chest, feel the warmth of the talismans.

"Why didn't I see that thing last night?" I ask.

"It comes with the daylight," she says. "It's a creature of the dawn."

She means I left too early yesterday morning. She's headed off through a bed of hibiscus toward the patio doors, swears as she snags on bougainvillea thorns. I take another look back toward the patio, take care to avoid the bougainvillea myself. I tuck my gun into the back of my waistband.

"Are those your kids?" I ask.

"My cousin's," she says.

At the doors, Izzy takes a last look around the patio. Light glints along the sharp line of her cheekbone, colors her shirt a frosty blue. There's no sign of the goblin now. She slips through the open doors, and I'm right behind her.

It's dim in the house, barely light enough to avoid the vague humps of furniture. Off to the right are the stairs to the second floor. Izzy heads up that way. In the upstairs hallway, she opens the first door.

"Akala?" she calls. "Daku? Wake up."

"Izzy?" says a sleepy voice from inside the room. It's Arthur.

"Daku," she says, "get up. We're leaving."

In the near darkness, he pushes back the bedcovers and she grabs him up, heads for the door again. With the boy on her hip, she opens the second door.

"Akala?" she says.

The girl isn't so easy. She fusses.

"Where's my bear?" she whines. "I can't go without my bear."

"Shh," says Izzy.

She puts the boy down. I snap on the Disney princess lamp by the bed to look for the bear. We've taken too long, made too much noise. The door slams back against the wall.

It's Traeger.

He looks about as human as the thing downstairs. He's half-naked, flushed scarlet with rage. He roars something incoherent, launches at Izzy. I hear her breath rush out as they fall. Akala screams, a sound that cuts like a knife.

They've hit the chest of drawers, fallen into the floor. Izzy is a tough, strong woman, but Traeger is on top of her. He beats at her face, and she holds him off. He's slobbering, snapping, trying to get at her throat with his teeth.

It's a savage, horrific fight. I grab up the princess lamp, jerk at the cord, club him with the base. One shot doesn't quite do it, so I hit him again.

"Don't hurt Elsa!" screams Akala.

I gather that's the lamp.

"Sorry," I say.

I set it back on the night table. Akala sniffles.

"Are you alright?" I ask Izzy.

She got a bloody nose. She shoves up and looks for a tissue, pinches at it.

"Yeah," she says. "Let's get out of here."

I've been along for the ride so far, but I need to sort his out. It does look like the Traegers are goners—whether from sorcery or their own ill luck. The adoption seems questionable to me, and I'm sympathetic to what Izzy is trying to do. Still, there are rules.

"This isn't going to work out for you," I say. "It's kidnapping, interfering with custody."

She looks at me for a long moment, holds her nose. There's blood spattered on her shirt.

"Wasn't that a bar downstairs?" she asks.

"Yes," I say. I've got a glimmer of what she means to do. "Don't touch the bottle with your hands," I say. "It'll leave fingerprints."

"Thanks," she says. "Good thought."

She heads off down the hallway. I hear the solid thump of her heels as she runs down the stairs.

"Izzy?" says Daku. "Izzy?"

"Shh," I say. "She'll be right back."

Izzy comes back upstairs carrying a glass and a bottle of whiskey wrapped in a towel. She partially fills the glass with whiskey, sets it on the chest in Akala's room. Then she dribbles whiskey on Traeger, pours some into his open mouth.

"Will that do it?" she asks.

She pulls out her cell phone then, calls 911. We head down to the living room with the kids to wait. Izzy sits on the couch, holds Akala in her lap. I pick up Daku and he snuggles against me in the chair. He's warm and wiggly. I take a breath.

"So," I say, "could a *galka* sorcerer call up something like Yara-ma-yha-who?"

Izzy turns her head, looks across at me. She's a shadowy creature herself in the growing light. Silence extends, fills the room.

"I don't know much about it," she says finally. "Maybe you could ask Johnny or Walt."

"Right," I say.

I expect Children's Services will be here with the police. Maybe the kids can get their real mother back soon.

Chapter 8

THE CURSE

This is supposed to be a real vacation, just for pleasure and no working. I've come to visit Joel Angstrom, who has ambitions toward degree in International Relations, and who's supposed to be studying in Dusseldorf this term—for however much that's worth. With Amsterdam so close, I couldn't pass it up, and now it seems I've got a problem.

It's three a.m. and I'm alone at the hotel. Joel went out hours ago for a couple of beers and hasn't come back. I've worn a track in the rug, pacing back and forth, and the clerk downstairs is so tired of me he's pretending not to understand English any more. He just shrugs at me now, his hands and shoulders quirking like he's got a tic. His eyes look bored—he's sure I'm just another stupid American bitch who's lost her boy lover to the local sex trade.

I do fine in Spanish, but my German is strictly rudimentary, and my Dutch is non-existent. We're at an impasse. I can't just sit still and wait, though. If something happens to Joel on my watch, his dad will kill me—we're already on bad enough terms. I head down the steep gangway stairs for the fourteenth time.

"*Polizei?*" I say, and the clerk shrugs like he doesn't understand German now, either.

My phone isn't working. I didn't buy a data package for Europe and there's no wi-fi here.

"*Telephon?*"

It's a picturesque old-style hotel, and there aren't any phones in the rooms. The clerk gestures finally, and I find a pay phone tucked away in the corner of the ornate lobby and the emergency number for police in my guidebook.

"Hello?" I say. "Does anyone there speak English?"

It's a bad start. Apparently not. At least, not at this time of night.

The guy on the line finally simplifies to pidgin German and I pick up the word '*morgen,*' which I gather means call back in the morning. I curse at him and then I gather he understands more English than he's admitted, because he hangs up.

"Shit," I say to the dial tone.

I try Joel, but the call just goes to voicemail. Then I go back to my room and try to get some sleep. If Joel's been murdered, it happened at least four hours ago. I'll probably come to the same end if I go out in a strange foreign city to look for him in the middle of the night.

I can't sleep, but I do lie in bed until daylight, watching stark moon patterns flow along the walls. The hotel serves a complimentary breakfast at seven, and I debate whether to skip it, but probably the day shift of police doesn't come on until after that. It's a cheap buffet of synthetic meat and cheese, plastic bread and lukewarm tea. After worrying all night, I'm starving. I wolf it down.

I wish for coffee, but there isn't any. Still, a little caffeine is better than none at all. I'm ready to attempt the phone again. I only have to wait fifteen minutes and feed coins to the phone twice before they find someone to tell me to come down to the station.

The address is in the Jordaan district west of my hotel and mercifully not far away. I'm tempted to take a taxi regardless, but I've already been here a week and I ought to be able to find the place on foot. If Joel doesn't turn up, I may have to stay here a while, and I'll need the rest of my budget to pay off the damn hotel. Maybe I should move to a cheaper place.

The Jordaan is the restored industrial district and mostly it looks good, but the police station isn't completely elegant. The waiting room has high ceilings and narrow windows and is furnished with gilt-framed portraits, antique tables and leather-upholstered chairs. Still, the floor and the wainscot show signs of wear and the plaster is cracked, the latest restoration wearing thin. Finally a constable shows up to see what it is I want.

He looks at my passport, listens to my story, and doesn't like it. He calls in somebody else, apparently an adjutant, and has me tell it over again. I'm already confused by the language, and now I'm having to deal with an obscure bureaucracy. The adjutant speaks excellent English, but he doesn't like the story, either. I can see it in the way his eyes flicker, the quick glance up and back.

"Ms. Detroyer," he says, "is this your correct age?" He holds up the passport so I can see it.

"Yeah," I say shortly. It's none of their business, and I don't mean to be sidetracked. "About my friend..."

"You do not look so old."

I understand how the man feels. I've had cases myself where the details don't match up. My looking twentyish is one of the results. I sigh.

"Look Adjutant," I say, "that doesn't have anything at all to do with why I'm here." His name is Peeters, and he's got a big nose and thinning, gray hair. The other one is Jansen, narrow-eyed and sporting a short, pale haircut that bristles like wire over his ears. I've got their faces recorded in memory, but I'd rather not try to say the names out loud until I want to be insulting.

"But your passport..." he persists.

"It's ligit," I say. "Check it if you want to." The worst thing about looking twenty is that people try to blow you off. "Meanwhile, I need to find my friend."

"Ms. Detroyer," says the constable. "This is Amsterdam. It is most likely that he only spent the night in the red light district."

"He just went out for a couple of beers," I say. "He didn't have that much money with him."

"Are you sure, Ms. Detroyer?" That's Peeters again.

"Cash and credit cards are all accounted for and in my possession," I say. "The women in the district don't work for free, do they?"

He looks irritated. I'm starting to wonder why they're not taking this more seriously.

"He's a good-looking boy," I suggest sweetly. "How many people get kidnapped and raped here every year?"

The adjutant looks even more irritated. "Ms. Detroyer..."

"Or killed?" I continue.

"It is too early to be so concerned," he explains.

Maybe I just don't look rich and influential enough. "I'll call his dad and tell him you said that," I say.

I'm getting pissed off, and I mean it. I'm ready to call Paul and tell him to get his butt over here on the next plane. Women are a lot easier to blow off than irate, well-off Nordic-type males. Much as I hate to admit it, Paul has gone into politics lately and he has the influence to cause people trouble. That'll get me off the hook, too. It might be the best solution all around.

But finally I've dented the adjutant. He doesn't want anybody else down here complaining.

"Ms. Detroyer, we will check around the neighborhood," he says. "But surely the young man will turn up. Perhaps he has only met some other students..."

I toss my best snapshot of Joel along the table.

"Here," I say. "I'll be at the hotel."

I start the hike back that way, slamming down the stairs and out onto the pavement. I stay pissed for about a quarter mile, stalking through the canyons of narrow streets. They're lined with embankments of six-story brick facades, three windows wide and crenellated by ornate gables. The houses are faced with trees. There are no cars parked in front of the apartment buildings, but boats are lined up along the canal. Finally a tin-can Citroën squeals and hoots at me as I trample into the crosswalk without looking, and I realize I'm going to get run over this way—or worse, get lost. I'm not paying attention.

Further along, I sit down on the abutment of a bridge to cool off, swing my legs over the water and lean on the lowest guardrail. The oil slick looks cloudy and faintly iridescent below me, but the canal is still pretty in the spring sunshine. Trees mask the parked cars here and a raft of ducks paddles by, disappears through the wall of houseboats moored along the banks. This is Princengracht, one of the major waterways, and it's lined with some of the better homes in the city. They're as tall and narrow as the other buildings, but ornate and well kept, spotted just now with reflections from the canal.

After a while my anger at the police drains off to a reasonable level, but then a nasty angst sets in. What the hell am I going to do? Sit in the hotel and wait for an obstinate and too-busy police force to come up with Joel? Yell for Paul?

Really, I'd rather not. Dealing with Paul will completely spoil my vacation, if this little fiasco doesn't—and also it's a matter of pride. Paul isn't happy with my relationship with Joel, anyway. If I call him to deal with this, I'll never live it down. I'll just have to think harder, instead.

We got our hotel far enough from the red light district and the sex shops along Zeedijk that we thought it'd be safe—at least enough so for Joel to go out and get us a couple of beers last night, but apparently we misjudged. I've been beating myself up for not going along, but it's questionable that would have helped. Whoever snatched Joel could probably have disposed of me just as easily. I'm convinced something happened. Joel has been here before and he's not likely to be sidetracked for so long by a chance gal of the night, or even a few long lost buddies. Plus, he's been making a sincere effort to make up for all the shit his dad pulled last year. I'm the reluctant party.

So how do I proceed? Well. There's no harm in asking a few questions myself.

I search around in my phone and come up with another photo of Joel. It's both of us this time, standing on the beach in Miami—not the best, but it's clear enough to show his face, and the rest of him, too, for that matter.

I dust off my jeans and start from the hotel, checking the various shops we've tried out in the last week. There are more around the block, so I make it a pattern, circling street by street, walking into the shops and showing the photo around.

"*Sehn sie?*" I ask.

All I get are headshakes, now and then a question. But I have to shake my own head then, because I can't understand it—I can't really deal with the language. Not that many people seem to speak English in this neighborhood. I grab a candy bar for lunch and keep slogging, but as the day starts to wane and rush hour traffic picks up, I start to get footsore.

"Dammit," I complain to the air.

I'm pretty far out toward the bad section of town now, and I ought to get back to safer ground before dusk. I head that way, dead tired and planning on an early dinner and collapse-into-bed at the hotel. I'm waiting at the light to get across the street when a car swerves to avoid an older woman on a bicycle. It misses narrowly, but the bike falls over anyway, right in front of me. The woman squawks, and packages fly. I jump down off the curb.

"Ma'am," I say, "are you all right?"

"Nah," she says in something like English. "I fall in zee street. Can't you see?"

She's old and black as Africa and drunk as a skunk. I can smell the juniper reek of genever on her breath, and hashish, too, in her clothes. I haul her up and she brushes off, apparently okay. She's wearing dark wool pants and a ragged coat, and has a gray felt hat pulled down over a scarf. It looks like there's blood on her knee.

"Um. Let me help you," I say. I go after the packages in the street. It seems I'm risking my life in the bicycle lane, but after all, the woman is elderly and could use the help.

She watches me suspiciously, counts the packages back into the basket.

"Could I help you get home?" I ask.

"You leave me alone," she says.

She starts off pushing the bike back the way I've come, and immediately trips and nearly falls. I don't ask again. I just move up on the other side of the bike and take hold of the handlebars. The old witch curses at me.

"Dammit," I say. "Shut up."

She does, but with poor grace. With all the packages heaped in the basket, the bike is heavy as sin, and soon I'm supporting it by myself and a lot of her weight, as well. She hobbles along leaning sideways, holding to my arm.

We're headed into the slums of Zeedijk, where the population must be heavily immigrant. The shops are faced with bright colors and signs that clearly aren't in Dutch. In front of one shop, a guy is passed out on a bench. Kids crowded on the street corners watch us go by. This is not where I ought to be heading just at dark. Still, I can always take a taxi home if I don't like the look of the streets when I leave. I'm not always known for doing the safest thing—and to hell with what anybody says.

"Where to?" I ask the woman.

"There," she croaks. She's limping more painfully now, and sounds almost civil, hardly sullen at all. Our destination is a run-down building with rusty bikes chained to scarred trees outside and stairs as steep as my hotel's. Luckily we don't have to go up those. Her rooms are on the first floor, so all we have to do is get up the steps from the street and in through the door, bike and all.

Someone who must be her daughter is at home, and the conversation becomes Dutch and incomprehensible—but then it's not, either. I can follow it just fine. Where have you been? Out drinking and smoking hash. Mother, how could you? Well, to hell with you!

The girl is dressed in jeans and a baggy sweater. She checks the cut knee and a couple of other bumps, and then she notices I'm still there, standing awkwardly inside the door and holding up the damaged bike.

"I guess I'd better go," I say then, and lean the bicycle against the wall.

The old lady says something in Dutch. The girl looks at her and then at me and says, "Wait, please! Will you stay for tea?"

I've impressed the old lady with my kindness—or something. She doesn't say a word to me, just points to a chair. As the daughter brings a basin and starts to clean up the knee, the old girl pulls out a panatela cigar and lights it up. I sit down obediently and try not to cough.

The apartment is close and cluttered, with cracked linoleum floors and worn chairs covered by throws. Plastic flowers spill over the table, and a wood stove seems to provide for both heat and hot water for tea. When the tea's ready, it tastes strong and herbal, and the packages I rescued turn out to include smoked eel and brioche rolls to go along with it. Tea with some of the city's least-affluent residents isn't something I expected, but I try to behave myself. They turn out to be Ma Ahfee, and her daughter Samma.

"You are from the U.S.?" asks the daughter—obviously a better conversationalist than the old lady.

"Yes. Are you're Dutch?" I ask, confused by the language. But no, they're from my own part of the world—Suriname, a few hundred miles south of Miami. It was a Dutch colony at one time, and like most of the Americas, it ended up with something of an African population—a little more rebellious than most, as I recall. Slaves escaped from the plantations carried on a war with the white settlers and eventually won a treaty that gave them full rights.

"Are you enjoying your visit?" asks Samma.

"I was until last night." I tell them about Joel leaving the hotel and not coming back. The old lady grunts.

The girl looks at her and then back at me.

"Where is your hotel?"

Her eyes are suddenly ominous. She puts down her cup, and the silence extends, becomes a palpable weight. I could get up and leave right now and never know what it is. But I won't.

"What's wrong?" I ask.

"Someone was killed near there last night."

She says it evenly, but then she realizes how I'll take it, waves her hands. "No. Wait! It was not your friend!"

Well, that's something. I push my heart back where it's supposed to be, close my eyes.

"How do you know it wasn't?" I ask.

"The man was well-known," she says. "A...a drug importer. Is that the right word?"

Dammit, Joel. What did you get into? It's the same as at home, likely—a drug fiasco, and the bystanders get wasted, too. Amsterdam is one of the major gateways to Europe, and Suriname has the Columbian connection. These women could even be part of the trade. But they must not have found his body, at least.

"Do the police know about it?" I ask.

"Of course," Samma says. "There was even mention in the paper this morning."

Dammit, again. I take a deep breath and put down my own cup. They're watching me, waiting, two pairs of onyx eyes, so similar, in different women's faces.

"Thanks for the tea," I say. "But I think I should probably go back to my hotel now."

The daughter sees me to the door. The old woman never says a word.

There isn't a taxi to be seen, so I have to hike home in the dusk. A shadow crowds me at the end of the block, but I snarl at the guy and he shies off. I must sound like a bona fide resident.

Back at the hotel, I make a call for Peeters, but he's not available. The night shift is on already.

"What the hell's wrong with you guys?" I yell into the phone. "Don't you the shit know what's going on in your own damn city? Or do you just hate tourists?"

They hang up on me.

I fume for a while and then go to find something to drink. About all I can do is wait for tomorrow again.

I wake up sprawled on top of the coverlet, still in yesterday's wrinkled clothes and hungover as hell. I tried out too much of the genever myself last night, I seem to recall. It was gawdawful stuff—but it seemed like the thing to do at the time. I can't even remember if I had dinner or not.

I drag myself up and into the shower, put on fresh jeans and a shirt at random. I'm willing to pay for real coffee this morning, as strong and black as I can get it. I'm in the dining room a long time working on my second cup. When I come out, a brown, fuzzy-headed kid is waiting in the lobby. Somehow I know as soon as I see him he's waiting for me.

"You come," he says, latching onto my sleeve.

"Where to, kid?" I'm trying not to seem completely gullible.

"To zee *wisiman*," he says, rolling his eyes.

What the hell. Maybe it's totally witless, but a gal's gotta take chances if she's going anywhere in this world. And one way or the other I'll get some attention from the police.

Early morning fog steams upward from the canals, eddies along the streets. In Dam Square a cold rain spits in my face. A cloud of pigeons circles and drops, avoiding the cars and littering the pavement with gray droppings. The Virgin of Peace stares blankly down at us from above. Further on, the landscape shifts as we enter the slums. Cold filters down through the clouds, darkening the abysses of alleyways. The wind casts trash into random drifts. The place we're going to looks rank and forbidding, an ancient craft house. Ma Ahfee is waiting for us there on the steps. The kid's eyes get bigger when he sees her.

"Here," he whispers, and darts away.

I look up at the woman, and she beckons like a phantom in the shadowy mist. I shiver, but I've come this far, and I plan to go on with it.

She pounds on the heavy wooden door, and it seems to echo to forever. The door opens and reveals another shadow.

"*Wisiman*," she says.

He's dressed in something long, colorful and sweeping. The glitter of a beaded cap flashes through the mist.

"Good morning. I'm happy to meet you, Ms. Detroyer," he says in clear English. He takes my hand. I think he's only offering a handshake, but he holds on, and suddenly I'm falling. His shadowy eyes are deep as wells, a rush of darkness rising to swallow me.

Maybe I should be trying to get my hand back, but instead I stand there like a dimwit. I gasp suddenly as he lets go.

"Please come in," he says, perfectly ordinary, "the weather leaves something to be desired this morning."

He turns to lead the way and I hesitate. Ma Ahfee is gone, ghosting away into the shadow in her gray coat and hat, and only the reek of her cigar lingers behind. I don't, for very long. I step into the dusky house and close the door behind me.

The interior is crude and ancient, with fire-stained beams and yellowed, crumbling plaster walls. The ceilings are low and claustrophobic, but beyond the entry a circle of lamplight opens up into a glowing landscape of Persian rugs and tapestries and tasseled cushions on the floor. Free-standing cabinets and pots are scattered around in haphazard order, and the place is scented with herbs and incense. A brass-clad water pipe glitters on a shelf, and I wonder if this is where Ma Ahfee gets her hash.

"Do sit down," the man says, and now I have a chance to look him over.

The robes and the beaded cap are African style, and so is he. I'd at first thought he was an older man, but now I'm not so sure. He's cocoa-skinned and dark-eyed, with straight hair that suggests Native American heritage. Slender and willowy, he folds onto the cushions with a litheness that suggests youth. He leans gracefully to pour me a cup of tea. But still age lingers in his eyes, a quality that's knowledge, maybe, instead of time.

"Ms. Detroyer, you are older than you seem," he says.

Maybe my own eyes look the same to him.

"Yes," I say, without providing any details. He doesn't ask, only offers me the cup of tea.

"What's in this?" I ask suspiciously, and he smiles. His eyes flicker darkly, catching the light.

"Nothing I will not drink with you."

To demonstrate, he pours another cup from the teapot and takes a sip. His English is very British and absolutely correct. The tea set is expensive-looking, hand-painted china.

"You are a private investigator in Miami, Florida?" he asks.

"Yes." I wonder how he knows. I haven't told anyone here what I do at home, and probably most people take me for a student, especially when I'm with Joel.

"Mr. Wisiman, why am I here in your house?" I ask, and his lips curve again.

"*Wisiman* is an occupation," he says, "not my name. And you are here so that I may correct a problem I have caused you." His voice is pure and velvety. It vibrates in the air like a chord.

"Huh?" I say. "I mean, I beg your pardon?"

"It was I who killed that man in the alleyway the night before last," he says. Then he smiles in earnest at my expression.

"Not personally, of course," he says. "I had only to wish it, and no necessity to soil my own hands."

"Oh," I say.

"You understand this?" he asks.

I'm not sure I do.

"Are you part of the…uh, local business network?" I ask.

"No," he says. "My interests are otherwise." A black cat drifts out of the foliage and picks her way daintily through he cushions. He puts down his tea and opens his hands so she can slide into his lap. She curls to study me with feline yellow eyes. "It was the result of a curse," he says.

It takes me a minute to sort through that.

"Oh," I say. "Then you're a…sorcerer?"

"A magician," he says. "In my heritage there is a difference." He raises his eyebrows, sitting like a statue of carved, exotic wood with the pale-eyed cat still watching me. She's his familiar, I decide. And there's another one. Now that my eyes have adjusted to the dimness, I can see a hunched vulture with a knife-edged beak and jaundiced eyes sitting on the arch of a carved wooden cabinet.

"This is Niger," he says, stroking the cat. "She is my eyes in the night, and that is Opete, my wings." He smiles faintly at my expression.

"About your friend, Ms. Detroyer," he goes on. "To practice *wisi* is to practice evil, in some ways—and evil moves outward like the ripples from a stone thrown into a pool. It encompasses all who cross the path of the *kunu*, the curse. I have caught your friend in the ripple pattern, as well as the victim, and you, plus the agency who actually committed the murder for me."

"And who is that?" I ask. I'm professionally curious.

He shrugs. "I don't know who did it," he says.

"If *wisi* is evil," I ask, "then why is it you cursed the man? Aren't you concerned about doing evil? Or is that any of my business?"

He gives me the quiet smile again, and his slender hands stroke the cat. In that moment, their eyes seem very similar.

"Opo," he says. "We are very different, you and I. I would not want to fight you. The spirit in you is not white, and not unbelieving.

"The man was my student," he says. "Power calls to power, and he came to me to learn the ways of it, but he broke the taboos I placed in order to enrich himself. He used his power in ways that were not permitted. The curse was then automatic. It was *misi-dede*, death from sin."

Amsterdam is the last place I expected to hear shamanistic delineations of good and evil, but his theology is obviously sound. He's identified the part of me that thinks so, too, that feels the reality of power misused—the part that's woman of color and spirit talker—though I've not told anyone about that here.

"So what can you do about Joel?" I ask.

"It is yet to be determined," he says

"How will it be determined?" I ask.

"My *apenti* will lead us," he says and gives the cat a shove. She takes off, and he reaches to lift a small, ornately carved drum from the nearest shelf. The sound he makes from it is hypnotic, nearly matches the beat of my heart. After a while, it captures the throb completely, masters the surge of my pulse. The bird ruffles its feathers on the cabinet and spreads its wings, seems to take flight.

The first time I worked a case with Paul, I had no idea he was looking for a partner. It was just a way to make a few extra bucks. I was waitressing nights and going to school days at Miami Dade, exhausted as hell and direly in need of some cash. Paul was just off the police force and trying to make his rep in private work. He needed a pretty girl, he said, to play decoy for him in a divorce case. He didn't mention he thought the guy had murdered a previous wife and a long line of one-night-stands. He said I had lots of smarts, but after that job he never seemed quite so impressed with me. We had an on and off relationship that lasted for fifteen years—at which point he must have forgotten about the brains, after all.

The contract we signed all those years ago had a clause for me to buy out the business. Paul got the idea to sell and go into politics. Maybe he did think I'd have some objection, because he neglected to tell me about his plans. Instead he aimed his kid at me as a distraction. I haven't yet figured out how Paul knew I'd take in the boy, but distractions or not, I was paying attention. Once I caught on, I sued for my option and bought out Paul's interest in the business. It was a big financial hit. I knew then I was through with the both of them—but it didn't quite work out that way.

The reason it didn't work out surprised Paul more than it did me, I think. So now relations are more complex. I haven't worked out exactly what I think about sleeping with Joel. What I feel is plenty clear, though. The kid is addictive.

The *wisiman* is shaking me. I'm groggy, even worse hungover than I was when I woke up this morning. The light has dimmed in the front windows, shifted far over to the west. It's nearly dark outside.

"I summoned the *luku*," he says, "the departed. You are a good vessel, Ms. Detroyer. The *yorka* spoke to me clearly through you."

"The what?" I ask.

It must have been the tea.

"The spirits," he says.

"Oh God," I groan. "What did they say?" I'm hoping it wasn't anything personal. I remember I've been dreaming.

"That we must hurry," he replies.

"Hurry?" I say. "What for?"

"Because the moon is full tonight, and it will rise in about one hour."

I'm not following him.

"Huh?" I say.

"It's an opportune time for appeasing a *kunu*," he says, "for anyone who has been cursed, or caught up in a curse. I cannot tell you more than that just now. I will make preparations." He scoops stuff out of the jars, mixes it in a mortar, decants into a mahogany box carved with signs and animal shapes. He packs it all into a kit, and then he's done.

"Are you ready to go?" he asks.

"Damn," I say. I rub my face, still groggy from the tea and the magic, whatever it is he's done.

He stops, stands up straight. The light glitters in his eyes.

"Do you need assistance, Ms. Detroyer?"

"No," I say. "I'm coming." I shove up out of the cushions, manage to sit upright and rake back my hair.

I remember it's cold outside, find my jacket and struggle into it. Maybe I should try to call the police again, but if they're like the Miami cops, they still won't be interested in this—they won't take the talk about curses seriously. And I don't like the way Peeters and Jansen looked at me—like I was a definite problem. It's occurred to me why. They're not real sorry this guy who was murdered is dead—and it's too bad about any bystanders that got in the way. They're just not going to look at it too closely.

"Is something wrong?" the *wisiman* asks, poised above me.

"No," I say, pushing up to my feet. "I'm ready."

Outside, the day is gone. The streets are dark and obscure, and I'm lost inside a minute. The fog is rising again, if it's ever really cleared. Vague clouds scuttle overhead, masking the stars. We're headed for the waterfront. I can smell the sea, the dank miasma of pitch, old wood and rotting weed that clings to the piers.

We seem alone in the mist, and the silence is eerie. My companion is a dark phantom of flowing robes hardly visible against the night. We turn at a corner, and a streetlight flares on the planes of his face. He looks at me.

"Are you frightened, *Opo*?" he asks.

"Not yet," I say, and then I shudder. There's no one else on the street. "Where is everybody?"

"Perhaps they can feel the evil," he says. "There is much of it abroad tonight."

I can feel it, too, as if the spirits of the dead have risen with the fog. They drift between the buildings on silent, stealthy feet—faint wisps not yet fully realized, ghosts from the past still clinging to the earth.

Our destination turns out to be a moldering ruin on the very brink of the harbor. It's a crumbling warehouse, tacked up with discolored notices in Dutch that have to say it's condemned. An old quay has fallen below it, and the sea rushes in over the broken timbers, eroding the pilings with the endless seethe of the tide.

"*Wisiman?*" I say. I'm shivering, even with my jacket zipped up tight. "Have they got him in there?"

"Yes," he says.

We're standing in the shade of another building down the street. The *wisiman* turns slightly, touches my arm with invisible fingers. Only his voice has any substance now.

"*Opo*," he says softly, "I must tell you now. There are many cults which believe that ill luck may be changed by bathing in blood and calling on the gods to share it. Using human blood strengthens the effects. They will plan to use your friend, who was captured at the scene of the murder, for a sacrifice."

"A sacrifice!"

"Shhh," he says. "Youth and innocence always strengthen the effects of the blood."

Images of Joel flicker past like a film: lithe and blond, meeting me at the airport in Dusseldorf. Surfacing from the blue Atlantic off Miami, his hair like pale silk. Sleeping quietly in my bed...

Paul's going to kill me if the kid dies.

Dammit. I'm shivering in earnest now. The cold has penetrated all the way to my bones.

"Who are these guys?" I ask. "Thugs? Religious fanatics? If they're so crazy, how do you know he's even alive?"

He shrugs in the darkness. "The *yorka* has said it."

"We're going in there?" I'm wishing now I'd called the police, after all. Wishing I had my gun—any kind of firepower. But there aren't any guns around here—only the police carry them in Amsterdam. "What the hell am I supposed to do?"

"Only stay with me." His fingers touch my arm again. "I will handle things," he says. "You must hide in a safe place out of sight. I will need you close so I have no problems with the boy."

"But..." I have lots of objections, but it's too late to argue. The bright smudge of the full moon is climbing up out of the harbor now. My teeth are chattering. "Okay," I stutter. "How do we get in?"

He's got a solid, practical-looking crowbar in that kit of his. He pries an official-looking padlock off a peeled, misshapen door, and breaks the panel for good measure— it's stuck in the frame. Inside there's a whisper of sound, a faint glow of light. He's got a pen light in his bag of tricks, too.

"The rite has already begun," he says, and leads off like a cat in the darkness.

The floor is uncertain, full of rotting boards. There are cracks between the planks, and the sea licks the pilings below, ready to catch me if I fall through.

"Wait there," the *wisiman* says, directing me to a frail ladder. I climb up, find it leads to a loft. I slide along the platform, clawing at cobwebs, wary of spiders in the dark.

There's a chamber below me like a scene out of hell. As my eyes adjust, I can see there are maybe a dozen figures, dressed in rag-tag clothes. They've formed a circle around a fire built in a metal drum, a blackened altar. They're writhing and chanting—a sound deadened to nothing by the heavy wood and rotted plaster above us, the restless wash of the sea.

The shadows are all dark but one.

It's Joel, slim and pale as a wraith in the flickering light. He's half-naked, and his hands are tied behind him. He's on his knees with his head hanging, and he's not making any fuss at all. He must be hurt, or maybe drugged, to be so still. I clench my hands then until the nails dig in—but I've said I'd wait.

The chant rises higher. One of them gestures—it looks to be a priest. Three of them grab Joel and lift him up. He struggles weakly then, but they only hold him down on the altar. The priest shoves his jaw over to expose the pale line of his throat. The man has got a knife, raises it high...

The fire explodes; the *wisiman* appears like a demon. He lifts his arms, screams out something powerful. They scatter magically. Everybody—including the priest.

Well, maybe it's just black powder and an impressive persona—or maybe it is real magic. I'm not going to complain.

Their disappearance seems only what he expected. The *wisiman* strides forward. He's got a blanket in his kit, too, and he throws it around Joel. The kid struggles weakly. Holding him, the *wisiman* looks up for me, where I'm still waiting, tense and uncertain, in the loft.

"*Opo?*" he calls.

I slide down the ladder, run toward them.

"Joel," I say. "Shh. It's Anna. Be still. Everything's okay."

I'm not sure he hears me. His eyes are closed, and his face seems slack and unresponsive. Still, he stops struggling when I touch him.

The *wisiman* cuts his bonds, lifts the kid in his arms. We head for the broken door. Around us the fire is spreading. It's spilled out of the drum, run along the floor while we weren't looking. It's infected the beams now, eaten its way into the columns. Suddenly it's hard to breathe—the heat is closing down on us.

I can't see where we're supposed to go. My eyes are watering. I'm starting to cough. The roar of the fire is deafening. Part of the loft crashes down. I'm choking, starting to panic now.

"*Wisiman!*" I yell.

"*Opo,*" he says. "This way."

I can hardly hear his voice over the noise of the flames, barely see his dark form through the flash and roar of sparks. I think we're lost, but suddenly the door is there. I lunge through it, close on his heels.

We're not safe yet. Something else collapses inside the warehouse—a wall. I can feel the vibration through the deck, through the air. Smoke roils across the water. Flames turn the sea into an ocean of fire. We keep going, careful of our footing in the eerie, shifting light.

Finally the air is better. We're back on solid ground now.

The *wisiman* stops, looks back for me.

"*Opo?*" he says. "Are you alright?"

I cough again. "I'm okay."

"This way," he says, leading off again.

We avoid an oncoming fire brigade, slip into an alleyway. The *wisiman* eases Joel down against a wall, shakes out his arms. The kid is solid, and he's got to be damn heavy.

"Is he all right?" I ask.

The *wisiman* is looking at me. "It is the father you want," he says.

I stare up at him. "The hell," I say.

"Anna?" says Joel. "Where are we?"

His voice is vague and blurred. I put one hand on his shoulder.

"Shh," I say. "Be still, kid. I'm here. Are you okay?"

He lets his breath out.

"'M okay," he says. "Listen. Anna, I saw…I think I saw a murder. Shouldn't we tell the police?"

I look up at the roiling, burning sky. I can feel the curse now. It's there—hanging, suspended, ready to fall.

"Kid," I say, "I think we need to stay out of this one."

Chapter 9

OTTER'S BRIDE

Alaska is a wild and desolate place. Flying into the airport, I've had an impression of snow-capped peaks and endless expanses of deep blue sea. People have carved out a safe space in Anchorage, but still the crushing peaks tower over the city, a reminder of how close eternity lies.

This is not a vacation—I'm here to work. My flight came in early in the day from Portland, so I've already checked into the hotel and gotten out for a brief look around. The place doesn't seem like much of a city, as those go—say as compared to metro Miami. To me this looks like a small town—except I know Anchorage the biggest city in Alaska. There are a few indications. For example, the store windows are filled with jewelry and art work I couldn't afford to touch with one little finger, much less buy and take home.

I'm not sending any post cards back to Miami on this trip, either. Since the *wisiman* in Amsterdam so uncharitably pointed out that it's Joel's dad I really want, I've been worrying even more about my relationship with the boy. My life has wandered into weirdness, and maybe I should be trying to get it back on track. I've made no actual move to do it, but still…

I don't have any trouble finding the place where I'm supposed to meet Caroline Driscoll for lunch. The visitor's center is a rustic log cabin roofed in sod, set against that towering skyline of snow-capped peaks. It looks like the grass on the cabin's roof needs cutting. Along the front porch beam, hanging baskets are overflowing with geraniums. It's May here and I'll be lucky if the temperature breaks sixty degrees. That's the dead of winter back home in Miami.

Just past the visitor's center is the restaurant I'm looking for. It has varnished log walls with cast iron tools hanging all around—I recognize the harpoons, but most of the trappings I can't even identify. Caroline is waiting on a bench just inside the door. She's white-haired and eightyish, but from the way she gets up, she's still an active woman. She's dressed in a flowered summer frock and carrying a bright straw bag.

"Mrs. Driscoll?" I say. "I'm Anna Detroyer."

She hesitates, then extends a delicate, arthritic hand.

"Thank you so much for the invitation, Ms. Detroyer," she says. "I don't get downtown that much anymore." She hesitates, smiles uncertainly. "Welcome to our city."

The menu features reindeer sausage.

"I do recommend it," Caroline says. "Though some might find it a little bit…spicy?"

"That works for me," I say.

The waiter leaves with our order. Caroline fluffs her napkin, spreads it on her flowered lap.

"So now, Ms. Detroyer," she says. "You're a private investigator? How is it you want me to help you?"

"I've been retained by Ms. Kathryn Sakharov," I say, "who is looking for her roots."

"Oh?" says Caroline.

"Ms. Sakharov's was adopted by a Russian immigrant family who lived in this area some fifty years ago, but later relocated to South Florida. The only thing she has from her birth mother is this necklace."

I take it out of my pocket and place it on the table. It's an Alaskan Native America amulet, an eagle motif carved in ivory and wound with copper wire.

"Oh," she says.

"The adoptive parents are both dead," I say. "Ms. Sakharov has already tried to get the adoption records unsealed, but there seems to be a snag. I'm here to find out what it is."

Caroline taps her fingers on the tabletop. The waiter drops off our plates. The sausage does have a nice tang to it.

"Mrs. Driscoll," I say finally, into the dead silence that's fallen over our table. "I'm really in need of help on this."

She's staring at the wall over my head. Her eyes look strange, enlarged and distorted by the split frames of her bifocals.

"Mrs. Driscoll?"

The bifocals flash down to me. "Ms. Detroyer," she says, "old records can be very hard to come by."

"I know that, Mrs. Driscoll," I say. "It's why I'm asking you instead of Children's Services."

She frowns, fiddles with her fork, picks at her pasta salad.

"If I may ask...How did you find my name?" she asks.

"Old letters," I explain. "You wrote to Kathryn's adoptive mother several times after they moved to Florida. You were friends?"

The woman frowns. Then she folds her napkin carefully, lays it alongside her plate. She leans back in her chair and quirks an odd smile.

"Dear, would you like to visit the museum?" she asks.

It turns out to be the Anchorage Historical and Fine Arts Museum. There's a lot about totems and whaling vessels and Native American art, but Mrs. Driscoll has a definite destination in mind. It's a balcony devoted entirely to the families that settled early Anchorage.

"All these families made their fortunes here," she says. She sits on a bench and folds her hands over her bag.

I think about that for a couple of minutes, and then I lean against a column and stare at her.

"You mean they've still got those fortunes?" I ask.

"Of course, there's some new money that came in with the oil pipeline a few decades back," she says, "but the older families still control most of the wealth. That means they have a lot of influence."

"Oh," I say. It must be contagious.

I walk along the gallery and look at the row of exhibits. The faces are uniformly white and very staid. None of them look much like Kathryn Sakharov. She has features that go with the carved ivory necklace.

"Do you mind telling me which family I'm dealing with here?" I ask.

Mrs. Driscoll flutters her hands, fusses with her handbag. I'm reminded how much like a small town Anchorage looks. My face has a cast similar to Kathryn's. Fifty years ago, I figure that wouldn't have been a good thing to have in one of these families. Actually, from the way Caroline is acting, there might still be issues about it.

I'm not going to let something like that get to me, though—or even slow me down. I'm bigger than that.

I turn to face her.

"I'll find out anyway," I say. "There has to be some clue in the public records."

"Drummond," she says, and glances away. "Dammit."

I'm surprised at her. She seems like such a proper lady.

Then she says, "Good luck, Ms. Detroyer."

She gets up from the bench and marches off down the gallery and into the elevator. I watch the doors close behind her flowered skirt and after a while I'm frowning, too. If there's something I've missed, I still can't see it. The obvious avenue is to contact the family. Regardless of whether it's a skeleton in someone's closet, I'm hired to do a job.

I stop at the desk downstairs.

"Hi," I say. "Are there any tours of historic homes in Anchorage?"

The man is young, thin and bookish, with heavy, dark glasses perched on his nose.

"Not really," he says. He pushes up the glasses, looks me over. "There actually aren't that many of the older structures still left," he says.

"I'm interested in people, and uh, the local history. Do any prominent members of the Drummond family still live here, for example?"

"Well, yes," he says. "Mr. Calvin Drummond still lives here in town."

I do a quick mental review of the exhibit I saw upstairs. "They were a mining family, weren't they?"

"Yes," he says. "Mr. Drummond and his sons still own the Dracher Mine. I'm sure you saw the photos of the gold-rush days."

"Are there any family histories available that might go into that?" I ask. "You know—the great Alaskan frontier?"

He raises his eyebrows.

"Not really," he says again. "We do have a flyer about the local historical society, though. Maybe you could check with them."

"Sure," I say, and take the sheet. "Thanks a lot."

At least I've got a full name to start with now.

Back in my room in the hotel, I check the phone book and locate Dracher Mining, Inc. They've got an office suite downtown. I've brought at least one pantsuit that looks professional, so I change out of my jeans and flannel shirt, ready to give the place a try.

The office building has old wood paneling and brass plates on the doors. It smells strongly of history, of tradition—and old money.

"I'm a private investigator from Miami," I tell the receptionist. "I'm working on an estate issue, and I need to speak to Mr. Drummond about it."

That's pushing the truth a little, but I'm playing this by ear. The woman is fortyish and well-dressed. She studies me over her reading glasses.

"Let me check with Mr. Drummond," she says. "He's expecting his grandson for an appointment—Mr. Yancy should be here shortly—but I'll see if he has a moment."

She taps on his office door, disappears inside. Right away she's back out.

"He'll give you five minutes," she says.

The door closes behind me.

Calvin Drummond is solidly built, with a shock of white hair and heavy, black eyebrows. His eyes are like flint when he looks at me. He doesn't stand up or extend his hand.

"What do you want?" he asks.

"I'm Anna Detroyer," I say. "I'm a private investigator from Miami researching the adoption of Kathryn Sakharov. She's looking for her birth family."

The man's face turns red.

"Get out of my office," he says. "Or else I'll call security to escort you out."

"Thank you for your time," I say.

I nod to the receptionist on my way out. At the front door to the building's lobby, I meet Yancy Drummond coming in. There's a strong family resemblance.

Well, damn. That wasn't very productive—or was it?

The man's response was way out of proportion to what I said. Of course, Drummond has a right to expect privacy for his family, but Kathryn has a right to know about her background, too—medical history, things like that. And certainly I have every right to ask about it. So how am I going to find anything out about the facts?

There's not much to go on, so I decide to read my brochure on the local historical society. I find a bench and have a look. They're based at the public library, and the address is right there on the flyer. It's only a short walk away.

"Hi," I say, at the reference desk, "I wonder if there's some way I could look up historical records?"

The woman smiles at me over her glasses. "Why certainly," she says. "We have a very well-preserved archive. What are you interested in?"

The service is great. They fix me up with a volunteer to help sort through the stacks of ancient microfiche—there is something to be said for small town friendliness, but not for their microfiche. It costs me the rest of the day and a bad case of eyestrain, but by four o'clock I've come up with a likely candidate: Marianne Drummond, born 1932 in Anchorage; died 1951 in Skagway, Alaska, of apparent assault. Survived by a two-week old infant. The infant seems to be the only Drummond born locally in that year.

I skim through news items, looking for details on the assault. It turns out a girl was also raped the year before by an unknown Indian male. Daughter of a prominent mine owner, it says, and doesn't mention any names.

I sit on the bench outside the library and stare at how the peaks cast shadows over the town. Marianne Drummond was nineteen years old in 1951.

Rape and murder may not be something Kathryn wants to hear about, but I'm into it now. Is this what people are hiding from me?

So where do I go now? Skagway?

It's better than trying to break through the stone walls around here.

It seems the way to get around in Alaska is to fly. I look through the phone book for bush pilots, turn down lots of offers for the grand tour. Finally I locate someone who will provide just the transportation. As a bonus, it seems he's ready to deal on the price.

"A trip up to Skagway?" he says. "What for?"

"I need to find out some information," I say. "How much?"

"How long will you be there?" he counters.

"I don't know," I say. "A couple of days, maybe?"

There's a silence on the line.

"Let's have a drink and talk about it," he says.

I kind of like the way this man is approaching the deal.

In person, he's Jeff Foxworthy, lean and lank, with thinning, gray-threaded hair and a yellow cast to his complexion. We meet for dinner at a place called Harry's, which is a bar and grill downtown. I notice that Jeff is into the hard stuff.

"I'm a private investigator," I tell him, "but I've not got a big budget."

I run my fingers through the frosting on my beer glass and watch the way Jeff goes through his bourbon.

"I've got to make enough to run the plane," he says.

The man looks like a borderline alcoholic and down on his luck. Likely he's desperate, or he wouldn't dicker like this for the job. Maybe I'm taking my life in my hands to hire the man, but somehow I like him better than all the smooth operators I've talked to on the phone earlier today. Under the alcoholic jitters, he looks tough as whipcord—somebody good to have at your back. If I'm going into unknown territory here, I want to be sure of who I'm going with.

"Do you know anything about Skagway?" I ask. "I might need some help in finding out what I want."

"Yeah," he says. "I know my way around the place."

"Can you go tomorrow morning?" I ask, and look pointedly at the drink in his hand.

He thinks about it, shoves the glass away.

"Sure," he says. "No problem."

We shake hands on it, and I head on back toward the hotel. It's well after ten o'clock now, and sudden darkness has fallen like a curtain across the peaks. It's a little bit of a walk to the hotel—I'm off the beaten path. The air is chilly. The stars are cold, bright points. At the end of the first block, I think I'm being followed.

I glance over my shoulder, see a bulky shadow turn the corner behind me. My skin crawls with a sudden unease. There's no one else on the sidewalks here; the shops and businesses are all closed and deserted for the night. I pick up my pace, headed for the next corner. I'm about half way there when another dark shape appears under the corner lights. I look at the purposeful way he's walking, glance over my shoulder. The shadow there is closing on me. That suggests I should get across the street—now.

I step off the walk. A car turns the corner. It's moving fast—cuts in front of me. I dodge back, grab for my phone. But calling 911 won't solve my immediate problem. I need the hell to deal with this. The bulky shapes have closed in; the car door opens. A dark silhouette towers over me.

"Anna Detroyer?" he says.

The car headlights spear the darkness, leave me blind.

It's not a situation to argue, or even make snide comments. He's got two bruisers behind me to make sure he's got my attention. They're close enough now that I can feel their breath on the back of my neck.

I'm feeling really stupid to get caught like this—it wasn't something I was expecting, though. It makes me think I might be onto something more serious than just a few old newspaper clippings.

One of the heavies grabs hold of my shoulder. I swing my arm up and bring my elbow down on his wrist, take off running. They might be big men, but that just means they're slower to move. As I dart around the back of the car, the tall man jumps back in, slams the door. By the time he's got the car turned around, I'm crashing through shrubbery. I cut through church grounds and stumble over a swale, come out three blocks from my hotel. I keep to the shadows in case they're cruising for me.

I should be shaky and scared, but instead I'm pissed-off as hell.

I was blinded by the light when the man got out of the car, but as he got back in, I saw enough to recognize him. It was Yancy Drummond.

So much for the charming, small town ambience. I've brought my .38 along on this trip, but I haven't been carrying it. When I get back to the hotel room, I dig it out of my luggage, make sure it's loaded, check my supply of ammunition. When I load my duffel for Skagway, I make sure the gun is right there on top. It makes me feel a little better prepared.

Then I sit on the bed and scrub at my face. I doubt very much if reporting this to the local cops will do any good. Caroline Driscoll warned me about the family's influence—likely there's corruption in the politics, as well.

I'm on my own here, with no one to back me up, and suddenly I'm missing Paul in a big way. I've been doing okay in the business by myself for the last year, but I have to admit I feel insecure without him. For fifteen years, he's been right there behind me, ready to back me up if there was any real trouble—but I've got nobody now. This makes me glad I'm leaving tomorrow with somebody that looks as tough and capable as Jeff Foxworthy does.

It's a long night. I lie awake thinking about Kathryn, and about what I'm missing in this case. I listen for steps in the hallway, start at headlights reflecting through the blinds. The alarm goes off just as I'm drifting into sleep.

It turns out I'm cranky as hell. Coffee doesn't fix it, either.

At nine o'clock Jeff is downstairs in the lobby to meet me. He's driving a rusted-out pickup truck that he's parked out front. There's mud crusted on the doors and the seats are ripped so stuffing pokes out here and there. Dust and cigarette butts cover the dash. I can hardly see through the windshield. I'm not going to complain, though. I'm happy to see Jeff looks steady, even though his pale eyes are a little bloodshot.

"You got any rain gear?" he asks.

"No," I say. "Nothing for this climate, anyway."

"I brought you a slicker," he says, and jerks his thumb at the truck bed.

The raincoat is almost as muddy as the truck, but I'm not going to complain about that, either. If there's a downpour, all that mud will wash off just fine. I toss my duffel into the bed on top of the coat and climb into the cab.

We take off from a lake somewhere to the north of Anchorage proper. The plane is a beat-up Piper Cub, a workhorse two-seater with pontoons and cargo space in the back. Jeff has pulled it up to the nearby dock. As the plane shifts and bobs on the chop, he works open the door, and I climb into the copilot's seat, stuff my duffel into the open space behind me. I'm glad Jeff knows what he's doing. The panels look indecipherable to me.

He works through a checklist, fiddles with the tanks, then climbs in and starts the engine. We rock and then even out on the waves, spank along the tops as the plane picks up speed. Once we're airborne, he banks to turn east, and then I get a bird's eye view of the local geography.

Anchorage is set on a delta that extends south and westward into Cook Inlet, and it's nearly surrounded by water. We're headed east along the coast toward the Chugach National Forest and what Jeff says over the headphones is glacier country. The vista is breathtaking, the craggy mountains jutting into the sky, the icecaps that slide in stone-crushing rivers down the slopes. I watch out the windows for a while, but it's going to be a long trip. After a while, I find a comfortable fit into the seat and sleep through the rest of the flight.

Jeff wakes me up when we're there. Skagway is in the vicinity of Yakutat and the Glacier Bay Park, somewhere in what looks like a complete wilderness of islands and sea. The plane loses altitude, banks. I see a scatter of streets, big, roomy slips at the town's waterfront.

"What's that?" I ask.

"For cruise ships," he says. "This town lives off the tourist trade."

Upriver, we skim along, touch down neatly and taxi up to a dock. The air feels colder and damper here. I think I'll be glad of the slicker. It'll cut the wind as well as the rain.

Jeff's right that he knows his way around the place. By that he means the bars. I check us into the only hotel and then we go out on the town.

The first stop looks like a saloon out of the Old West. The room is long and narrow, high ceilinged, and it's paneled with dark wood that must have been put up in the late 1800s.

A haze of cigarette smoke drifts across the ceiling, and the old bar rail shines with a faded brass patina.

I order a beer. Jeff gets a bourbon, takes a look around the place.

"Jonesy is who you need to talk to," he says, "but she's not here yet. Let's get a table and wait."

He sees some guys in the back he knows and we take a seat with them, where I get filled in on all the local fishing yarns. About ten o'clock a woman shows up at the door, seventyish, with hair that looks like pink cotton candy. She's wearing a blue polyester jog suit and actually smoking with a cigarette holder.

"There she is," says Jeff.

Jeff gets up and waves, and she makes her way through the scatter of tables to ours.

"Hi, honey," she says to Jeff. "Buy a girl a drink?"

"What'll you have?" asks Jeff.

The bar clientele is thinning out by now, and we've got the table to ourselves. She sits down. It's a few minutes before we get through the pleasantries.

"Yeah," says Jonesy. She narrows her eyes, knocks her cigarette ash onto the floor. "I remember that story. I was just a kid then. Let me think about it."

She thinks through nearly a bottle of gin. I've switched to the hard stuff myself by then. I'm wondering how much it takes to put Jonesy down.

Maybe Jeff is thinking the same thing. He gets the bottle, screws on the cap.

"Okay, Jonesy," he says. "We need to call it a night. What do you think about that story?"

Then woman squints her eyes again, concentrates hard.

"The girl's name was Marianne something," she says. "The family tried to hush it up. They owned a mine out this way and the girl ran off with an Indian kid or something, married him, got pregnant." She takes a drag off her cigarette. "I don't remember his name. The gal died later on."

That sounds a little different from the newspaper account. Still, this shouldn't cause the kind of response I got from Drummond last night.

"What about the baby?" I ask.

"I never did know any details," she says. "You oughta go out to the Tlingit village. Somebody there will know the boy's name and what happened to him."

I raise my eyebrows at Jeff. He shrugs.

"Forty-five minutes to an hour," he says. "We can do it tomorrow morning."

It's pouring rain in the morning. I gather that's nothing unusual. The locals go about their business. By noon it's stopped, and Jeff knocks at my door.

"Ready to go?" he says.

"Five minutes," I say.

It's running late for the trip by then, but Jeff is sure we can still be back by dark. I have to remind myself that's not until ten p.m. this time of the year.

We hike out to the plane and get the gas tanks topped off, and then we're in the air again. The cloud cover is low and glowing with light. Mist rises from the trees in slow tendrils like smoke. Jeff flies down the coast for a while, and I watch fir-capped islands slide beneath us. A stray shaft of sunlight sparks off the iron gray waters below. This is the Inland Passage—rainforest country. Eastward, the mountains rise in hazy, ever-sharper layers, and the dark crowns of firs begin to alternate with birch. There's no visible sign of habitation for miles and miles around.

Finally Jeff slows our air speed, heads in for a landing. He jiggles the rudders. The scenery slides by faster as we come down, skimming over the waves. The nose of the plane tilts up, the pontoons reaching for the water, and then there's a crack that sounds like a gunshot.

The plane flips, and we're tumbling across the water.

It's night. Joel and I are walking on the beach. Behind us the lights of Miami's high rises light up the sky, bright enough to blot out the hard points of the stars. Phosphorescence paints a pale line at the edge of the surf. We splash each other with water and laugh. A wave breaks over us and we fall, roll through the surf in a tangle. We wrestle, still laughing, and he comes up on top. He's a shadow against the sky above me, an outline of pale shoulders and light-colored hair.

"I win," he says.

"Not yet," I say, and he laughs.

The wave recedes, leaves us lying skin to skin. He drops his head, kisses me, and then his lips start to drift. It's slow and sweet, his warmth a comfort against the night, his lips like fire against my skin. For a moment I think I'm going to have what I want from him, but then the surf breaks over us again.

I yelp as the cold water splashes down. We roll and he pulls me up to my feet, still laughing. When I look up at him, it's not Joel standing there. It's Paul.

I know I'm dreaming then. People don't transmute from one to the other that way. Still, I want to hold on to the feeling I've had, to the warmth and pleasure. I want to stay in the dream, but I know I can't. Dreams like this aren't real.

I take an easy breath, open my eyes. I'm in some kind of structure, wrapped in a blanket and lying on a plank floor. There's a primitive fire pit in the center filled with glowing embers. It's dim in the house, but the firelight reveals support poles lashed together above my head. Large bunches of fragrant herbs dangle from the rafters, drying in the heat. There's got to be a smoke hole somewhere above me, because the air where I'm lying is fairly clear. There's a pattering on the roof that must be rain.

I turn my head carefully. Along the walls, the space is divided into compartments with sleeping platforms. Above each cubicle a wide shelf holds storage baskets and what must be rolled blankets and robes. The place has a pungent scent, a blend of smoked salmon, dried berries and cedar wood.

Since turning my head worked out okay, I try sitting up. My first attempt doesn't work out, but the second try does it. Still, I feel the need to hold my head in my hands for a while until it quits spinning. My clothes and hair are damp. It takes a while to remember what happened—the flight, the shot, the plane tumbling. I'm guessing it maybe broke up and sank, and that's how I got wet. But then, why aren't I dead at the bottom of the Passage? And also, what happened to Jeff?

After the spinning stops, I look around. I can see painting on the end wall of the house. Squinting at the designs, I manage to make out Raven, but there are other figures I don't recognize. It's enough to identify where I am. This is a Native American longhouse, built in an Alaskan design.

The house has a misty, ethereal quality because of the humidity and the wood smoke. The air is chilly, so I'm glad of the fire and the blanket. I pull it closer around me, notice it's real wool—it smells like a wet sheep. I'm wondering again about how I got here, when a door opens in the end of the house and the answer walks into the room.

My host looks very young. He's medium-tall and has wide cheekbones. He's carrying firewood, and he's dressed in a cedar bark rain cape and a woven rain hat. No shoes. When he sees me sitting up, he doesn't say anything. He just drops the firewood into a pile, begins stacking it neatly onto other wood already there against the wall of the house.

I wait while he finishes. When he's done with it, he takes off the rain hat and cedar cape. I'm a little concerned he won't have anything on under it, but he's wearing a gee-string and brief loincloth. When he looks at me, his eyes have a dark, liquid sheen. A mass of black hair falls around his shoulders. A necklace with an abalone amulet catches the firelight, sends out glints of bluish radiance as he moves. He sits down cross-legged across the fire from me.

"Welcome," he says. "This is Land Otter House, and I am Sees-through-Mist."

"Anna Detroyer," I say.

"How are you feeling, Anna Detroyer?"

"Alive," I say. My voice is a hoarse croak, and I clear my throat. "I can't say much beyond that."

"It's enough," he says. "Are you hungry?"

"I…" I'd meant to say no, but actually I'm starving. "Yes. I am," I say.

"I have some stew cooking," he says.

It's in a cooking box. He checks the box, adds a crumble of dried seaweed. Then he pours in a bit more water, adds hot stones from the fire pit with a pair of tongs. A cloud of steam hisses up. He closes the box and covers it with a mat.

Through the steam he looked like something else, but I couldn't quite see it. I feel dizzy again, hold my head for a second.

"Are you alright?" he asks.

"Sure, I'm okay," I say, but now I'm wondering if I should eat any of his stew.

If this is a traditional Native American home, there should be a village outside, other people. I can't remember seeing any villages from the air as we flew in. I look around again, at the walls, the rafters, the ceremonial paintings. The house is quiet and empty.

"How did I get here?" I ask.

"I saw your plane crash into the water," he said. "Your pilot got out okay, but you sank with the plane. I got you out and brought you here. The water was very deep and cold."

That doesn't quite clarify where 'here' is, but it does explain why I feel like a drowned rat.

"Thank you," I say. "I'm sure I'd be very dead without you."

I have that second of dizziness again, as if he's shifted but I didn't quite catch it. There's a flicker of motion at the corner of my eye. A white owl drops down from the rafters, settles on his shoulder. It whispers something into his ear, and Sees-through-Mist glances at me. I wonder what they're discussing.

"You can see it?" he asks.

"What?" I ask. "The owl?"

"Spirit talker," he says. "I'm glad you can see it."

The owl takes flight, disappearing above us somewhere. Maybe it goes out the smoke hole, or maybe it's going to perch in the rafters to watch over us during the night.

Sees-through-Mist may have identified me, but I know what he is, too.

"You're a wizard?" I ask.

"Yes," he says.

Maybe that's why he tends to shift slightly in the edge of my vision, but then, maybe there's something else wrong. I might be looking at a mask for something else. He checks the cooking box.

"The stew is done," he says.

He serves out a bowl for me, hands it over. I take the painted wooden bowl and spoon from his hands. It's a fish stew, smells enticing. My empty stomach growls—still, I hesitate.

He serves out a bowl for himself, notices I'm not eating.

"It's safe to eat," he says.

"How do I know?" I ask.

"You don't," he says. "You'll have to take my word for it."

It's a standoff. I'll have to make a judgment call. I'm sure he's not what he looks like, but I'm not feeling anything cold or terrifying about him. I'm actually warm and comfortable and having a hard time holding on to thoughts about evil. I wonder vaguely if I hit my head when the plane went down.

I spoon up a cautious bit of the stew and sniff at it, but everything seems to be fine—it doesn't smell rotten or decayed. I try a cautions sip and it tastes fine, too. I give up and eat the whole bowl, and then a second one.

"So," I ask when I'm done. "Am I your creature now?"

"Yes," he says. "But don't worry too much about it."

He wipes out the bowls with shredded bark and cleans the spoons.

"Would you like to sleep?" he asks. "There will be guests coming in the morning to celebrate your arrival."

"Wait," I say. "You were expecting me?"

"Not exactly," he says, "but I was hoping you'd come. I've been waiting a long time."

It's mystifying, but again, I can't deal with it right now—I'm feeling lightheaded, drowsy. The partitioned compartments are bedrooms. He shows me to one and gives me a fur robe to wrap in. Presumably he beds down in a different spot, somewhere along the quiet walls of the house. Rain patters quietly on the roof as I drift off into sleep.

I start awake to noise and light—people talking. The main door of the house is open. Filtered light flows into the rafters from the smoke holes above. I worry the question of where I am again. Maybe this is a ceremonial house that they only use now and then.

I'm at the far end of the house from the noise. I pull the fur robes tighter, planning to ignore it a few moments more—but someone has been watching, waiting for me to wake up. I start as she appears suddenly in my field of vision.

"Welcome, Anna Detroyer!" she says. "I am Blackbird."

I shove up to a sitting position on the sleeping platform and have a look at her. She's a tiny bit of a woman, not more than five feet tall. Gray-threaded hair plaits hang over her shoulders. She's wearing a traditional wool robe and glass beads that catch the light, flash it back in red and yellow glints. There are a couple of girls behind her, looking maybe twelve years old.

I push back the tangled mass of my hair.

"Uh. Thank you," I say.

"These girls will help you dress," she says. "I will come back when you're ready for the ceremony."

I look at the girls. They're in native dress and waiting solemnly, big-eyed, as if tasked with something important. All I can do is throw back the fur robes and try to achieve some kind of dignity as I struggle up.

They've brought water for me to wash in, which gets the remains of mud off my face. I strip off the damp, wrinkled jeans and shirt I slept in, take the embroidered deerskin dress they've brought for me to wear. I see them look at the medicine pouch I wear under my clothes, but none of them offers to touch it—even the strap. I don't take it off, either—by now it's like part of me. One of the girls combs and braids up my hair. When they're done, an older man comes and decorates my cheeks with painted designs.

Once I'm properly dressed, Blackbird is waiting to introduce me around. There must be at least fifty guests in full Native American finery already arrived at the other end of the house. There are black wool robes and painted cedar hats, flashing amulets and beads. I've been to contemporary Native American festivals in Florida and Oklahoma, but this is different—very serious and heavily traditional.

Besides that, I catch glimpses of things I'd rather not see out of the corner of my eye. There's a flash of vertical pupils. A forked tongue flicks out, catching my scent. For some reason it doesn't seem all that terrifying. I've sort of realized I'm in another reality by now. I'm just hoping I'm not really dead.

"Come this way," says Blackbird. I follow her through a throng of people, and she indicates a seat right in the center front. It seems a little exposed.

"Can't I sit in the back somewhere?"

"No daughter," she says, "you have to sit here. The celebration is in your honor."

In my honor?

I give it up and sit down. Sees-through-Mist appears and sits down at my left. He's dressed in finery this morning, too—a fringed *chilkat* robe and a cedar hat carved in an animal design. His abalone amulet shines above the robe, catching the light. His face is painted with an otter design on either cheek. He gives me an inscrutable glance.

There are speeches about welcome and thanksgiving that I somehow understand, even though I don't speak a word of Tlingit. Then there are huge amounts of food: salmon, whitefish, vegetables, fry bread. Later on there are gifts. I recognize the ceremony then. This is a *potlatch*, the gift-giving feast of the Northwest. Normally it's held to commemorate a birth or a death—I'm just not sure which this is.

Somewhere during the gift-giving ceremony, Sees-through-Mist has disappeared, but the party continues. There are dancers and singers who perform traditional songs. When they finish, more food arrives. I'm thinking the party may last for a while.

The atmosphere is all twilight and mist, flashing color and rhythmic, hypnotic chants. I feel comfortable, honored to be part of it—I could stay here forever. But something is nagging at me. I frown, lift my hand to touch the medicine pouch under my clothes. It's heating up, the talismans burning against my skin.

"Blackbird" I say. "What's this all about?"

"To thank you," she says.

"Why do you need to thank me?" I ask.

"Because you have brought Sees-through-Mist his heart's desire."

I need to understand this. Somehow, it's important.

I glance at her and she looks back with dark, beady eyes, very much like her namesake. My vision shifts and for a second I see a real blackbird sitting there—it cocks its head, snaps its beak at me. In front of us, a new troupe of dancers begins a chant. I fumble through the fog in my brain. Finally I remember what Jonesy said about the Tlingit.

"Tell me about Marianne Drummond," I say.

"Ah, yes," says Blackbird. "That one. She was such a beautiful girl. Sees-through-Mist was very much in love with her, and she was carrying his child. We have not seen her in many seasons, though. We heard that she is dead."

Things come into focus.

"She was married to Sees-through-Mist?" I ask.

"Of course," she says. "The wedding feast was held in the village over the hill. I was there myself."

"But he's not old enough," I say.

She only looks at me. The singers continue their chant. I've forgotten this is another reality. Urgency jabs at me. This is not a good place for me—I need to be somewhere else.

"How did she die?" I ask.

"Her father came for her," says Blackbird. "He tried to kill Sees-through-Mist, took the girl. He is responsible for her death."

"Her father?"

Calvin Drummond—it's not that hard to believe. The old man I met in the office was hard as nails. He wouldn't have stood for a scandal. He must have put the child up for adoption. Maybe when Marianne objected, he hit her a little harder than he'd meant to.

I've still got my hand clutched tight around Grandpa's medicine pouch. I close my eyes.

"What have I done to bring Sees-through-Mist his heart's desire?" I ask.

"Drummond's grandson has followed you," she said. "It was he who shot down your plane."

Followed me? Suddenly I know where Sees-through-Mist has gone. While I'm occupied at the *potlatch*, he's taken off his mask and gone hunting.

I push to my feet.

"I've got to go," I say.

She only stares at me. It won't be that easy to get back to where I came from. I'm trapped here by sorcery, and I don't know how to break free of it.

Or do I? I had Marianne's amulet with me in the plane. It was a ward against sorcery, wrapped with copper wire—it was in my pocket.

I work my way past the seated guests, heading back to the cubicle where I changed my clothes. A few of them glance around at me, but most are absorbed by the singers and dancers. No one tries to stop me.

I'm lost, confused by the haze and the compartments, but finally I find the right one. My jeans, shirt and jacket are there, neatly folded, along with my shoes. I search through the pockets. There's no amulet. Dammit. That's why I've gotten caught like this—I've lost it.

But I've still got my medicine pouch. Maybe the talismans will give me the power I need to break away. I jerk the dress off over my head, pull on the jeans, tie up my shoes. The singing and dancing are still going on out in the main hall. A few guests look up as I hurry past them, jog toward the door. It opens into a deep mist, as if there's nothing beyond it at all. A breath of eternity drifts inward, cold fingers stroking my face, sliding around me in an icy embrace.

Suddenly I'm breathing hard—I can feel the sorcery now that holds this place out of space and time. If I can't get out of here, I'll be dead for sure.

I take a cautious step out, feel for solid ground. It's there under my foot, so I take another step, then another. I've walked into a dead silence. The beat of the drums and the singing have cut off like they never existed. I touch the medicine pouch, feel it warming under my fingers—the fetishes inside are hot as coals. I wish I had a stick to feel for the ground in front of me, but there's nothing. I take another step and fall flat on my face.

It knocks the breath out of me. I cough, retch, curl up. I want to give up, to lie there and let the cool mist flow over me, to drift into oblivion. But I'm feeling that urgency again. I groan and roll over painfully, feel for what tripped me. It's a piece of driftwood with a thong caught in it. At the end of the thong is Marianne's amulet.

I wrap it around my wrist, push up to my feet. The mist swirls, grasping at me with icy fingers. I clutch at the amulet, take another step and fall into water this time.

It's cold and deep. For a second I'm panicked, but I'm a certified diver—I know how to float. What I should do is relax.

It takes forever. My lungs are bursting for air. The pressure rings in my ears. Finally my head breaks the surface of the sea. There's gray sky above, an expanse of water, a dark mass of forest beyond. I gasp and look around. I'm not that far from a rocky shore—I take off swimming.

A lot of time has passed for me, but in the here and now, it looks like the plane has just gone down. There are debris in the water, a spreading, iridescent oil slick. I hear someone shouting, look that way.

It's Jeff. He's yelling at me from the shore across from where I'm headed, waving his arms. A rifle cracks and a bullet skips across the water in front of him. He ducks behind some rocks. The next bullet skips to the right of my head. I duck under the water, swim as far as I can. When I come up, I can see Yancy Drummond on a low rock promontory, framed by sweeping spruce and hemlock trees. He's cocking his high-powered rifle for another shot. He's not staring at me, though. There's something else in the water.

I turn my head, look for it.

It's a big animal, at least five feet long, solid, man-sized—a sea otter? As I watch, the creature reaches the shore, starts to scale the rocks. There's a shimmer of unreality about it, a shifting, magical quality. Drummond works on the rifle—it seems to be jammed.

Suddenly the name of the house where I've been rings a bell—Land Otter House? This is a *kushtaka*, a creature that takes the drowned. And sometimes the living.

You can't kill one with a rifle.

"Drummond!" I yell. "Get out of there!"

He looks up at me, snarls something. He goes back to struggling with the gun. I take off swimming in that direction.

Drummond has seen the otter coming for him now. The creature is climbing the rocks, its claws long and sharp, its back flexing in a graceful curve as it leaps up the slope. At the top, its whiskers pull back to reveal sharp fangs. It shimmers again, and for an instant I can see the man—the sleek body, the dusky skin, the mass of raven hair.

Drummond must have seen it, too. Panic contorts his face. He screams, upends the rifle. He tries to club Sees-through-Mist with the stock. The otter shifts, lunges at him. They teeter on the point, tip over. It's a slow motion fall, a graceful, halting plunge against the backdrop of craggy rocks and wild, misty shore. Then they crash into the water, throwing up a spray that showers back like rain.

I try to dive after them, but there's no way I can catch a creature like that in the depths of the sea. All I can see is the dark shape of their outlines—Sees-Through-Mist and his captive, disappearing downward into the murky depths.

And, of course, there no way I can find my way back to Land Otter House, either. I'm out of breath, out of luck, and I'll have to give it up.

I rise to the surface, swim for shore. I'm shivering with the cold now, find my teeth are chattering. By the time I get to the rocks, Jeff is there and waiting for me. He extends a hand, pulls me up on the bank. He's soaked through, and he's got a trickle of blood running down the side of his face.

"My God," he says, "did you see that thing? It just pulled him down into the water…"

I shove back my wet hair, hug my aching ribs.

"I did," I say. I'm panting, out of breath from the dive, the frantic swim. "There's nothing we can do."

"Who was that?" he asks. "And why was he shooting at us?"

I hesitate, wondering if I should say the name. This is going to be trouble.

"It was Yancy Drummond," I say. "He followed us from Anchorage."

"Drummond?" Jeff says. "Drummond?" He rubs both hands over his face, smears the blood onto the front of his shirt. "He's wrecked the plane—it sank. We'll have to get to the Tlingit village for help," he says. "It's a little ways east."

He holds out a hand, helps me up. I hurt in a few places. I'm limping.

Jeff reaches for my arm. "Hey, are you alright? You were down there a long time."

So, was it a dream, a vision? Or was I really in the house of the *kushtaka*?

"I'm okay," I say. "There must have been trapped air in the plane."

"Can you walk?" he asks.

I'm bruised and aching. My left knee hurts, and I've definitely got something wrong with my ribs. Still, I'm upright, breathing. I reach up, touch the medicine pouch under my wet shirt. It's still warm and alive, burning with the magic that's gotten me safe out of the water.

"Yeah," I say. "I think so."

"Then let's get out of here," he says. He looks around at the gray surface of the sea, the dark forest. There's no sign of anything there. "Damn," he says. "That thing gave me the creeps."

I hope Jeff has got plenty of insurance on the plane. Besides that, someone else has to know Yancy Drummond followed us here. I'm thinking it's about time the old man Calvin Drummond had a comeuppance—at least a civil suit. I follow in Jeff's footsteps as he starts off, but I have to turn and take a last look at the sea before we enter the trees. It's still and luminescent from the clouded sky—empty of anything but reflection.

I've still got the thong to Marianne's amulet wrapped tightly around my wrist. I touch the yellowed surface, trace the copper wire as we walk.

There's almost a feeling of peace about it now—long overdue, I think.

Chapter 10

CROSSROADS

"Now all my damn goats are disappearin'," says Eleanor Jorey. "I can't even breed 'em fast enough. Hell. I gotta do somethin'."

Eleanor has got her hands stuck in the back pockets of her ragged jeans, and she's swinging along with a deceptive, ground-eating stride. She's taking me on a tour of her pint-sized ranch just outside the Miami city limits, and talking about her prize Nubian goats. They're miniatures, black and lop-eared, and the kids are gamboling along after us like overgrown pups. The nannies watch us suspiciously. I already know to avoid the billies. They think humans need odor-adjustment, if not a good butting.

Eleanor's fiftyish and freckled, a red-head darkened to cinnamon and blasted by sun. She's clearly partial to boots, western shirts and black Stetson hats. She's run this farm for years, supplying livestock for God-knows-who in the way of stock enthusiasts. I had no idea there was even a market for pygmy goats. But then, they must be more popular than I'd realized—now somebody's hijacking them.

My first thoughts about that, I keep to myself.

"Is there any pattern to the thefts?" I ask.

"They're always at night," she drawls. She squints into the sun, and deep crows-feet crinkle at the corners of her eyes. "Course," she says, "that's standard for rustlers, ain't it? I've heard the dogs barkin' a coupla times, but when I get out to the corral, there ain't nothin'. They're always gone."

I'm visualizing a stakeout, for weeks maybe, inside that barn. I've had cases that were more fun.

"Did you call the sheriff?" I ask.

"Yeah," she says. "Shore did."

"And?"

"He's got bigger fish to fry than my little goats."

Dade County cops have got the standard case of burnout, regardless of whether they're with the city or with the county.

"Son-of-a-bitch," she grumbles. "After all the taxes I pay, now I gotta hire a private dick."

That's me, Detroyer and Angstrom, P.I.'s, except Angstrom's not part of the deal any more. He went into politics and made good. Now he's one of the local commissioners.

Eleanor and I are finishing up the tour, coming up to the house again. The ranch is clean and well-kept. Pine trees line a drive that winds off toward the Tamiami Trail, makes a Y-shape at this end with one branch leading to the house and another to the stock pens. It's a clear shot from the house to the barn, maybe three minutes for Eleanor at a dead run. Mostly the brush is cleared from the pasture, but once somebody made it to the trees, they'd be damn hard to catch. There's a sign out by the road that identifies the place clear as day. Eleanor's got horses, too, but nobody's been messing with them. Just the goats.

"Any trouble from your ex?" I ask.

"It ain't his style," she says, and kicks at a stand of thistle with her heavy boot. "He never did like this damn ranch—like he might git shit on him. 'Sides," she says, and shrugs, "he's married again, got a passel of kids. I ain't heard nothin' from him in a while."

So, it's back to the stakeout plan. Unless I can figure this some other way.

We're headed for my rattletrap Chevette now, parked out in front of the house. I've seen the works, including the barn. I scrape miscellaneous off my shoes onto the bahia grass clumps by the drive.

"Well, thanks for the look around, Ms. Jorey..."

"Eleanor," she says.

"Eleanor," I repeat. "I'll ask around, see if I can turn up anything about it."

I get in the car and she leans to look in the window, tips her Stetson like a man.

"Thank you, Miz Detroyer."

"Anna," I say, and crank up the car.

The drive back into Miami is sweltering. It's September, and too close to gridlock this time of the day. The AC in my car only half works, and once I hit the traffic lights, I have to crack the windows to help it out. Back at the office, I've got messages on the voicemail. The first one is from Joel Angstrom.

"Was that Dad's SUV at your apartment last night?"

Damn.

"Anna, about last night...." It's Paul this time. He stops. "Let me know what you decide," he says, and hangs up.

Shit. Like I'm supposed to know already.

I don't even want to think about it. I'd rather fight the traffic instead. I've got work to do on Eleanor's complaint and it's not five o'clock yet. I don't want to stick around the office where people can find me. I climb back in the car and head north for the Metro Justice Center. Maybe I can catch the day shift custodial staff before they leave.

I've spent so much time testifying in this building that the super's an old buddy of mine. She's back in her office just now, checking time records for the night shift about to come on.

"Hey, Bernice." I drop into her extra chair and stretch out my legs, cross one athletic shoe over the other. "You're a Protestant, aren't you?"

She's African American and from up north somewhere, but I want to make sure before I ask about the goats. You never can tell.

"Yeah," she says, squinting at me over half-glasses. She's stout and intimidating in her tight polyester uniform. Her hair's done into an elaborate coif, woven with red and blond braided extensions. "Baptist," she says. "What's it to you, honey?"

"Don't want to step on any toes." I take out a picture of Pinky, the latest of the missing goats, and toss it over. "Ever see this animal before?"

She picks up the snapshot. In the photo Pinky is getting an award, and he's brushed and shined, standing broadside to the camera with all his black, glossy lines on perfect display.

"Can't say's I have," Bernice says. "But then, they all look the same to me."

"The owner will pay a reward for a live goat on this one," I say.

"Hah!" she says. "Good luck, honey." She doesn't see many live ones.

I sigh.

"Well, keep an eye out anyhow, will you, Bernice?"

"Sure, Anna," she says. "I'll let you know."

I wink at her and pull up my feet. "'Preciate it."

I get out of her way and start off south again. My next stop is Little Havana. I make a circuit of some of the stores, ask questions, hand out the photo and mention the reward. It's getting dark by then. The office is already locked up for the night, so I pass on by and pull in at my apartment.

There's a doll on the doorstep that looks like a pincushion. It's split open and has an oversize phallus stuck in the appropriate spot. I've hit pay dirt already—but I don't like this kind of notice.

I slide inside with my gun out, just in case somebody's there. The place looks fine. Couch, dinette, miscellaneous clutter. The bedroom is bare. The bathroom is empty. I toss the doll in the trash, then on second thought, fish it out again and toss it on the table. If I have the kind of accident it threatens, my friend Gloria can check it for prints.

I pop a beer and drop into a chair, lean back and think about Paul Angstrom sitting here last night—willing to really talk to me, maybe for the first time in his life. It's funny how things happen. I've always wished for a real communication with him, but under the circumstances, it's a downer in every way that counts.

I'm thinking of another beer, or maybe something stronger, when footsteps trample along the outside deck. I could get dramatic, shut out the lights and fling open the door—thirty-eight in hand. But the footsteps sound stubborn and determined. Who's at the door is no surprise.

"So," he says. "Are you and Dad getting back together?"

"I don't know," I say.

Joel stares off at the lights from the pool. "Can I come in?"

"Sure."

Once inside, he falls into a chair.

"Dad's dating a nineteen-year-old trophy blonde," he says. "Is that what I am to you?"

"Want a beer?" I ask.

I don't wait for the answer, just get a couple of bottles out of the fridge and hand him one.

"What's with the doll?" he asks, jerking head that way.

"It's a gift."

"Like hell," he says.

"Well, you know how things go," I say.

"Anna..." he says.

"Did you say what you came to say?" I ask.

"Yeah," he says, and he looks at me straight. That look is harder to meet than all the anger in the world.

"Well, I still don't know," I say. "But kid, I'll keep you posted."

The door slams behind him.

I wake up early and can't go back to sleep. Paul Angstrom is stuck in my brain. That's what's keeping me awake, I decide, and it's what made sleeping so hard last night. Shit. About six thirty, I give it up. I balance last night's tossing with three cups of black coffee, and then I move out for the office. I'm hoping it will be quiet this morning, so I can think.

There's a chunk of bloody liver nailed to the office door. It's not the best come-on to encourage new clients. It doesn't do much for the wall, either. Runnels of dark blood stain the paint, trail down to pool on the scuffed terrazzo floor. The building's custodian has left me a note already. Somehow I don't think this is going to improve our relations.

Then Bernice calls about eight. She's found Pinky.

The poor damn goat. That's just what I needed to make my day. I can tell Eleanor what's going on now—but it'll be hell to stop.

The maintenance staff is scrubbing a dark bloodstain off the Justice Center steps. They've got the goat in a body bag, and Bernice unwinds the twist-tie for me to have a look. Pinky's legs are tied with a cord and his throat has been neatly slashed with a sharp knife. He's got white powder sprinkled over him that looks like ash. Bernice hands me the bag.

"Okay," I say, holding it out to keep the blood off my jeans. "Uh. Thanks a lot, Bernice."

As I expected, Eleanor is not pleased.

"So what the hell am I gonna do about it?" she yells.

We're standing out in front of her barn. Pinky is lying between us in the black trash bag, and I nudge his corpse with my toe, look away.

"I don't know," I tell her.

Eleanor jerks around to stare out over the field, and I think she's going to cry. Dammit. This is like telling somebody their lost child has been killed.

"Look," I say. "I'll keep working on it. Maybe I can come up with something more."

She's still staring into nowhere as I pull out into the drive and head back for Miami.

At the office there's a brown paper bag on the doorstep with a candle burnt down inside. It's been cut out like a demon's face and circled with salt. I step over it, leave it for the custodian. At least there's no blood this time.

There's a message from Paul on the machine. "Anna," he says, "listen. Don't leave me hanging like this. We've got to meet somewhere..."

I've got a divorce case to work on, the one that's gotten me into this trouble with Paul. I fiddle with the files for the rest of the afternoon, but I don't accomplish squat. Instead I decide maybe is time I had a talk with my friend, Sophie Corrales. She forty-six, waitressing tonight at a *cantina* near where I was handing out photos last night.

The *cantina* is a great place for a private talk. The music drowns out conversation even a foot away, and all the regulars have got to be deaf. I wave at Sophie and slide into a booth. When she comes around I scream my order for dinner and coffee. Then I yell, "When can you take a break, Sophie?"

She holds up a single finger. I drink coffee for an hour and listen to the *salsa*, watch people dance. Then she slides into the opposite seat.

"How's Cataldo?" I ask.

I helped her husband out of a drug rap a few years back. He's a lot older than she is, a Marielito who wanted to go straight in the U.S. but ran into some opposition from his friends. He still lives on the edge, maybe, but at least he's not in jail.

"Bueno," she says. She's brought a plate along with her, starts scarfing down a sandwich. "The place is busy tonight, Anita. I cannot talk long," she says. She's got her mouth full, and it makes lip-reading tough, but I catch the general drift.

I tap the edge of my fork against the table. "Sophie, I need to see a *babalau*," I say.

She looks startled. "A priest?"

"Yeah," I say. "And a friendly one." I tell her about the doll, the liver and the bag.

She's forgotten about her sandwich. It's stalled right in mid-air.

"*Madre de Dios, Anita...*" she says, and stops.

"I know, I know," I toss the fork onto my plate. "Look, Sophie. The reaction is all out of proportion. All I did was ask about a damn goat. I need to know what else the hell's going on."

She stares at me, stares at the band, at the couples dancing across the floor. Finally she drops the sandwich back on the plate, leans closer.

"Give me a couple of days," she says.

"Thanks, Sophie."

I slide out of the seat, search my pockets to pay the check.

"Anita, be careful," she says.

Her eyes are too intent. They stab at my back as I head for the door.

My next impulse is to get blind drunk. The need has been forming up over the last couple of days, a gut reaction to things I don't really want to know, things running out of control. Drinking myself senseless isn't a great idea just now, what with the threatening messages, but still I need to unwind.

Or maybe I just need to see a friendly face.

The Katze Klub fits the bill. It's dark and not overly busy, a perfect spot for brooding. I slide onto one of the bar stools and my buddy Harve the bartender bellies up to the other side.

"Hey, Anna," he says. "What can I get you?"

"A double," I say.

Harvey's a bald, chunky guy, forty-something. He raises both eyebrows.

"That bad, huh?"

I show my teeth, but it's not a grin. "You know me too well, Harve. I'll have to find another place pretty soon."

He sets the drink down in front of me, leans both elbows on the bar finish.

"What's wrong?" he says.

"I'm finding out things I don't want to know about people," I say.

"Don't you always do that?" he asks.

"Don't get funny on me, Harve. I feel grim."

"I could tell," he says, and slaps the bar. Someone else has come in the door. "Let me know when you want another."

It's nearly ten by the time I get out the door. In spite of my determination to stay in control, I'm almost too buzzed to drive. Probably I should have taken a taxi home and gone back for the car tomorrow. I pull the Chevette into the parking space at the apartments and sit there leaning on the steering wheel for a few minutes, staring into the glow of the lights. The moon is invisible tonight. A brief spatter of rain passes by, moisture swept in from the sea. Pale droplets on the windshield catch the light. The alcohol hasn't helped with my troubles. It's left me maudlin, instead.

I shove the door open finally and get out, heading past the humped shapes of silent cars toward the stairs. I haven't completely forgotten the possible dangers, but when it happens my reactions are slow.

I'm passing the shrubbery by the pool, and a shadow moves behind me. I catch the shift in the corner of my vision, jerk sideways far enough to keep the guy from breaking my neck. Still, he gets his arm around my throat.

This is not good. He's a big guy. I claw at his arm, drive an elbow into his ribs. I've got no leverage. He's holding me off the ground, and already things are going dim.

Another shadow hits us from off to the side. I get a quick rush of breath as the guy's arm loosens. Then he heaves me against the fence. I bounce off the chain link, land hard on the concrete and lie there gasping.

I've got to get up. It's Joel there in the lights, and the guy's whipped out a knife. They're circling on the sidewalk. I heave up fast and jam one heel into the back of the guy's knee. As he goes down, I kick him in the jaw.

I'm not exactly encumbered with ideas about sportsmanship. I've got my gun out now, but the guy doesn't move.

Joel's leaning over, both hands braced on his knees. I can smell blood, and it's not my own.

"Are you okay?" I ask.

"Yeah," he says. "But I'm bleeding. God." He straightens. "Do you want to call the cops, Anna?"

"No," I decide. I let the gun sights fall, catch him by the arm. "Let's go upstairs."

He's got a shallow cut on the inside of one wrist and he looks white, but not faint. I wash the blood off in the bathroom sink, decide the cut doesn't need stitches.

"You've got a chain link bruise on your face," Joel says. "Anna, are you sure you don't want to call the cops?"

"I'm sure," I say. "Press on the cut. Sit down."

He drops onto the toilet seat.

"Why not?" he asks.

"There'll just be another one along tomorrow."

"Dammit," he says. "What's going on?"

I'm rummaging for gauze and tape.

"I don't know," I say.

"You don't know?"

I cinch a gauze pad around his wrist, tape it up tight.

"Yeah," I say. "Just all of the sudden life's gone to shit."

"Yeah. Right," he says. "As usual."

"Lie down," I say. "You look pale."

In the other room he kicks off his shoes, falls onto the bed. I clean up the mess in the bathroom, and then I'm feeling a little shaky myself. I crawl in beside Joel.

He wakes me up sometime in the middle of the night. He's got one hand up inside my shirt and he's tugging at the catch to my jeans. For a moment I feel cooperative. I roll against him, search for his mouth. Our hands start to drift, to slide along in familiar ways.

And then there's an image between us. It's Paul's face, stuck in my brain like he was last night, and it hauls me up short. What the hell have I been doing all this time? I've wanted Joel's dad for years, but it just never worked out, so I've been sleeping with the son instead. Now, Paul's back in my head. Anna, what are you going to tell the kid?

I don't have to tell him anything. He can feel the difference.

"Shit," he says. He rolls away from me and out of bed, fumbles in the dark for his shoes. The bedroom door slams behind him.

I bury my head under the pillow, figuring he's gone for good. Still, when I stumble out into the living room the next morning, there's a blanket folded on the couch and half a cup of expresso abandoned in the sink. I start another pot and lean on the counter to wait for it to drip. To be truthful, I feel better that he was here all night. That guy on the sidewalk might have woken up pissed.

Things seem to be looking up down at the office. There's no mess in the hallway this morning, and the message light is blinking already. It's Sophie.

"Anna, I got you an appointment," she says. "*Calle Ocho* at two o'clock this afternoon. There is a list of things for you to bring..."

Santeria has emerged from the shadows. The devotees won a Supreme Court victory a few years back that lets them practice their religion right out in the open, and the altars don't have to be hidden away any more. The temples sit right out on the street like any other church. After all, this is the U.S. of A., with freedom of religion and all that.

With Sophie to recommend me, I can walk right in and buy sorcery to counter whoever it is that's after me. And I'm reassured by the list of offerings I've been told to bring. This could be a lot worse.

I've got sorcery pegged as the source of my troubles. The culture imported with the Marielitos has always depended heavily on magic for protection from police and rival gangs, and believers are expected to make payments to the priest who handles things for them. In the secret days the religion had a bad name. There were rumors of drug dealers sacrificed along with the donated animals. The result was a flurry of religious discrimination around South Florida—until that Supreme Court case, anyhow.

Now the kinder ceremonies are visible, too, like rituals to assure a healthy baby, long life and so forth. For the offerings some folks go down to the Safeway supermarket for animals that are already dead.

The name of the temple is painted on the big glass windows of a storefront half-way down Eighth Street. The sidewalks look perfectly busy and safe. No shadows lurking in the alleyways. Still, I'm skittish. The tone of those messages hasn't been fun.

Bells rattle on the door as it swings shut behind me. I glance around for signs of Palo Mayombe—skulls with a candle on top, black cauldrons full of artifacts, slugs, crucifixes, knifes, dolls, snakes—but I don't see any of that. Instead there are statues of saints in the dim light, strings of bright-colored beads. This looks like an Abaqua temple, and fairly benevolent. It feels clean of evil spirits. But I expected that. Sophie owes me.

As the bells clatter, a guy comes out through curtains that screen off the back. He's Cubano, of course, and younger than I expected—maybe all of twenty-five.

"I'm Anna Detroyer," I say. "I have an appointment."

"Ah, yes," he says. "The *mujer* of the crossroads."

"Huh?" I say. "I mean, pardon me?"

A smile touches his eyes.

"Only come into the back, *senorita*."

He holds the curtain aside for me.

There's no assistant. This is the priest, black and *Indio* and Hispanic all rolled together into a nut-brown, blade-sharp slenderness. He moves with a macho, swaggering grace. Long, wavy hair falls around his shoulders. His shirt is unbuttoned to the waist, and gold chains and strands of colored beads glow against the dark, smooth skin of his chest. He's wearing tight jeans. His black eyes narrow at my hesitation—another smile beginning.

"Uh, here," I say, and offer the bag I've been carrying. "Do I give this to you?"

He reaches out to take it, and I duck through the curtain past his arm.

I've passed into candlelight. It takes my vision a few seconds to clear. The walls are draped in darkness, the floor muffled in dark rugs. The air is close and scented of incense and herbs. When I can see, I notice two chairs set face-to-face with a small table between. The altar is lit up with a soft, flickering glow of electric candles.

"Sit down," the man says. "I am Javier Curandero."

I decide to be direct. "Aren't you a little young to be a priest?"

He's unloading my bag onto the table. "Of course," he says. "But I have been called to the profession. How can I refuse such a thing?"

I can't really tell how to take that in the candlelight. The flames glance off his eyes, catch the sharp arch of his cheekbones as he turns his head. The light reveals nothing.

The bag is empty now. The man's shadow drops into the other chair.

"So," he says. "You are Anita Detroyer, and you have had some problem with sorcery."

"That's right," I say.

The chair I'm sitting in has an upholstered seat and wooden arms. It's fairly comfortable, so I lean back and cross my ankles.

The offerings I've brought for the Orishas sit on the table between us: rum, candy and cigars. Curandero's shadow moves. A lighter flares. The sweet scent of perfumed tobacco joins the herbal scent of the room, and then he hands the cigar to me. I gather I'm supposed to smoke it.

He lights another for himself and sets it in an ashtray on the table. The glow flares off the rum bottle as he opens it. He pours two eight-ounce glasses full. Again, it's one for me and one for him. He lifts his glass to the altar and then takes a healthy chug, like maybe it's iced tea or cola—then a hit off the cigar.

"Today I will call upon Eleggua," he says.

Is this a challenge? The rum I can handle, but I'm not so sure about the cigar.

"Tell me about your problem," he says.

I tell him about Eleanor and her goats, and about how I've been getting those messages since I started inquiring around.

He thinks about it, his lean, dark face masked in the scented haze of smoke.

"You're right," he says. His voice sounds flat and close in the darkness, absorbed by the thick fabric of the draperies. "There is more to the problem than a few questions about missing goats. You must search for the actual root to your difficulty."

"Well sure," I say. "That's why I'm here."

I'd expected some kind of mystical song and dance, actually more than I've gotten so far. Nobody who sells this kind of service wants it to look too easy.

"What other things are happening in your life?" he asks.

He's offering therapy, now. I don't especially want to tell him all my personal problems. If I tell them to anybody, it'll be Harve.

"Huh?" I say.

The tip of Curandero's cigar glows like a burning star. I feel queasy from mine, like I'm getting sick, but the rum helps. The darkness has taken on a certain ambiance. I'm feeling the spirits move now, the faint drift of things I can't quite bring into focus. There's one behind the priest—a child. But no, it's an old man instead. Then it's nothing— only a brief vision.

"Is your love life going well?" he asks.

"What?" I say. "Oh. Um. Not especially."

"And your work?"

"Not too well this week."

"Ah."

That's all the man has to say for a while. I do have to admit he's put his finger on the crucial intersection—a crossroads, did he say? Work with love life. The tip of his cigar travels in a glowing, languid arc.

"There are other women involved here that you don't see," he says. "Two of them."

"Oh?"

"One in your work and one in your love life, I think, but it's hard to be sure. The two seem very closely tied just now."

"But I don't know any..." I begin.

"One of the women is vindictive," he interrupts, "and the other is completely unaware of you. In order to have what you want, you must deal with these women."

I have to think about that. It doesn't help.

"And the messages?" I ask.

"They will disappear when the other problems are solved."

My cigar is burnt down now, and my glass is nearly empty. I wonder vaguely if either one is a true gauge of how long I've been here in this room—in this place in Miami, Florida. Damn. Am I really just a few blocks from home? It seems a million miles, somehow.

"How do I know what it is that I want?" I ask.

"You want power over others," he answers.

That rouses me.

"No, I don't."

His shadow moves vaguely against the candlelight. Maybe it's a shrug. "It's what everyone wants," he says.

"Is this psychoanalysis?" I ask.

"It's cheap at the price," he says.

My mind is too slow, working through what he's said in the darkness. Finally I remember why it is that I've come.

"Um. About the goats…" I say.

Curandero exhales a final cloud of smoke and stubs out his cigar. "I recommend that your friend should invest in white goats. They will not be so attractive for sacrifice."

I stare at him through the darkness, searching for a glimpse of his eyes.

"Well, damn," I say, and blink at him. "I'll tell her that."

His shadow shifts and rises. The spirits are fled. The interview is over. I stub out the butt of my own cigar and shove carefully to my feet. I'm relieved to find the world seems steady. I'm startled to feel Curandero next to me.

"For protection," he says.

He's close enough that I can feel the warmth from his bare skin. He's got something in his hands, slides it over my hair. It's strands of beads that fall and lie cold against my throat.

The man moves away from me then, and a shaft of light stabs into my eyes like a knife. He's opened the curtains.

Outside on the street, I think for a minute I'm going to throw up, or maybe to faint from the damned cigar. Afternoon shoppers stare at me, give me plenty of space. After a while the sickness eases off, and then I lean against the stucco wall and laugh. White goats. Under all that mysticism, Curandero is sharp as a tack.

Back at the office, I give Eleanor a call.

That's one case wrapped up, and for sure I got my money's worth from the rum and cigars. But for all that the session solved the goat problem, it didn't do much to straighten out my head. In fact, I'm likely to have hell of a hangover before it's even dark. I sit there as the afternoon dims outside and stare at the walls, wait for it to happen. Instead, I get to worrying about the crossroads that's supposed to be my problem.

Hell. I can't see any women in the picture. All I can see to deal with is Paul—and I might as well get on with it, regardless of whether I know what to say to him. I was full of self-doubt last spring, not sure how I could get along without him. Now I've got a different perspective entirely. He's not at home when I call, but I leave a message on his voicemail mentioning I'll be at his house by eight. Then I lean back in my chair and close my eyes, hoping to decide what to do.

I barely jerk awake in time to make it by eight. Sitting in my beat-up car outside his well-lit, upscale new house, I still don't know what to say. I'll have to play it by ear.

Paul opens the door himself when I ring the bell, and I just stand there looking at him. He waits, and somehow I feel the world slide and rearrange.

Until this week, I've not seen Paul face-to-face for a couple of years. But it's Joel who's only a shadow now. Paul is the one who's solid and tangible and real, standing there in front of me in a glowing white shirt against a spotless white expanse of shag carpet. He's wearing a halo of lamplight.

"Come in," he says finally, when I don't make a move.

I make an effort, get in through the door.

"Do you want a drink?" he asks.

He looks tanned and fit, with light crow's feet around his eyes and hair bleached out pale by the sun. Physically he looks about the same—tough, sexy and handsome. He's not the same, though. There's something different about his eyes.

I'm making us both uncomfortable, but right now I can't do anything else. I manage to look away.

"No thanks," I say.

Paul's always been one to take short cuts. No telling how long he's been into corruption, but I accidently got a recording of him doing it. It's that divorce case I've been working on, a rich woman that hired me to follow her husband around, thinking he had a mistress. He wasn't buying a woman, though. As it turned out, he was buying a commissioner. Paul was setting up kickbacks from the city contracts.

"I hope you don't mind if I have one," Paul says.

"Go ahead." I glance around at the house while he gets fortification from the bar.

The living room is done in monochromatic shades of pale. There's a fireplace, even though you'd have to run the AC on high to use it, and an array of leather sofas. Light shimmers off a pool through a glass wall in the back. The place is architect designed, and not just your ordinary suburban tract house.

I make myself at home on one of the sofas.

Paul brings his drink and sits down across from me.

"How did you get the recording?" he asks.

"I was trolling for Moreno's mistress," I say.

Paul takes a hit off his Scotch, sets the glass on a side table.

"Yeah," he says. "I know her. Hot little tamale named Carlotta."

"Marielita?" I ask.

"Her grandfather," he says.

Well, likely that's one of the women. Paul closes his eyes.

"So now what do *you* want?" he asks.

Then suddenly I know what it is Curandero was talking about—that hunger for power. Having that recording gives me something I've never had before—a real mastery over Paul Angstrom. There's a sweetness about the idea—a seduction. And maybe I understand this man better now than I ever have before. I close my eyes. The child vision is there waiting for me, over by the fireplace, Eleggua, Lord of the Crossroads.

"I think I need a drink after all," I say.

Paul gets up to make it for me. I watch the line of his back as he moves, the way his shoulders flex as he mixes and pours. The priest is right about human nature, but damn—this kind of power is going to be ashes. When I was younger, I might have gone for it, but now the time is long past. I don't know when it happened, or where it happened—but somehow I don't have the desire any more to fool myself, or to even try to make this work out.

"Here," Paul says, and hands me the glass.

He pivots to stare at the fireplace.

"Do you want to get married?" he asks.

"Paul..." I say.

His voice turns suddenly fierce.

"Isn't that what you've always wanted from me?"

"Dammit. No," I say.

He swings around.

"Is this thing with Joel out of spite?"

I grit my teeth.

"Not my part in it," I say. "You'll have to ask Joel what the hell he's been doing it for."

Paul stares at me like that idea has never occurred to him. Then he jams his hands in his pockets and jerks around to stare out at the pool.

"So what's the kid got that I haven't?" he asks.

"Shit, Paul."

He swings around sharply.

"Is this jealousy?" I ask, inspecting his expression. "It's a little late for that."

He glares.

I let out my breath, put down the drink. "What are we going to do here?" I ask. "Air out fifteen years of disappointments?"

"I'd rather not," he says.

I have to sigh. The response is standard for him.

"I figured," I say.

"So what do you want from me?" he repeats.

I glance up. "Huh?"

"Do I have to spell this out?"

"Sure," I say. "Go ahead, Paul."

"I want to make a deal for the recording," he says clearly and distinctly. "What do you want from me?"

That's always the way the man thinks. And he's right, of course. Everybody can be bought for the right price. You just have to be careful what you end up paying. Luckily I've done my cost analysis.

"Get out of politics," I say.

I've surprised him. He blinks, stares at me a long moment.

"That's pretty tough, Anna."

I shrug, reach for my glass and bolt half the drink.

"It makes sense, though. I've caught you this time, and that deal won't go through. I won't check to see what else you've done so I won't have to make any moral decisions. But look, Paul, if I found this out, somebody else will, too, just as easily. You'll get snared eventually, and once it hits the press, you're done. You'll go to jail. Take what you've got. Get out now while you're ahead."

He stares at me.

"Take it or leave it," I say.

"That's all?" he asks.

"Get the mistress off my back," I say. "And her priest."

"What?"

"I've been getting these messages," I say. "And somebody tried to kill me yesterday."

He frowns, thinks about it.

"All right." His blue eyes turn narrow and calculating. "What else do you want? Money? Sex?"

I've decided what I want from him is peace.

"Nothing." I shove up off his leather couch. "I'll keep in touch to see what you do about the politics. You'll need to put in a resignation."

The ghostly child Eleggua has disappeared into nothingness—the room is empty of spirits now. I let myself out, and then I'm back in my car, headed home. I'd expected this would hurt, and it does, but still maybe I've got what I needed. Above me the sky is empty and washed-out by the city lights, and nothing is ever as clear as you want it to be.

The familiar, angular shapes of apartments rise up out of the night, then the dark humps of cars in the lot, the tousled heads of palms by the pool. The stairs to my door are worn and familiar.

I've got a bad taste in my mouth. I start to get a beer from the fridge to wash it out, but I decide on cola instead. It goes better with the faint, lingering tang of rum and smoke in my hair.

I kick off my shoes and sit down on the couch to check the news, but then I notice a backpack thrown against the chair. Hell. Maybe the Coke could use some rum, after all.

When the drink's gone, I go and check in the bedroom. Moonlight cuts through the window, highlights a rumpled shape. I sigh and drop my jeans, slide in beside him.

"Anna?" he says.

"You were expecting someone else?" I ask.

"I just didn't know if you'd come home tonight."

A car pulls into the parking lot outside. Light slides down the walls, highlights his face with faint color.

"Well, it's like this, Joel," I say. "I've settled things with your dad. We're not friends, but hopefully we're not enemies, either. So, are you going to take off now?"

He lies there so long I'm starting to get pissed. But then I catch myself. This is something I've suspected all along. If it's true he's using me to spite his dad, at least I can let him work up to telling me.

"No," he says finally.

"What?" I'm actually surprised.

"What do you mean 'what'?" he says.

"Shit," I say.

"What?" he says.

"Ah. Nothing." I let my breath out, roll over and bury my nose against his chest. "Dammit, Joel, what does the man want?" I ask.

He throws an arm across me and pulls me up tight, nuzzles against my ear.

"My mom," he says.

"Shit," I say. "Why didn't I ever figure that out?"

About the Author

Lela E. Buis is an award-winning artist and writer. She couldn't decide on a career, so ended up working as a waitress, a gas station attendant, an engineer at Kennedy Space Center and as a teacher of various subjects and levels. She began writing as a child and leans toward genre fiction, having published mainly science fiction and fantasy stories and poetry. When she's not painting or writing, she looks after a disabled cat and a couple of part time dogs.